I0576469

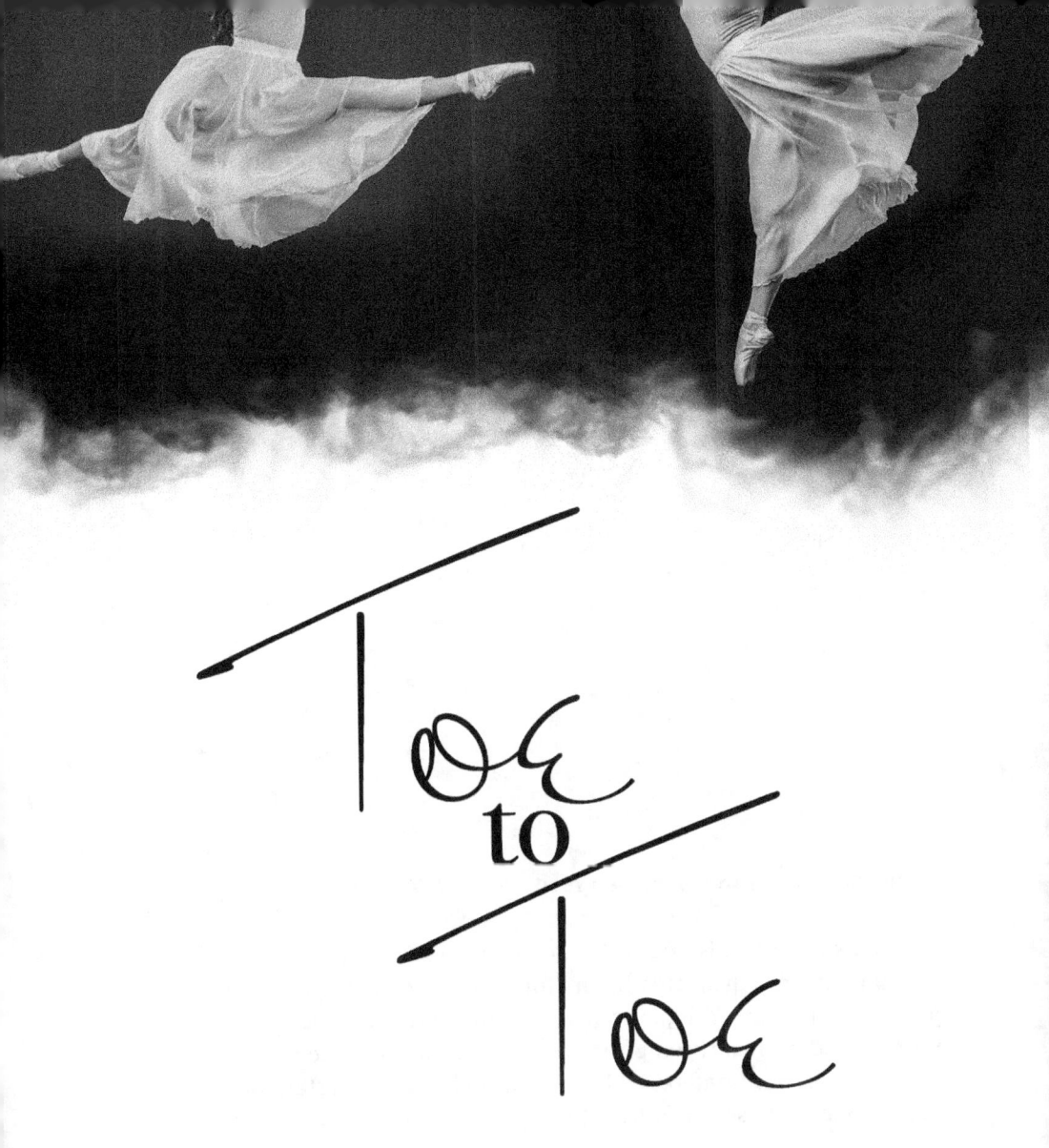

Toe to Toe

PENELOPE FREED

Toe to Toe

Copyright © 2021 by Penelope Freed

All rights reserved. No part of this publication may be reproduced, distributed, or transmitted in any form or by any means, including photocopying, recording, or other electronic or mechanical methods, without the prior written permission of the author, except in the case of brief quotations embodied in critical reviews and certain other noncommercial uses permitted by copyright law.

This is a work of fiction. Names, characters, businesses, places, events and incidents are either the products of the author's imagination or used in a fictitious manner. Any resemblance to actual persons, living or dead, or actual events is purely coincidental.)

Editing by Caitlin Fitzgerald and Saxony Gray
Cover design by Vanilla Lily Designs
Interior design by Stephanie Anderson, Alt 19 Creative

ISBN 978-1-7364893-0-7 (print)

To Molly & Melissa
My two girls

CHAPTER 1

Hannah

"GOOD HANNAH! Use your head! Quicker spot, quicker spot!" Ms. Parker shouts over the music. I jump higher, trying to whip my head around even faster to keep from getting dizzy. I manage to make it across the room before I lose my balance completely. I hold the last pose for a half a second. Two weeks until auditions. Three weeks until competition. The mantra running through my mind is the only thing keeping me from collapsing.

"Olivia! Do *not* touch your leotard!" Ms. Parker yells to someone behind me. I can picture Olivia giving a quick tug on her leotard just before her turn, like always. I grab my water bottle off the floor and take a quick sip as I watch the rest of my classmates. Olivia finishes with an extra flourish of her arms, grinning at herself in the mirror. I smile, not surprised, then move down to make space for her on this side of the studio.

"My legs are *so* dead," Olivia complains under her breath as Lisa loses her balance on the quick turns, almost crashing into the wall. I nod in silent agreement, pushing my water bottle back against the wall and grabbing Lisa's while I'm at it. Lisa's annoyed face relaxes as I hand it to her and we all do our best to catch our breath as Katy and the rest of the class take their turns.

From the minute she started class, Ms. Parker hasn't given us a break for longer than the time it took to put on our pointe shoes. I wasn't the only dancer who glanced at the clock when we started jumping, dismayed at how much time we still had left. I wasn't sure if my legs were going to hold up until the end of the hour and a half class. But I only have two weeks to be ready, no time to rest now.

Twenty minutes later, we stumble out the door of the studio, legs quivering. The studio lobby is crowded and loud, dancers trying to get into class crashing against those of us exiting. Parents are standing around waiting, having their own conversations while bored siblings noisily complain about wanting to go home. A couple of little girls dressed in pink weave through the crowd to hug us quickly before heading into the studio we just left for their own class. I follow Katy into the narrow dressing room that is the unofficial domain of the senior dancers, and breathe a sigh of relief when Olivia slips in, closing the door behind her. The dressing room is hot and crowded with all of us in it, but at least it's a place to relax before our next class. I hunt through my dance bag, nose wrinkling at the smell of old sweaty feet clinging to the inside of the bag, searching for the granola bar I tossed in there this morning, grabbing my phone as I search.

I lay down, putting my feet up against the wall as someone plops down next to me. I turn my head to see Olivia laying there with a bag of M&M's on her chest, already scrolling through the phone in her hand.

"Is anyone else sore?" Katy asks as she sits in the corner. "I'm *dying*."

"I foam-rolled my legs while I was doing my homework last night." I was prepared to be sore yesterday after my first class back after Winter Break and two weeks of no dance. Foam rolling last night was painful, but worth it so I felt better today. I don't have time to waste getting ready for the next few weeks.

Ignoring our conversation, Olivia butts in from her spot on the floor. "Hey, Banana, can I sleep over next Saturday? My dad and Martha are going to Santa Barbara for the weekend and won't let me stay home by myself." She turns to me with pleading eyes. "Please?"

"I don't know, Livvy, the Pacific Sound Ballet audition is the next day. I need to be ready."

Olivia pops an M&M in her mouth, the pleading look gone from her eyes. "It's okay, I'm sure Megan or Allyson will let me stay."

My chest tightens a little at the mention of her squadmates. "No, it's fine. I'll just text my mom and make sure. You could come to the audition with us the next day. You are auditioning right?"

I tap a quick message to my mom while I wait for Olivia to answer. "I don't know. I mean the summer intensives are just so... intense. I kinda want a normal summer, you know?"

"Come on, Livvy. It'll be fun. Besides, we haven't had a sleepover in ages." Honestly, I can't remember the last time Olivia slept over.

Olivia cranes her neck to look at Lisa and Katy. "Are all of you planning to go to the audition? We should totally have a sleepover at Hannah's if you are." Okay, I was not expecting that, but it does sound like fun. "We'll have fun." Olivia shudders dramatically, "Well, not at the audition—bunch of old people watching us dance, waiting for us to make a mistake." I steal one of her M&M's and toss it at her face. Olivia just laughs. "But the sleepover will be!"

"Is your mom still okay to take me?" Lisa asks.

"Of course," I say. Truthfully I forgot to ask my mom, but Lisa is practically a permanent plus one for us whenever we have competitions or auditions. Pacific Sound Ballet, or PSB, has one of the best summer intensives in the country. Unfortunately, Lisa's parents think spending the summer doing ballet all day is a waste of time, no matter how prestigious the school.

Katy looks up from her phone. "I wasn't going to go to the audition but if it means a night away from my idiot brothers, count me in."

Lisa already has her phone out and is typing. "I'm just checking right now but it should be fine. I was going to carpool with you anyway." She looks up, biting her bottom lip. "Han, can your mom text my mom…" Lisa trails off, but I understand. Lisa has never broken a rule in her life, yet Mrs. Hamasaki always believes she's up to something. I tap out another text to my mom. She still hasn't seen the first two.

Lisa's version of fine and my version of fine are very different. With Mrs. Hamasaki involved, it will likely take three phone calls from my mother just to convince her that Lisa isn't imposing on us or sneaking off to get into trouble with boys.

"Does anyone have an extra granola bar? I'm starving." Katy looks hopefully around the dressing room.

"I don't think so," I shrug. "But you can hunt through my bag."

"I think there's another bag of M&M's in mine, you can have it if you want it," Olivia calls from her spot on the floor.

"Do you know how many calories are in a bag of M&M's?" Lisa asks from the other end of the narrow space. She is—somehow—already doing homework, proving why she gets straight A's.

"Don't know, don't care. Chocolate calories don't count!" Olivia laughs. "We're sixteen Lisa, we're supposed to eat crappy food and make dumb choices."

"And how many dumb choices have you made today?" Katy asks, her words muffled as she searches in my dance bag.

"Hmmmm…" Olivia plays along, counting on her fingers. "Let's see. I *chose* to hit snooze too many times, so I *chose* to run late for school, which made me *choose* to park in the way back of the parking lot. Which made me *choose* to not look where I was going while I ran to class, so of course I *chose* to run headfirst into Tyler Stanley." Olivia pauses dramatically and sighs. My breath catches in my throat at the mention of his name. "Tyler *chose* to help me pick up all my stuff, and while he was helping me, he *chose* to ask me out to a movie this weekend. And I *chose* to say yes." Olivia finishes with a smirk. "So…none," she adds, sticking out her tongue at Katy.

"Tyler Stanley asked you out?" Katy's voice cracks. Tyler Stanley is gorgeous. Like, perfect-sandy-blonde-hair-that-never-quite-gets-in-his-hazel-eyes, perfect. If our life were a movie, he would be the cool, super popular guy with a secret heart of gold that the dorky girl has a crush on. And yes, I would be that dorky girl. And yes, I have had a crush on Tyler since sixth grade, I suppose Olivia forgot.

"I guess it's true, cheerleaders always win." Katy mumbles.

"You know half the school is in love with him, right?" Lisa adds, still working on her homework. "Good luck with that."

I take a big bite of my granola bar, filling my mouth so I have an excuse not to join the conversation.

"I'm aware," Olivia deadpans, glancing at me. Maybe she does remember my crush on Tyler after all. "The girls have already threatened to kick me off the squad for taking him off the market."

Of *course,* Tyler would pick Olivia. If Tyler was the cool guy in a movie, then Olivia was the "popular girl" who ruled the school. Okay, to be fair she doesn't *really* run the school, but she is pretty, popular, and on the cheerleading squad. She's naturally blonde with blue eyes, a perfect chest-waist-hip ratio, and always looks perfectly styled. When we were kids she was always the one plotting elaborate adventures while I tagged along for the fun, piping up with the occasional suggestion so we didn't get into too much trouble.

Hearing that Tyler asked her out sends a bolt of lightning through me. Lightning that feels a lot like jealousy. "So, what movie are you going to see?" I ask, hoping my voice doesn't betray my feelings.

"I think that killer robot movie that's coming out. I don't care, I'm not planning on watching the movie anyway," Olivia grins. "Come on, don't want to be late for class. Ballerinas are never late," she adds in a perfect imitation of Ms. Parker. I hang back as she scurries out with her jazz shoes.

Lisa shoves her math book in her cubby and follows. "Don't worry about her. I'm sure she didn't mean to rub it in. You know how she is."

Of course I know Olivia, she's been my best friend my whole life. She had to remember my long-time crush on Tyler.

"It's fine," I tell Lisa. "I just need to find my jazz shoes. I'll be right out."

"They're right there," Lisa says, pointing to the top of my open bag.

"Right." I grab them and follow Lisa back to the studio for our last class of the night. It's not like I have time to date anyway. Auditions for summer intensives are coming up. I don't have time for boys.

"*S*WEETHEART? Is that you?" I drop my dance bag and backpack to the floor just inside the kitchen.

"Yeah." I slip the Lancer's keys onto the Batman keyholder, already making a list of all the homework I need to finish before I go to sleep.

"Your dinner is in the fridge. Just need to heat it up."

"Thanks," I call through to the living room where I can hear the TV.

Reheated dinner is just one of the perks of my glamorous ballerina lifestyle. So is not getting to start my homework until 9:30 p.m. Algebra questions, research for my US History essay, re-writing my Biology lab notes, reading a chapter in that English book that I've already forgotten the name of. Shoot, did I bring it home? I'm heading back to look for it in my backpack when a folder on the table catches my eye, a post-it with my name stuck on the front. Abandoning the hunt for the book, I flip through the folder until the microwave pings. Mom's tiny cursive writing on the tab reads Summer Intensives. A quick flip through the folder tells me Mom has all the paperwork filled in and ready to send for the upcoming auditions. Relieved she took care of it, I put it aside and scroll through my phone while I eat, dreaming of the day I might join the ranks of a ballet company like the ones filling my Instagram feed.

Procrastinating starting my homework, I take the file to the living room and plop down next to my mom on the couch. "Thanks," I say, waving the file in my hand. "What are you watching?" I ask.

"Oh, you're welcome sweetie. Just catching up on *Arrow*." I rest my head on her shoulder, stealing a moment to relax. "How was class? Are you feeling ready for the auditions?"

"Class was good. I'm less sore today so that's good. Foam rolling last night helped. I broke my pointe shoes in class today, I need to sew the ribbons on my new pair." My phone buzzes and I glance at it.

> **LISA:** Guess who got into my room and stole all my highlighters?
> **KATY:** At least your brother doesn't fart on you for fun.
> **LISA:** Thank god I only have 1.
> **ME:** Thank god I only have none.

Seeing Katy and Lisa complaining about their siblings reminds me. "Did you talk to Mrs. H?"

"Yes, I got everything sorted out for Lisa and Katy." Mom pauses the tv, giving me her full attention. "You and Olivia haven't had a sleepover in ages. What brought this on?"

I shrug. "Her dad and Martha are going out of town."

"Good for them."

"It'll be nice to see Olivia. All I see of her now are her dad's Facebook posts. She looks just like her mom."

"You always say that."

"It's true. The two of you remind me so much of us when we were your age." Mom looks wistfully at the photo of the four of us on the mantle. Olivia and I are just toddlers, fated to be best friends because our moms were best friends. At least until Olivia's mom died. It's been four years but there is still a hole in our lives where Olivia's mom used to be. While she's distracted by her thoughts I peek at my phone, but there aren't any new messages.

"I was surprised she said she'd come to the audition—ballet isn't Olivia's 'thing' these days, you know? I don't think she's planning to go to a summer intensive at all. I heard her tell Ms. Parker she was going to stay here and have a 'real summer,' whatever that means." I'm pretty sure it means going to the beach with Tyler Stanley and getting a killer tan, but I don't think my mom wants to know that.

"Well, either way, it will be nice to have her and the other girls over. The house is so much quieter without her around. Do you have homework to do?" She kisses my head before I get up off the couch, her hand reaching for the remote.

"Of course," I sigh. "It never ends. I better get started," I say, standing up. "Night Mom, love you."

"Goodnight sweetheart, don't stay up too late," my mom calls as I head upstairs to my room.

I check my group chat with Lisa and Katy before I pull out my math book, hoping for an excuse to put it off for five more minutes.

> **KATY:** Seriously, pity me.
> **KATY:** Also…

A photo from Katy of the disgusting blister on her pinky toe that ripped open in class tonight pops up in the group chat. She doodled neon green slime oozing from the blister and dripping onto her biology textbook.

ME: That's disgusting.

Sometimes I wonder how Katy even ended up in ballet. Her oldest brother Cole is a sophomore at UCLA on a basketball scholarship. Her twin brothers, Jack and Hunter, are juniors at our school—Jack plays football and something-else-ball, and Hunter runs track. They're one of those sporty families who watch football on Sundays and have burping contests after dinner. I know, I was there once.

I reply with a gif of a cat vomiting rainbows.

LISA: Is that how you feel about Katy's blister or Olivia's news?
ME: Both?
KATY: Both is valid. I'm sorry she surprised you like that. You ok?
ME: Yes. No. I don't know. I mean, it's only a first date, right? It could be nothing.

I'm not okay, but I'm hoping that if I keep pretending I am, eventually it will be true. And they haven't even gone out yet, maybe it'll be a disaster. Even though I don't want to, I text Olivia to ask her about the upcoming competition. She doesn't respond so I put on some music and pull out my Algebra book, out of excuses. Stupid "normal high school experience" homework that my parents insist is good for me. I don't care about school, I just want to dance.

CHAPTER 2

Olivia

ALLYSON: Uniforms tomorrow?

MEGAN: Yes. I just checked with Coach

I CATCH UP with the squad group chat as I eat my dinner. Thank god football is season over at least. Juggling Friday night games, pep rallies and practice with my dance schedule this fall had been ridiculous. I laugh to myself as I scroll through the conversation. It drifts from which uniforms we're supposed to wear tomorrow (long sleeves, thank fuck) to a discussion of which basketball player is the hottest. Allyson called dibs on Mark Spencer, even though we all know Madison has wanted him for ages.

ME: As long as everyone keeps their mitts off Tyler I don't care. I licked it, it's mine.

I add a gif of a baby licking a window for good measure before loading my plate in the dishwasher. I tiptoe past the other bedrooms as I go upstairs, not wanting to wake anyone up. Once in my room, I pull out a bottle of neon purple polish and start working on my nails.

> **HANNAH:** Mom wants to know if you're going to stay with us during YIGP? Or is your dad coming for the whole weekend?

How am I supposed to know? The Youth International Grand Prix competition isn't for another couple weeks or something, I have no idea if my dad will make the time to come with me or not. Ugh. Freaking Hannah and her super organized mom, always making plans. I don't do plans, plans are for dorks. I have a hard enough time juggling my life without planning things a month in advance. Unlike Little Miss Perfect, my dad is always at work and my useless stepmom has her hands full with Aiden and Marie, they don't have time to organize my life too. Which is fine, I'd rather do it myself anyway.

> **ME:** don't know if he's coming or not yet

I toss my phone on my bed and go back to painting my toenails. The bright purple nail polish is doing a great job of hiding the disgusting bruised toenail on my right foot. You would think it was from the hours I spend standing on my toes at dance, but you would be wrong. My stupid little brother—stepbrother to be precise—dropped my Spanish book on my toe this morning.

I glare at said Spanish book where it's sitting on my desk, mocking me. I still have homework to finish for tomorrow but I'm not going to bother doing it tonight. I already finished everything for my first two classes, I'll do the rest in class before it's due. My AirPods hum along to my bops playlist and I concentrate on not getting any nail polish on my comforter.

My phone buzzes again beside me and I smudge my pinky toe polish when I glance at it. "Shit," I say to the world in general.

> **TYLER:** hey Liv, got a problem on Sat. My dorky cousin Trevor is still in town. My mom says he has to come with us or else we have to hang at the house. Know anyone who can come with and keep him occupied?

Well fuck that, I pout. It's taken *ages* for me to get Tyler to finally ask me out, not to mention I was almost late to class this morning since I waited around to "bump" into him, and now this?

> **ME:** to babysit?
> **TYLER:** dude, he's a junior

I hate being called dude. I'm a fucking lady thank you very much. I sigh and try to think of someone who will do it. I could take one of the girls on the squad, maybe Megan? No, she keeps trying to flirt with Tyler.

A year ago, I would have asked one of the dance girls, but since I joined cheer they don't bother to include me in anything anymore. It stung at first, but I'm over it now. I rack my brain—who can I trust to come with us that will keep his cousin occupied but won't distract Tyler from me?

ME: Hannah would do it.

TYLER: Who?

ME: Hannah O'Brian? I'm sending you her number so you can ask her

TYLER: Why do I have to ask her?

TYLER: I don't even know her

ME: Because if I ask, she'll say no. No way she'll turn you down, trust me.

I smile to myself as I send her number to him under "*Hannah— nerd friend for Trevor.*"

This will be interesting.

"VIIIIIIIIIIIIIIIIAAAAAAAA!!!!!!!" Aiden is flopping around on the floor, wailing at the top of his lungs. "Not that dino! Other dino!"

What. The. *Fuck.* I bounce Marie on my hip and take a deep breath before I strangle my brother. "What other dino, Aiden? These are the only kind in the freezer." There is literally only one kind of dinosaur-shaped chicken nugget in the entire world, right? I put Marie down and scrape Aiden up off the ground. "Marie, don't move." I glare at her, praying she doesn't magically learn how to crawl while I deal with this meltdown.

Aiden hiccups, tears and snot running down his face. Honestly, he'd be a pretty cute three-year-old if he wasn't such a little shit most of the time. I was kind of excited at the idea of having a sibling when my dad and Martha started dating, Aiden was a really cute baby, but the reality of having two siblings who require constant monitoring so they don't accidentally kill themselves is not what fourteen-year-old me thought I was signing up for. I suppress my revulsion and pick him up so he can see for himself there is only one kind of chicken dino in the freezer. "See buddy, these are the same dinos as always."

"Same, same?"

"Yeah, buddy, the same." He squishes up his face like he's thinking about it really hard. "How many do you want?" I try, praying he eats them.

"Ummm…fwee? Want fwee." He holds up three sticky fingers and nods his head. I put him down so I can pull the box out and make these monsters their dinner. I really hope my dad and Martha bring home some leftovers. I strategically agreed to babysit tonight so they could go out on a date. I've learned that offense is the best defense when it comes to babysitting the monsters—if I volunteer to do it at regular intervals, they don't ask me to do it when I really don't want to. Tomorrow night is my first date with Tyler Stanley, I'm not risking anything getting in the way of it happening.

I pull out the box and dump a handful of nuggets on a baking sheet before sticking them in the oven to cook. Aiden is still sniffling back tears but at least he isn't screaming anymore. Marie is sitting patiently on the floor by my feet sucking on her fist and drooling everywhere.

"Come on monsters, let's go watch tv," I swing her back up onto my hip, narrowly avoiding the string of drool that's hanging from her chin. So gross. I grab a tissue on my way to the living room and wipe off her face before I plop her on the floor at my feet with her toys. "What are we watching Aiden?"

"Pirates!!!!" He yells, running in circles around the room, tears forgotten. I flip the tv on and find the show he wants before I pull out my phone.

> **TYLER:** Hey beautiful, how's the monsters?
> **ME:** Loud. Annoying. Weirdly wet. Pick an adjective.
> **TYLER:** Need some company?
> **ME:** Can't, my dad and Martha will kill you if you're here without them knowing. And me, they'll kill me too. I'm too pretty to die.

I fluff my hair, purse my lips and take a selfie of myself laying on the couch. Then I angle my phone to include the drool monster on the ground and Aiden running amok in the background and take another. I post the good one to my Insta, but send both to Tyler. Perception vs. reality is a real bitch. I toss my phone aside and pretend to pay attention to the monsters.

"Ouch!" I cry when my hair is suddenly yanked from my head. "Son of a…" I stop myself before finishing that thought out loud. Marie has a handful of my hair in her wet, chubby fist and she's using it to pull herself up to standing. I guess I'm washing my hair tonight.

"Come on, baby girl," I pull her up to sit on my chest on the couch. She squawks and wiggles around, her chubby legs straddling my stomach. Her brown curly hair and eyes are exactly the same as Aiden's. They both look just like Martha, except that Marie and I have my dad's nose.

We pass the time with Marie bouncing up and down on me, Aiden chattering away about whatever this pirate is up to and me praying no one loses an eye and the dino nuggets cook quickly.

When my dad and Martha walk in the door two hours later, the monsters are fed, bathed, in pajamas and sleepily watching Finding Nemo on the couch. I even loaded the dishwasher, like the angel I am. "Thanks, pumpkin," my dad says, dropping a kiss on my head.

"Thanks," Martha mouths to me as she gently picks up the almost asleep Marie. I smile, because I know this just bought me at least a couple weeks before they ask again. My dad picks up a grumbling Aiden and follows Martha up the stairs. I watch them go, running my fingers through my hair, feeling the familiar burn of jealousy in my chest. I absently pull at the tangles Marie made, letting the pain tugging at my scalp replace the pain in my chest.

It's not fair. That should be Mom walking up the stairs, not Martha. My mom, not their mom.

With a sigh, I roll off the couch and tiptoe up to my room so I can shower the food and drool off me before I go to bed. All I want to do is sleep in tomorrow, but nine am ballet class calls. I skipped on Monday and tonight, so I absolutely can't miss class tomorrow. Ms. Parker will give me another one of her patented guilt trips and Hannah will look at me with those disappointed eyes and make passive-aggressive comments about what I missed in class earlier this week.

Excuse me if I decided to try something new and made a commitment to the cheer squad. They're all so big on following through on your commitments and blah, blah, blah. Well, look at me, I committed to something and I'm following through. They just don't like it because I didn't commit to *ballet*. Well, guess what? I didn't want to commit to six days a week of ballet this year, I wanted to be a normal high schooler.

I check my phone when I finish my shower. My Insta post from earlier has over a hundred likes and comments already, sweet. And then there's this gem of a text.

> **HANNAH:** are you coming to class tomorrow? Ms. Parker wants us to stay for an extra 30 mins to work on Sleeping Beauty since we couldn't run through it earlier this week. Also, entry fees for YIGP are due tomorrow. She asked if you were coming and I said I didn't know.

For fucks sake, Hannah. You're not my personal assistant, why do you keep letting people assume you know my life? I shake my head and toss the phone on my bed. I'm not even going to answer her.

CHAPTER 3

Hannah

ONE BY ONE the girls in my class slink into the studio, curling into our sweats and hoodies as we slowly get our shoes on and start stretching before class. Ballet class at nine o'clock in the morning is hard, no matter how much you love dancing. Even Ms. Parker can be a little grumpy on Saturday mornings before she's finished her coffee. Still, Saturdays are my favorite—the one day a week that feels like old times, the day everyone is guaranteed to be in class.

I like to get there early to help with the baby class that starts half an hour before ours, it always puts me in a good mood for my own class after. The babies are so cute in their tiny tutus and itty bitty ballet shoes. I've become a pro at tying the strings on those little shoes. Olivia and I were that small when we started dancing together, our moms signed us up for class almost before we could walk. No surprise there, since that's where they met as kids.

Lisa joined the studio when her family moved here from San Francisco when we were nine. Then, after her old dance teacher retired, Katy joined us a year later. The four of us, Olivia, Lisa, Katy, and I have been dancing together ever since—although this year feels more like the three of us with the occasional appearance by Olivia. For the last three years, since we joined the senior class, Saturdays have meant being together at the studio all day long for rehearsals and classes, no matter what else is going on in our lives.

I'm already laying on my back, my right leg hooked under the foot of a portable barre, my arms pulling my left leg up to my face, when Lisa and Katy wander into the studio. They come join me at our usual spot—the heaviest barre, placed just to the left of center. I don't even have to think about where I stand, I always take the front spot on the right, Lisa right behind me. Katy puts herself right in the middle of us on the opposite side, not saving any room for Olivia.

"Morning," I say to Lisa as she plops down next to me.

"Morning," she mutters, her hands wrapped tightly around her hot tea. "Need a hand?" She offers, nodding at my leg. Katy drops down on the ground beside her, my water bottle in her hand, I must have left it in the dressing room.

"Sure." Lisa grabs my left foot and pushes it down. My thigh presses against my shoulder as Lisa pushes my foot all the way down to the floor behind my head. Katy wiggles the water bottle, getting my attention, then puts it on the floor near the barre next to me. "Thanks," I grunt to both of them.

"Hannah, your feet are so freaking good, it's not fair. Why can't my feet be bendy, gorgeous bananas like yours?" Lisa takes another sip of her tea, pushing my leg further behind my head. "It's so not fair, you got great feet and you're super flexible. This is why we can't be friends." I crane my neck to see if she's kidding or not and see her grinning from behind her cup. I stick my tongue out at her and wink.

"You have good feet too," I point out. I may have been blessed by genetics in some ways, but so was Lisa. "And you have longer arms than me Katy, so there," I add, switching legs.

"My arms are longer because I'm taller. My turn," Katy says as I finish stretching so I roll over onto my stomach and reach for her foot. Lisa has her feet together in a butterfly stretch, her cheek resting on her feet.

From my vantage point on the floor I see Olivia slip in the door just as Ms. Parker finishes her coffee and gets that look on her face, the one that guarantees we'll be starting our morning with more than just pliés.

"Morning ladies!" Ms. Parker is entirely too cheerful, maybe that was her second cup of coffee, not her first. "How about we wake up with some jumping jacks?"

KATY IS WAITING for me in the doorway after I gather up my stuff at the end of class. "What did you bring for lunch?" she asks. We get an hour for lunch after class and I know Katy wants me to drive her to go get lunch at the taco place down the street.

"Sorry Katy, I packed my lunch. I think Olivia is going to Taco Stop though,"

"She's taking food to the football team, probably to see Tyler. Saturday is my day to get away from my brothers, not spend extra time with them." She wanders off to see where Lisa is as I go outside.

The strip mall where the studio is located has a little courtyard in the middle with tables and chairs. The coffee shop and the dog groomers that are on either side of the courtyard provide some excellent people watching. And good coffee. The coffee shop, not the dog groomers. I find a table big enough for the three of us and scroll through my phone while I wait for Katy and Lisa. I wonder if Katy asked Olivia to take her to Taco Stop after all, despite not wanting to see her brothers.

I look up when I hear the scraping of chairs. "She already left, I'm getting something from Beans 'n Things, anyone want anything?" Katy walks backwards towards the coffee shop, watching to see if Lisa or I want anything.

"Black iced tea?"

"No sweetener?" Katy checks with me before disappearing inside after my nod.

"Did you see Marianela Núñez's post last night?" Lisa pulls it up on her phone so I can see the gorgeous Argentinian dancer all four of us idolize. I dream that one day I'll be that good, that I'll get to dance in a company like The Royal Ballet in London or the Classical Ballet Company in New York City.

Katy comes back with my iced tea and her iced coffee while Lisa and I are entranced by Nela's adorable cats. "You know she didn't even wait to see if anyone wanted to go with her? She just took off." I share a look with Lisa, not responding to Katy's comment. "How did she know I didn't want to go say hi to my brothers?"

"Because we all know you would never voluntarily spend extra time with your brothers." Lisa laughs and scoops up a forkful of the pasta she brought for lunch. "Or the football team," she adds, saluting Katy with her fork before taking a bite. She doesn't say it, but I can imagine Lisa adding "or Olivia," in her mind.

Eager to change the subject before our lunch hour is spent talking about Olivia, I steal one of the potato chips off Katy's plate with a grin. Olivia has been my best friend for as long as I can remember. Talking about her behind her back, especially with Katy and Lisa, feels wrong. Even if maybe sometimes they have a point. Especially when they have a point. Would it have killed Olivia to see if any of us wanted to go with her?

We chat and eat, enjoying the chance to rest our bodies before the next couple hours of dancing. We're arguing good-naturedly over which teacher at school is worse—Lisa's AP Chem teacher or my hard-nosed US History teacher—when Katy throws a piece of her uneaten sandwich at Lisa. I can't contain my laughter at the smear of mustard streaked across Lisa's nose and the pile of lettuce that went down Katy's front as she lobbed it. I wave as they rush back into the studio to clean up before rehearsal, leaving me to finish eating alone.

I pull out my phone to check the time as I finish the last few bites. There's a text from my mom asking what I want from the store for dinner tonight and a text message from a number I don't recognize. Who on earth is texting me?

UNKNOWN: Hey Hannah, I got your number from Olivia. I have a question for you, text me back -T

T? Who is T? That can't be T for Tyler can it? My breath catches in my throat. No. It can't be. I glance at the time it was sent. Over an hour ago? I type out my response, one excruciating letter at a time.

ME: Hey, what's up?

I can't ask who it is can I? That would be so lame.

UNKNOWN: I wanted to know if Olivia had left yet, we needed her to get more food. Don't worry about it.

It must be Tyler. But why did Olivia give it to him? Why would she do that? I need to respond without betraying the panic coursing through me.

ME: Oh, sorry. I only just saw your text.

Dare I? *"How's practice going?"* I type, but then quickly delete it. Tyler just wanted food, he's not trying to have a conversation with me, stupid Hannah.

TYLER: Like I said, don't worry about it.

See, not trying to have a conversation, it was just about food. Then I see those three little dots. My heart leaps into my throat. Wait, what else is he typing? My palms get so sweaty, I'm afraid I'll drop my phone. Why am I so nervous? I stare at it, willing the text to come through.

TYLER: What are you doing tonight?

I gasp and drop my phone. It lands in my lap and slides down my slippery tights before hitting the ground. Thank you baby Jesus, it lands on top of my dance bag. I pick it up and stare at it. What am I doing tonight? Sewing ribbons on my new pointe shoes and dreaming of you? I want to reply. Easy tiger, one thing

Toe to Toe

at a time. My thumb hovers over the screen, unsure of what to type. I take a deep breath and type.

> **ME:** Nothing, just chilling at home.

I hit send before I can think about it. Chilling? Wow, way to sound cool. Now my heart is really thumping in my chest. Why is Tyler asking what I'm doing? Isn't he going out with Olivia tonight? Did she cancel on him? But she's bringing them food, why would she bring them food now and not go out with him tonight? None of this makes any sense. This must be a joke. Maybe Olivia put him up to it. No, Hannah, that's mean. Olivia wouldn't do that. Would she? Wait, Tyler said she wasn't there yet. Get it together Hannah. My phone buzzes again, interrupting my runaway train of thought.

> **TYLER:** My cousin is in town and my parents won't let me ditch him tonight. Olivia said you might be willing to come with us tonight so we can still go out.

My heart sinks. They want me to babysit the cousin so they can have their date? I can babysit, I guess. Olivia must have remembered our failed attempt at forming a baby-sitters club. The extra spending money would be nice, but I can't deny I'm disappointed. I don't know what I thought Tyler was going to ask, but that wasn't it.

My phone buzzes again.

> **TYLER:** Olivia said to tell you he's not ugly. He's chill, I promise it won't be awful.

Not ugly? Why would it matter if he's ugly? I'm glad Tyler thinks he's chill though, I hate babysitting crazy, hyper kids. I wonder where his parents are going. I guess it doesn't matter.

> **ME:** Sure. What time do you want me to come over?
> **TYLER:** 7
> **ME:** Cool, see you.

Putting my phone down I take a deep breath. I stare at the table, suddenly overwhelmed by sadness. All my fantasies of Tyler secretly liking me back, just like in a movie, are crashing down around me. The reality of Tyler and Olivia going on a date hits me. Can I keep wanting him if he's dating my best friend? Doesn't that make me the worst best friend in the world? But it's only a first date, right? Maybe that's all it'll ever be.

CHAPTER 4

Hannah

PHONE, SEWING KIT, pointe shoes, check. Ribbons, check. Elastic, check. Book in case I finish sewing before they get back, check. I grab my phone charger, just in case. I scan my room one more time, making sure I have everything I need before heading over to Tyler's house to babysit.

I stayed for an extra hour after rehearsal to work on my solos for competition with Ms. Parker. I was so tired by the time I got home, I took a quick shower and dropped onto my bed to take a power nap. I threw on some leggings and a big comfy sweater when I got out of the shower but I'm not changing—the sweater is a little bit holey but I don't think this kid will care. I wasn't going to put on any make up, but at the last second I decided to put on some concealer and mascara so I don't traumatize the kid. I throw my damp hair up in a messy bun and head out the door. "Bye Mom! Bye Dad!" I call as I head to the door, stopping in the hallway to grab a jacket.

"Bye honey!" Mom sticks her head out the kitchen, "have fun, I hope they don't keep you out too late."

"I know, I'll be fine." I reassure her. I'm really hoping this kid just wants to watch a movie or something so I can relax. I hop in the car and head to Tyler's house. Pulling up to the curb I hop out, grabbing my big purse and swiping on some chapstick. My pointe shoe sticks into my ribs and I wriggle to get more comfortable. First priority is to get ribbons sewn on.

"You came!" Olivia says, sticking her head out the door. She glances over her shoulder and drags me a little way from the door, letting it shut softly behind her. Olivia could be one of those fashion influencers, she always looks cute. Tonight she's wearing skinny jeans that perfectly show off her slim legs, a perfectly off the shoulder burgundy sweater, ankle boots that perfectly coordinate, and a smattering of dangly necklaces and earrings, all topped with her freshly washed and curled hair. I look like the homeless version of her with my messy bun, stretched out leggings and Converse. "I wasn't sure if you would come, you never go out, but I couldn't think of anyone else who would want to hang out with Trevor for the whole night," she says, glancing back at the house. How annoying is this kid? "So Trevor is, like, really into comic books and superheroes and stuff like that. And books and shit like that." Okay...not sure why I need such a run-down on this kid, it's one night. "He's kinda a gangly white guy." Olivia adds, "I guess he's cute, if you like that nerdy look." Obviously Olivia doesn't, but I still don't understand why it matters if Trevor is cute. I'm babysitting him, not dating...

Crap.

Is this a double date, not a babysitting gig? Ummmmm...how do I play this cool and figure it out? I think quickly. "Hey, uh, how old is Trevor? Um. Tyler never said," I add, dumbly. Okay, I think I saved it. Crap, I have pointe shoes in my bag and I look a hot mess.

"He's seventeen," Olivia chirps. "His family live in Seattle, they were here for Winter Break. I guess they go back home tomorrow." Tomorrow? Oh well, I guess my lack of attractiveness won't matter, he'll be gone. Oh god, but Tyler will be there all night, staring at me and my no makeup and messy hair. Crap, this sweater has a hole in the armpit. Note to self Hannah, do not under any circumstances raise your arms.

"Cool," I manage to say. I don't want to stay and watch Tyler and Olivia all night long. I want to go home. I thought I was babysitting. I never would have agreed to come if I knew I was going to be going on a date. Not just any date either. My best friend and the boy of my dreams going on their first date? This is the stuff of nightmares.

But what would Tyler think if I back out now? And what would his cousin think? That would be so rude, wouldn't it? I would be mortified if that happened to me. Fine, I'll stay. "What time does the movie start?"

"Oh. I dunno, we're leaving in just a second. I'll go get the guys. I just wanted to warn you first. I didn't want you to think that I thought you were only good enough for Tyler's dorky cousin, I just didn't know anyone else who would be nice enough to keep him distracted for me." I guess I am babysitting. A seventeen year old. Who thinks this is a date.

As Olivia heads back inside, I run back to my car and toss the pointe shoes and sewing kit inside. Maybe I have some makeup in my bag? I scramble through my purse, looking in every pocket. Jackpot! There is a black eyeliner and some powder in the bottom. I quickly swipe on a little eyeliner and get rid of my extra shiny forehead. Okay, I feel slightly better. At least now Tyler won't be blinded by my face. I debate taking my hair out of its bun, but since I don't have a brush I leave it. If I take it out now it'll dry all frizzy and weird.

I look up and see Olivia and Tyler walking out the door, Olivia leading him out by the hand. She's already holding his hand? I feel my heart break a little inside my chest. They look so perfect together, her blonde hair bouncing as Tyler follows her to his car, his sandy hair flopping just so, perfectly framing his perfect face, his green shirt just tight enough to make me notice the defined muscles of his arms.

"Hi, I'm Trevor," someone says from above my head. "Thanks for being a good sport about this, Olivia was determined to make this date happen, I guess."

I look up into a pair of warm brown eyes, the curly brown hair above it a little greasy, but not gross. Trevor's nose is a little too sharp to say he's super cute, but it's not bad. He kind of reminds me of Tom Hiddleston or Benedict Cumberbatch—he shouldn't be cute, he's not really cute, but he's attractive anyway. He's wearing a gray shirt with a big red, white and blue target with a big white star in the middle. It's tight enough to show that he has some muscle, although nothing like Tyler's, maybe that's what Olivia meant when she called him skinny. It takes me a second to realize it's the Captain America symbol on his shirt. Oh, that's right, he's into that comic book stuff. I'm not such a bunhead that I've never seen the movies, my parents have dragged me to see a few of them, I just don't care that much about them either way.

"Oh, yeah. Uh, hi," I stammer. Jesus Hannah, get it together. "Yeah, I'm Hannah, nice to meet you. So how come we're having to go on this date with them?" Oh god, that sounds awful, I cough, stumbling over my words. "Sorry! I meant, not that I don't want to go, I just, uh, wondered, uh…why." Way to be cool Hannah. I can feel my cheeks turning bright red, my ears on fire. Curse my fair Irish coloring. Luck of the Irish my butt.

Trevor grins. "My family and I are going home tomorrow morning, and Tyler had to spend all day at practice. It was either cancel the date and hang out with our parents and my little sister tonight, or bring me along. I guess Olivia wasn't interested in having me along as a third wheel." When he smiles his eyes sort of crinkle up, it's cute. "So I guess your friend took matters into her own hands."

"Didn't you have to go back to school this week? We did."

"Na, I go back on Monday." I see Olivia beckoning us over to Tyler's car and I walk over to see what she wants.

"Ready? The movie starts pretty soon," Tyler says. "We can all ride in my car." Tyler's black BMW is spotless, the envy of pretty much every guy, and girl, at school. The little red Mitsubishi Lancer I share with my mom? Not so much.

"I think I'd rather drive my own car. I can't stay out super late," I hear myself say.

"It's cool, I'll ride with Hannah," Trevor says, and starts walking back to my car. Olivia looks ecstatic, this is obviously going even better than she imagined. I hurry to catch up, Trevor is easily six feet tall and my 5'4" legs have to jog to keep up. Sliding into the driver's seat, I hurriedly shove everything back into my purse off the passenger seat. A pointe shoe tumbles to the floor and I dive for it just as Trevor starts to sit down. My arm slams into his thigh and my forehead lands with a thunk against his shoulder. That is a solid shoulder.

"Ow! Oh god are you—"

"Are you okay?" Trevor asks, concern written all over his face. His dirty Vans are currently crushing my shoe and my head is spinning. I sit back against my own seat, eyes closed, and wait for the world to stop.

"Yeah, I'm okay," I say, pinching the bridge of my nose. "Can you get my pointe shoe please? You're squishing it." My shoe. I pray he hasn't crushed it. My old shoes were too dead to wear anymore and I haven't saved up enough money to buy another new pair, buying this pair cleaned out all my Christmas money. "I'm okay, really," I add, opening one eye.

Trevor is busy rubbing his shoulder and examining his thigh. I hadn't noticed that he was wearing shorts. Who wears shorts in January? "Do you have a Band-Aid?" he asks, turning his head to look at me. That's when I notice the bright red line running down his thigh. "I don't think it's too deep," Trevor hurriedly says. I am so mortified, my nails must have cut his leg as I was reaching to save my shoe. If my cheeks weren't scarlet before, they are now.

But Band-Aids I know I have. I grab my purse and start rummaging through it. "Yeah, I do, somewhere," I say, head buried in the bag. I keep my head down while I look, willing my face to go back to its normal ghost-like white. Something flies over my head and lands on the backseat with a thump. It must be my shoe. "Here, I found one." I hand it over, still embarrassed.

"Thanks," Trevor says, taking it from me. He carefully peels it open and puts it over the deepest part of the scratch. It's pretty long, about 3 inches really, but only one section is deep enough to be bleeding. My head feels better so I start the engine and buckle my seatbelt. As I start to pull away from the curb Trevor chuckles and says, "I mean, if you really didn't want to go on the date you could have said something, you didn't have to stab me."

I blush again. "No no, that's not it. I just didn't know. Um." One day, one day I'll speak in actual sentences. "I, uh, thought you were younger." I fizzle, hoping Trevor won't guess the truth.

"Younger? Like, fifteen? That's not that bad is it?" Trevor asks.

I swallow. "Um, a little younger than that." This is so embarrassing. I'm gonna kill Olivia when I see her.

"Younger? Why would Tyler and Olivia go on a double date with...Oh!" Trevor starts laughing, getting louder and louder. Okay, it's not that funny. My ears are burning again and my cheeks are on fire. "You thought you were babysitting me?" Trevor keeps laughing as my shoulders creep up to my ears, embarrassment coursing through me. "Disappointed?" he asks.

Honestly, I kind of am. I was looking forward to sewing my shoes for tomorrow and earning some money. I can't tell Trevor that, he already thinks I'm a clumsy idiot. "Not really." I say, checking for cars at the stop sign. Tyler and Olivia are way ahead of us, not having to bandage each other up before they left the house.

"Not really? Geez, I'm flattered." Trevor chuckles, but I think he might be a little mad. His laugh sounds a little fake. Not that I blame him, I would be mad.

"Sorry, I'm sorry, I didn't mean it like that!" I say quickly. "I just meant, I was planning to sew my shoes and I'm really tired from dance today." I must sound like such a dork to Trevor. "I mean, this is fine, I just wasn't expecting it. That's all," I finish lamely.

"Hey," Trevor's voice is quiet, "it's cool Hannah. I wasn't exactly planning to go out on any dates while visiting my family for Christmas. So, how come you're so tired from dance?" he asks, changing tactics.

"Well, normally on Saturdays I have about six hours of class and rehearsals, plus I had an extra hour of coaching after everyone else. I have a really important ballet competition in a couple of weeks, plus auditions for summer intensives. I have to be ready for them," I relax a bit, relieved to have a safe topic presented to me. "Olivia is competing too, but I don't know if she's going to any auditions." I add.

"So, you basically worked out for seven hours today? Damn, that's a pretty good reason to be tired." I glance at Trevor. He eyes me with a mix of disbelief and respect. "What's a summer intensive? Is it like ballet summer school?" Trevor asks.

I don't answer until I've gotten onto the freeway. I've had my license for about six months and I'm a pretty good driver, but the freeway still makes me a little nervous. "Yeah, it's pretty much like ballet summer school. Most of the really major companies and schools run three- to six-week programs. The really good ones make you audition to get in. A couple of the best schools around the country have year-round programs. Getting into the summer program is the best way to get invited to stay for the year-round program. But they only take the best of the best year-round," I explain.

"And that's what you want? To stay instead of coming back here in September?" Trevor asks.

"Yeah. If you can get into a year-round school, then you have a good chance of getting into a company. The best schools in the United States feed into the best ballet companies. Same with the competition, you can win scholarships to some of the summer intensives and sometimes they even offer people a spot in a year-round program just from the competition. That's why the next few weeks are so important to me," I add.

"You think you're good enough to get in?" I can't tell for a second if Trevor is being sarcastic or asking me a genuine question. I decide to assume he's serious.

"Maybe." I shrug, "I think if I have a good day, I might. I won the top prize for my age division at the same competition when I was ten. Plus, I've been working my butt off all year for this. I mean, I'm not bad, my teacher thinks I might get into one of the top schools." As long as my nerves don't get the best of me, and my shoes aren't ruined. And I have a good bun, and the right leotard, and the right tights. As long as everything goes perfectly, I'll be fine.

Winning that award six years ago was still one of the best moments of my life. Of course, not winning it again the next year had been crushing, feeding the anxious thoughts in my brain. It's hard to live up to your potential on a daily basis, especially when you aren't the same adorable red-head you were at age ten.

"You don't think she's just telling you that to make you feel better?"

Why is Trevor such a buzz kill? "Maybe, but I don't think Ms. Parker would do that to me. She's pretty brutally honest with us. Besides, she knows what she's talking about—she used to be a principal dancer at the Classical Ballet Company and she went to their school. CBC is one of the best ballet companies in the world, she was a big deal in her day. She told some of the other girls in my class they could go for the experience, but she didn't think they should plan on getting in. She makes us all go to a bunch of auditions every year, for the experience. Last year was the first time she told me I should think about going, if I got in anywhere," I add.

"Did you?"

"Get in? Yeah, I got waitlisted for CBS, and I got into San Francisco Ballet School, and State Street Ballet in Santa Barbara. Ms. Parker talked me into going to the State Street Ballet intensive. It's a much smaller school and Santa Barbara is only a two hour drive from Camarillo, plus their intensive was only three weeks long." Ms. Parker thought it was a good place to go for my first intensive, not too far and not too long. I couldn't seem to get her or my parents to understand that I was fully prepared to move to New York the day I turned thirteen, but they insisted I go somewhere smaller for my first time. I explain all this to Trevor as we drive to the movie theater. I park the car and start to climb out.

"Hey," Trevor grabs my arm, stopping me from climbing out of the car. "Are you okay?" he asks.

"Um, yeah. Why?" I ask, surprised.

"Well...you seem a little nervous or something," Trevor replies. Oh. I guess I have been talking a lot. *A lot.* I do that when I'm nervous. Why am I nervous? I don't even like Trevor, I like Tyler. Tyler, what will he think of this, think of me? I need to be charming and funny and put together. Yeah right.

I pull my arm free and climb out of the car. "I'm fine, really. Like I said, I wasn't expecting to be going out on a date tonight. I'm just a bit frazzled, I guess."

Trevor smiles. He has a pretty nice smile. "Well, don't think of this as a date, okay? We're just hanging out, seeing a movie. I'm not interested in a date either." Well fine then, maybe his smile isn't so nice. I glance up at him. Yeah, it is. "You don't know me from Adam, I don't know anyone here at all. I'm going home to Seattle tomorrow and you're off to New York to be a prima ballerina, we'll probably never see each other again. It's just a movie, after all." Trevor throws his arm around my shoulder and leads me towards the movie theater where Tyler and Olivia are already waiting. "Did you hear about how they did the CG for the dinosaurs in this?" He looks down at me. My bewilderment must be obvious. "So, they put motion capture on...."

The movie is okay. A lot of dinosaurs running around and eating people, which seems dumb to me. Why would these people even go to a dinosaur park in the first place, that just sounds like a bad idea. And who thought it was a good idea to recreate giant, dangerous, flesh-eating monsters anyway? I don't get it. I spend more of the movie watching Olivia and Tyler together than focused on the screen. Every time there is a scary moment, and there are lots, Olivia jumps and clutches Tyler's arm until he finally puts his arm around her shoulder, at which point she buries her face in his chest and stays there for the rest of the movie. What an actress. I remember sneaking downstairs one time when we had a sleepover at her house to watch *The Shining* when we were ten and she never jumped once. I was the one hiding behind the couch.

By the time the movie is finished, I'm sad, tired, and want to go home. Trevor is nice enough, and pretty funny, but watching Olivia and Tyler snuggling and flirting is just too much. I glance at my watch—10:00. I think I could make an excuse to go home now without looking like a total loser. "Hey guys," I say, "I'm gonna head home, I have a headache."

"Now?" Olivia asks. "But we were going to go get frozen yogurt!" We were? "Just stay a little longer, please?" Puppy dog eyes. Why is Olivia so good at those puppy dog eyes? Olivia pulls me aside while Tyler and Trevor talk about some motorcycle they just spied in the parking lot. "Please Hannah? If you go home then it's just the three of us… Come on Banana, please?" Ugh, how can I say no to that? When we were little Olivia thought my name was Banana, not Hannah. She only calls me that when she wants something, but I can't say no to it.

"Fine." I sigh. "But only until eleven," I add quickly. "I'm serious Olivia!" I call to her back, but she's already skipping off to join the boys. I can tough it out for another hour. It's not like they've even kissed or anything, right? Besides, I don't want Tyler to think I can't be just as fun as anyone else. So instead of going home to cry and be miserable alone, I decide to stay and fake not being sad and miserable here. "Fine, frozen yogurt and then I'm going home," I tell the air.

We walk over to the frozen yogurt place nearby, Olivia skipping along between Tyler and Trevor. I trail behind, picking at my nails and trying not to stare too obviously at the back of Tyler's head. If I was smart, I would get over this crush. I've had a crush on Tyler for four years and not once have I had any reason to think it would be returned. This is the longest time I've ever spent with him and we conversed awkwardly for all of five minutes while we waited for Olivia to use the restroom after the movie. If only it was so easy, to just tell myself to get over it and I would.

It's one of those self-serve frozen yogurt places, my favorite, and we each grab a cup. I fill just the bottom of my cup with chocolate and vanilla swirl then top it with some strawberries. Olivia has her cup filled with a rainbow of colors and proceeds to see how many kinds of sprinkles and chocolate she can fit on top. Tyler and Trevor's cups are towering mountains of yogurt. Tyler's is a trio of chocolate, vanilla and something neon green. I watch him try to get crumbled candies to stick to the sides. Am I ridiculous to think that it's adorable how hard he is concentrating? And the cute way his tongue is peeking out because he's concentrating so hard?

"I get it now. No wonder you didn't want to come." Trevor says quietly, sneaking up behind me.

"What?!" I jump, startled.

"You okay?" Olivia asks, looking up from her sprinkles. "Trevor, you sly dog! Behave!" she adds with a wink.

Trevor's hand on my shoulder forces me to turn around and face him. "Hey, it's okay, I won't tell anyone," he says with a smile. "I get the whole unrequited thing, trust me." My face is burning, and I don't know where to look. How could he have guessed? I thought I was being subtle. I squeeze my lips together and focus on putting another dollop of chocolate vanilla swirl in my cup. If I don't say it it won't be true.

"Hey." I feel a little push against my hip. "Hannah, it's okay really." I shake my head, silent, too mortified to answer. "Alright, I get it. The strong and silent type. Well, Bruce Banner," who? "As long as you don't turn big and green on me, I'll leave it alone. But your secret is safe with me." Trevor takes my cup and walks off to the cash register with it. I stay where I am, staring at the ice cream machine in front of me.

This is unbearable, I should have gone home. I fumble in my purse, looking for my keys. All I want is to go home and be left alone. I'm having a hard time finding my keys because tears keep blurring my vision. I look up, hoping to see where the restroom is. Olivia is sitting on Tyler's lap, helping herself to his frozen yogurt. Trevor is walking towards them, thankfully no one is looking my way. I hurry down the hallway towards the restrooms when I see one of the employees struggling to pull a large trash bag out the back door. Perfect.

"Here, let me get the door for you," I offer, rushing ahead of them to push the back door open. He grunts and pulls the big black bag out the door behind him, not even looking back to say thank you. Rude, but I don't care, I just want to get out of here before they miss me. I jog back to my car, wiping my eyes and sniffing. Olivia is supposed to be my best friend, how could she do this to me? Why did I stay once I realized what this was? Stupid move, Hannah. I shouldn't even have agreed to the babysitting—I was just so excited that Tyler had even known who I was and was texting me. And then, the chance to be out, on a date, with him there? It seemed too good to be true. I should have known Olivia would be the center of attention, she's always the center of attention, even when she's not.

I glance back at the yogurt place—Trevor is standing outside, holding both our cups, looking at me. Not saying anything, just watching me ditch him. I'm sorry, I'm sorry for just leaving, but I can't watch anymore. I hope Trevor understands, but it doesn't matter, I'll never see him again anyway. I climb in my car and drive home, my heart weighing a thousand pounds.

CHAPTER 5

Olivia

HANNAH IS such a buzzkill. I watch her sneak off to her car, thinking we can't see her, but Trevor and I are both watching her go while Tyler is talking about some football game happening tomorrow. I have no idea what he's talking about, but I nod and "mhmm" as if I'm paying attention, my fingers playing with the hair on the nape of his neck.

I raise an eyebrow at Trevor, wondering if he did something to piss her off, or if Hannah's natural lameness sent her scurrying home. I knew she wasn't going to like being on a date with Tyler and me, but I honestly didn't think she'd get this upset. He shrugs at me, holding two cups of frozen yogurt in his hands, then kicks a chair out from the table we're sitting at and settles into a seat.

"...so yeah, fuck the Patriots. I swear, I'm not even gonna watch the Super Bowl if they end up playing again." Tyler is completely oblivious to my silent conversation with Trevor. I blow out a frustrated breath and try to pay attention to what Tyler is saying. "Hey, where's what's-her-face?" Tyler asks suddenly, looking around. "Did she ditch us?" Uh, duh. I know it's hard to believe that anyone would leave our majestic presence, but it's true. Not that I say this out loud, I finally got my chance for this date and I'm not going to blow it.

"I think so babe," I purr.

"*Hannah* said she had a headache so she was going home," Trevor offers up with a shrug. I smirk to myself at his emphasis on her name. I wonder if Trevor actually likes her. I also wonder if he clued in to the fact that Hannah has a crush on Tyler. Interesting that he covered for her so quickly, I know Hannah well enough to know she probably snuck away when we weren't looking. Too bad for Trevor, he never stood a chance.

Okay, I'm not a completely heartless bitch. Hannah needs to get over this crush, it's been four years—Tyler is *never* going to notice her. I'm doing her a favor, really. The sooner she gets over her one-sided obsession, the better off she'll be. Then she can go off to New York and live out her ballerina fantasy and meet hot dancers out there guilt-free. Really, I'm a saint. Well, saint-ish.

"More ice cream for us," Tyler laughs. Trevor grins, clinks cups with Tyler and starts to dig into both their frozen yogurt concoctions. Gross.

Or maybe she needed to go home to mommy, I think uncharitably when Tyler starts chatting to Trevor instead of me.

Tyler ends up eating half of mine but that's fine, I'm not that hungry anyway. Trevor isn't totally annoying, he's actually pretty funny, so I guess it's not a complete fail. I mean, honestly I'd rather he wasn't here, but I wouldn't make out with Tyler on the first date anyway—gotta keep him wanting more—so I don't mind too much. At least Hannah stuck out the movie before she bailed.

Once we get back to Tyler's house, I give Trevor my patented "evil cheerleader" stare and he hightails it inside, finally leaving me alone with Tyler. "I had a good time tonight, Tyler," I tell him, twisting a lock of hair around my finger. I lean towards him, just close enough for him to catch a whiff of my perfume, then I bite my lower lip and look away. I'm not shy, but I don't want to intimidate him. I peer up at him through my eyelashes. "Did you have fun?" I ask, just in case he didn't follow. He plays football, I don't know how many times he's hit his head.

Tyler steps forward, so close our chests are almost touching. After a quick glance back to make sure no one's peeking at us through the windows of his house, he trails a hand along my arm until his fingers twine with mine. Okay, that's pretty smooth, I'll give him that. Maybe he's more than a pretty face after all. "Yeah, I did. Wanna do it again soon?" Our clasped hands are gently swaying, our arms brushing against each other with the movement. He bends down and presses a soft kiss to my cheek. "I'd really like that, Liv," he adds, smiling.

It's the smile that does it—turns my brain right off. It's small, a little lopsided, a little unsure of my response. At school, Tyler is confident, loud, says whatever dumb-ass thought flits through his mind. This Tyler is a little more vulnerable, a little more sweet. I grin up at him, "Text me," I say and rise up on my toes to kiss his cheek before I spin around and skip back to my car. I give him a little wave as I climb in, then crank up the music for the drive home.

I don't bother being quiet when I let myself into the house since my curfew isn't for another forty-five minutes. Goody two-shoes Hannah Banana is good for one thing, at least. When I told my dad she was coming with us he laid off on the Spanish

Inquisition about where I was going, smiled, and told me to be home by midnight. I guess having a reputation for always following the rules will get you that kind of response. I should remember this trick and use it again.

"Hey Dad," I call out as I walk past the kitchen. He's got his head in the freezer, probably hoping he can find some ice cream. At least it's not Martha, she's probably in bed already. I swear, she goes to bed almost as early as my monster siblings do.

"Hey pumpkin, have fun?" he asks, emerging with a carton of cookies 'n cream. "Want some?" I shake my head.

"Nope, we had frozen yogurt," I pat my flat stomach. "And yes, we had fun. Night Daddy." I kiss the top of his head and make my escape. I think I hear my dad start to say something about babysitting Aiden and Marie, but I'm already halfway up the stairs so I pretend I don't hear him. I tiptoe into the monsters' room, kissing each of those drooly, disgusting sweethearts on the head before heading to my own room.

I flop onto my bed, face buried in my pillow and give a little squeal of happiness. I really like Tyler. He's so hot, and strong, and we will look so good together. He's also not totally dumb, so we may be able to have some actual conversation. Bonus: having a boyfriend gives me a built in excuse to get out of babysitting.

I finally unlock my phone to look at the texts that were buzzing in while we were on our date. I didn't want to check my phone while we were out, I figured if I did then Tyler would think that was okay. And that is *not* okay with me. If I'm going to have a boyfriend, you better believe he is going to pay attention to me when we are on a date. Gotta train 'em right from the beginning.

MEGAN: So...how good a kisser is he?

MADISON: Ugh, Megan don't be such a whore.

ALLYSON: Don't call her a whore, slut.

ALLYSON: JK, you know i love you!

MEGAN: I hate you bitches.

MADISON: No you don't. You love us. Cause we may be bitches but we are the queen bitches

MEGAN: Better bow down when we walk by

ALLYSON: But seriously, Liv. How good a kisser is he?

I love those bitches. Kinda hate them too. I start typing a response when my phone buzzes again in my hand.

HANNAH: Sorry I bailed. Headache.

Sure, Hannah. A "headache." More like your old crush on Tyler reared its ugly head. Well guess what, I won this round. You may have won the family lottery, but this time I'm the one who got the best. I stick my tongue out at an imaginary Hannah and start typing while I change into my pajamas and wash my face.

ME: You may be bitches but you're MY bitches. I don't kiss and tell…..but it was…

I attach a gif of fireworks and explosions. They can take that however they want. They don't need to know if I've kissed him or not. Let them think he's already completely mine, then maybe they'll back off and hook their claws in someone else.

CHAPTER 6

Hannah

"OH MY GOD, my feet hurt so much!" Lisa says, pulling off her pointe shoes. "I have a huge blister, look!" I gag as Lisa thrusts her sweaty foot in my face so I can examine the quarter-sized blister on her heel.

"Gross!" I laugh and shove her foot, knocking Lisa over into Olivia and Katy who are busy packing up their bags too. "I have epsom salts, you can soak it when we get to my house." I add. After a long week at school and an even longer day of rehearsals, I'm excited to hang out with the girls all night. We've been so busy it seems like we hardly see each other, even when we spend hours together at the studio. I can't remember the last time I hung out with Olivia.

I'm trying hard not to think about how the next three weekends could make or break my dreams too much. Even though I know in my head how much hard work I've put in, I can't shake the feeling that one bad day could ruin everything. I'm hoping that the sleepover tonight will keep me distracted so I don't psych myself out of a good audition tomorrow.

"Bye Ms. Parker!" I call out as we leave.

"Bye girls, good luck tomorrow! And don't stay up too late," she calls back from where she's locking up the back of the studio.

"Meet you at my house?" I call to Olivia across the parking lot. Katy swings her bags into my trunk, next to mine and Lisa's, sliding into the backseat while Lisa slides into the front with me. Olivia looks up from her phone and waves.

"I'll be there soon, gotta swing by my house first," she calls, head still down, typing furiously on her phone. She smiles at something on the screen, then hops in her car and pulls out of her parking space.

"Hi Mom!" I say, as we crash through the front door, giggling over the story Katy was telling in the car. "What's for dinner?"

"Hi Mrs. O'Brian!" Katy and Lisa parrot, peeking into the kitchen with me. "That smells yummy, what is it?" Katy adds. The kitchen smells like garlic and yeast and spices.

"Is that falafel?" I ask, peering over her shoulder. Seriously, my mom is the best cook. "Olivia is coming soon, when can we eat? We're *starving*."

"Dinner will be ready and your dad will be home in about twenty minutes. Why don't you go upstairs and I'll call you when it's ready," my mom says, pushing us all back out the doorway and out of our tiny kitchen. We grab our bags and head upstairs to my room. I flop on my bed and plug my phone in to charge while Lisa and Katy grab their chargers out of their bags and plug their phones in too. All our phones are dying because we spent half of our lunch taking pictures and videos of ourselves dancing and posting them on Instagram. None of us have very many followers, except Olivia of course. I'm more of a lurker than a poster. I was trying to get a video of me doing a really hard fouetté turn sequence, but I kept laughing in the middle and messing it up.

"Hey, I have an idea, give me your phone for a second," Katy says. I hand it over and she starts scrolling through my photos. "You should just use the good part of those turns, it will look so cool!" Growling in concentration Katy fiddles with my phone for a minute. "There! How awesome is that?" She tosses my phone over to me and I look to see what she's done. She's made a little clip of me turning, the way she's clipped it I just keep turning forever and ever.

"That's super cool, thanks Katy," I say and post it to my Instagram.

"Is it weird that I'm nervous for tomorrow?" Katy's busy braiding her long brown hair as we talk. "I mean, I know it doesn't *really* matter how I do, since I'm not going to go anyway." She shrugs. "But I don't want to do badly either."

"No, it makes sense." Lisa shrugs, laying out a sleeping bag and pillow on my floor. "Even though you'll be going on all those college visits this summer, you still don't want to embarrass yourself at the audition."

"Where are you going again?" I toss an extra blanket to Katy for her bed. My full size bed is big enough for two people, but I assume Olivia is going to crawl into it with me like usual.

"Colorado State, Alabama, Florida State and University of Arizona. Pity me, I'm going to be stuck in a car with my entire family for three whole weeks, even Cole is coming. Just shoot me now." Katy mimes it dramatically and falls on the floor, writhing.

"Hellooooo!" Olivia calls from downstairs, interrupting our laughter. The lilt of her and my mom's voices drifting up the stairs reminds me of how much simpler life used to be. They chat for a minute before her blonde head comes poking through my door. "Your mom says dinner's almost ready. Your dad was parking right when I got here. Let's go, I'm starving!"

"Are you girls excited for the audition tomorrow?" My dad asks once we're all sitting at the table. I take a helping of salad and pass it to Katy next to me.

"I am," Lisa says, taking a piece of naan bread and passing it to my mom. "Do you remember the audition from last year, Hannah? The class was so fun, even though it was hard."

Katy looks around the table. "It's just a class, right? I didn't go to any last year, remember?"

"You've never gone?" Olivia looks surprised. "It's just a class, but with a bunch of old dudes sitting there judging you the whole time." She laughs as she takes a couple of the falafel off the serving platter and passes it to Lisa.

I grimace at Olivia's joke. "That's not really true." I turn to face Katy, her dark brown eyes throwing irritated glances Olivia's way. "Okay, yes there are people there judging you, but it's not just a bunch of 'old dudes,' they usually have one of the teachers from the school give the class, and a panel of other teachers watch."

Katy ignores Olivia, talking to Lisa and I instead. "We don't have to learn choreography or anything, right?"

"Nope," Lisa answers for us. "Well, I've never been to a summer school audition where we did. Maybe for some of the more contemporary programs, but we didn't last year at the PSB audition."

"Don't stress about it Katy," Olivia adds, helpfully. Katy's shoulders stiffen at the sound. "They just want to see who is paying attention to corrections and if you have decent training. You'll be fine."

After kitchen duty, Olivia insists on taking a shower, so we all scramble around and take showers after her before getting into our pajamas. I finish before Katy and Lisa and am surprised to see Olivia blow drying her hair when I get back to my room. "Um, why are you drying your hair and putting on makeup?" I ask, confused.

"Why not?" Olivia asks, with a shrug. "Hey, we should all do our nails," she adds, walking over to my dresser drawers, looking for my nail polish collection. Not that I have that much. I don't usually wear nail polish, if I do it's just a pale pink or clear. I definitely wouldn't want to wear anything crazy tomorrow at the audition.

I tell Olivia that which just makes her laugh. "Banana you are such a bunhead, it's almost gross." Lisa and Katy walk into my room just then, freshly showered and in their pajamas too. "Please tell me one of you has nail polish? Hannah only has boring colors," Olivia asks, winking at me.

"I think I have some, hang on, let me look," Katy says, reaching for her bag. She pulls out a small makeup bag and dumps it out on my bed. "I have red and purple. Who wants what?" She holds up two little bottles and we proceed to paint each other nails. I refuse to put anything on my fingers, but the purple does a great job at covering up my bruised toenail. Olivia has been checking her phone constantly, which buzzes almost non-stop.

Once everyone's nails are dry we tumble downstairs to watch a movie and pile up on the couch. Olivia sits on the floor in front of us, holding up her phone. "Smile girls!" she says, snapping a pic.

"Wait, wait, do it again, I look bad!" Lisa cries as we look over Olivia's shoulder at the picture. We try a couple more times, until everyone is satisfied with the picture. Olivia taps away at her phone while Katy and I debate between watching Center Stage (for the thousandth time) or going really old school and watching White Nights. I can never decide if 1980's Mikhail Baryshnikov or 2000's Sascha Radetsky are cuter. But what girl doesn't want two amazing dancers to have a dance-off over her? Center Stage it is.

I'm getting the movie ready to play when Olivia runs upstairs. She comes back down a minute later with all her bags, dropping them by the door. "What's up?" I ask. "Did you forget something at home?"

"Uh. No. Yeah, so I think I want to sleep in my own bed. You know." She looks away. "So I can get a really good night's sleep. But, if anyone asks, I was here all night, okay? I'll be back before we have to leave in the morning." Her eyes flash with defiance as she looks at each of us in turn.

"What? But I thought your dad and Martha were in Santa Barbara? Isn't that why you were staying here tonight?" I ask, feeling stupid and more than a little disappointed she's not staying. Why would anyone ask? And why wouldn't Olivia actually be here? A pair of headlights light up my front windows, a second later Olivia's phone buzzes in her hand.

"Gotta go! Say you'll cover for me, please Banana?" Olivia looks up at me with those dang puppy-dog eyes. Ugh. Why can't I resist her?

"But where are you going? And who is that?" I ask, holding onto her arm, not willing to let her go. "Seriously Olivia, who is that and where are you going?" I add, getting worried. Why wouldn't she drive herself home if that's where she's going?

"Relax, it's just Tyler," she laughs. My heart jumps just a little at the mention of his name and I let go of her arm. I can feel a little piece of my heart stabbing me in the chest, thinking about him taking her out so late. "We're just going to go hang out for a little while and then I'll go home and go to bed. Promise. Don't worry Banana, it's fine." Olivia opens the front door and starts to walk out but turns back quickly, "Hey, is the spare key still underneath the old rock?"

"Uh, yeah," I manage to say. Just as Olivia opens the door to Tyler's car I call out, "Text me when you're back, just in case, okay?" Olivia waves and slides in, leaning over to kiss Tyler's cheek. I lean hard against the door jam and watch them pull away. I can feel my eyes getting tight and hot, my throat closing up. I take a second to let the cool night air wash over my face before I close the door. After a moment, I plop onto the couch next to Lisa just as Cooper Nielson is pulling up on his sexy motorcycle and all is right in the world again.

"Did she seriously just ditch us?" I look over and see Katy propped up against the side of the couch, her arms crossed over her chest. I shrug.

"She said she wanted to sleep in her own bed."

"I thought the whole point was that her parents didn't want her to stay alone overnight?" Lisa says, distracted by the dancing on screen.

"I don't know," I huff defensively. "You know what she's like…"

"Yeah. We do." Katy's voice is flat. "You know she probably just used us as a screen so she could be home alone with Tyler?" I gasp, glad the noise is muffled by the movie. I had been kidding myself, deliberately not thinking about her and Tyler together right now. Another stabbing pain in my heart has me curling around the pillow in my lap, holding myself together physically and emotionally. I don't respond. I can't. Lisa pats my knee. I give her a small smile before pointedly watching the movie, chin resting on my knees, heart breaking a little more with each breath.

We're about halfway through the movie when my phone buzzes, jarring me from the movie. It buzzes again, again, and again. What the heck? The only people who would be texting me are in my house right now. Except Olivia. I grab my phone, having visions of her in trouble. I can hear Lisa and Katy's phones buzzing too. Okay, that's weird. Olivia never texts those two. I swipe the screen open and see notification after notification popping up from Instagram. What is going on?

I open up the app and discover that Olivia posted the pic she took of us on my couch with the caption "Dance sleepovers are the best! @hannahbananaballerina @lissssadancer and @kdpops love you!" Our phones are buzzing from all the comments being posted by everyone at school. I guess Olivia had more followers than I thought. I start reading some of the comments, but after the twentieth one saying "guuuuurl! U so gorg!" I drop my phone and go back to the movie. Katy and Lisa have done the same thing. Our phones keep buzzing periodically, which honestly is starting to get a little annoying. I grab my phone to put it on Do Not Disturb, then realize I can't in case Olivia texts me. I bite my lip, starting to get worried, it's almost 11:30, I hope she texts me soon.

"Hey, who's @marvelousStanLey? That's not Tyler is it?" Lisa suddenly asks, looking at her phone.

"What?!" I cough and try again. "I mean, huh? No? I don't think so, pretty sure he's @footballstudStanLey." I pretend not to know, like I haven't stalked him on Instagram for ages and know all of his social media handles by heart. Or that he mostly posts pictures of his abs, pictures at the gym, or lately pictures of him and Olivia. Nope, I don't know that at all.

Lisa stares at me for a second over her phone, one eyebrow suspiciously raised. I smile weakly and pretend to watch the movie. "Um, why?" I ask. Be cool, Hannah. Wait. "Seriously, why?" I ask, curious.

"Cause he just said you're cute!" squealed Katy, throwing a pillow at my head. What?! Katy shoves her phone in my face, "See, right there!" I look and there it is, right in the comments:

MARVELOUSSTANLEY: Hey @hannahbananaballerina, nice pj's. No babysitting tonight?

Oh, that must be Trevor. "He did not say I was cute, Katy. He's teasing me about my lame pajamas." I say, tossing the phone back to her. I try to laugh, hoping to hide my disappointment that it wasn't Tyler. Tyler is probably making out with Olivia at this exact moment, why would he be commenting on her post? I cringe.

"Who's Trevor?" Katy asks, grinning at me. "Wait, is that Tyler's cousin, the one you went on the accidental date with?"

"Yeah. But whatever, he thinks I'm a nutcase," I shrug and grab my phone, hoping to stop some of the notifications so I can concentrate on the movie. "Oh!" I gasp, almost dropping it when I see a follow request from @marvelousStanLey.

"What?" Katy and Lisa both ask, as I throw my phone across the couch in panic. Katy picks it up and looks to see what spooked me. "Oooooo, he wants to follow you? Yeah Hannah!"

"Gonna slide into your DM's, huh?" Lisa laughs.

"Oh my god, Lisa, who says that?" Katy laughs, almost falling off the couch.

"What? No! I mean. What?" I stutter, not sure what to do. Okay Hannah, stop being an idiot. "He's just being nice. I bet he follows, like, thousands of people, it doesn't mean anything." Lisa just looks at me, one eyebrow raised. "What?" I ask, slouching down into the couch. "It's nothing." I add, for emphasis.

"Uh, yeah, no." Katy says looking at her phone. "He follows, like, fifty people. You are special," she adds, with a ludicrous wiggle of her eyebrows. "Hannah has an admirer!" she sings, tossing a throw pillow at my head. I shriek and roll off the couch onto the floor, covering my head with my arms, my phone clutched in the air above my head. Lisa snatches it from my hand before I can protest and starts tapping at it.

"What are you doing!" I cry and try to grab it back, but Lisa holds it out of my reach and Katy grabs my arms, preventing me from taking it. "Please tell me you aren't writing to him?" I beg.

"All I did was accept his follow request and sent him one back, calm down." Lisa says, handing back my phone. "You know you would have done it eventually, I was just saving you time and a panic attack over it," Lisa added, sticking her tongue out at me.

Oh.

Well. Okay. I guess that's true. And I guess Lisa is right, I *probably* would have done it eventually. And she's right that I would have had a panic attack over deciding if I should or not. Whatever. It's still rude. I stick my tongue out at Lisa and Katy, cross my arms over my chest and ignore them, pretending to watch the movie.

Of course, we've missed most of it and I'm only just in time to see the final scene, my favorite scene. "As a boyfriend…you kinda suck!" Lisa, Katy and I all say in sync with the movie a minute later, laughing. I love these girls, even if they're a pain in the butt. I guess I'll miss them when I'm gone.

We clean up our mess and tiptoe up the stairs to my room. It's past midnight and we need to get some sleep for tomorrow. Lisa and Katy grab some blankets and pillows and sprawl out on my floor. I check my phone anxiously one more time, hoping to see a text from Olivia. What I see instead is another Instagram notification.

(HANNAHBANANABALLERINA): marvelousStanley sent you a post by royaloperahouse

What? I mean, I follow @royaloperahouse, that's the Royal Ballet in London's account, of course I follow it. I click on the DM and see he's sent me a clip they posted back in December with some of their principals rehearsing a section of the Nutcracker pas de deux. I remember this one but watch again anyway, enjoying the gorgeous dancing. I don't bother to turn the sound on, I can hear the classic Tchaikovsky music playing in my head. When it finishes, I look back at the message he sent with it and frown.

MARVELOUSSTANLEY: Looks pretty superhuman to me, are you sure you aren't a superhero?

I don't understand, I thought I was pretty rude to Trevor on our "date." I mean, I ran away and ditched him. See, this is why I'm not even going to think about boys. I should be sleeping right now, I need to be ready for tomorrow. The audition tomorrow is way more important than wondering why a boy is messaging me.

I mean, he's a cute boy. And he was nice.

No. Stop it Hannah. No boys. Go to sleep.

I lay on my back and stare at the ceiling, but I'm too wound up to sleep. What is Oliva doing? Should I have let her go? I glance at the time on my phone.

12:31. Why is my left foot itchy? I try to rub it against my shin to sooth the itch without being loud. Lisa and Katy are already asleep. How can they sleep so easily? I close my eyes and picture myself relaxing against the mattress. My comforter is pulled up over my ear, almost covering my face. It's toasty warm.

12:46. Okay, now it's too warm. I can't breathe. I push my nose out from under the blanket and take a deep breath of the cool air in my room. Which leotard am I going to wear? The teal long sleeve one? I love the long sleeve one, it feels so elegant, but then I get the visible sweaty armpits. But what if they want to see that I'm sweating, so it proves I'm working hard?

12:49. Nope, I'm wearing the long sleeves. Yesterday I saw that Insta post from PSB and a bunch of the girls had long sleeves and it looked so good. I'll just be sweaty.

12:53. Go to sleep Hannah.

12:55. Should I have responded to Trevor's message? What would I even say?

12:57. I don't know what to say that won't sound stupid. I'll do it later.

12:58. Seriously Hannah. Go to sleep.

CHAPTER 7
Olivia

I HADN'T REALLY lied to Hannah last night, I really did go home to sleep in my own bed—after Tyler and I watched a couple episodes of Stranger Things and made out on the couch. I kicked him out at two in the morning though. Not because I'm some goody-goody and "saving myself" for someone special or some other BS like that. Nope, I just don't want Tyler thinking he gets to decide when and where we actually do have sex. It turns out Tyler is a pretty good boyfriend. He hasn't pressured me yet and I plan to keep it that way for at least a little while longer. Surprisingly, I like him more than I thought I would. And before anyone accuses me of using Tyler to gain social popularity, I'll have you know I've been used by more than one guy to get in with the popular group at school. I'm not so full of myself that I think a dozen different guys would ask me to homecoming for my sparkling wit and charming personality.

If I'm truly being honest, I may have set my sights on Tyler when I realized that if we were dating, we could protect each other from the constant string of people trying to use us to get a foothold in our social group.

No matter how unromantic my reasons for pursuing Tyler were, I have no intention of becoming one of those Hallmark movie "high school sweethearts who live happily ever after" couples. Like my parents were. Well, like my parents were supposed to be. I'm not going to be the cheerleader who dates the quarterback and gets engaged right after we graduate. I have plans and they don't include staying here. I just want to have fun and enjoy being sixteen. Besides, Tyler isn't even the quarterback, he's a running back.

I silently close the O'Brian's front door behind me and breathe a sigh of relief that the house is dark and silent. It's just after 5:30 in the morning and I was half afraid that Mr. O'Brian would be up already. He's always been an early riser.

Tiptoe-ing through the silent house brings back memories of all the times I spent the night here as a kid, especially when my mom was sick and my dad would stay at the hospital with her. I had a hard time sleeping, so I would sneak downstairs to watch TV in the dark. Mr. O'Brian would take me to get donuts for everyone—plus one extra to split on the way home. Then we'd watch Saturday morning cartoons together while we waited for everyone else to wake up.

I put the pink donut box I picked up on my way over on the kitchen counter. Hannah's probably going to complain about how donuts have too much sugar in them and we should have a healthier breakfast before a big audition, blah, blah, blah. Just as I pull a coffee mug out of the cabinet I hear a light switch on behind me.

"I see you beat me to breakfast," Mr. O'Brian says. "I didn't know Dan let you drink coffee?"

"Um, yeah." I shrug. I don't really know what to say. Mr. O'Brian and I used to be able to chat about anything and everything, from school to clothes to cartoons. I think I talked to him about my mom's illness more than anyone else over those donut and cartoon mornings.

"How are you, Olivia? Still up before the sun I take it?"

"Oh. Uh. yeah. I'm good. Busy you know, school is so much work. But I'm okay." I stumble. The coffee maker is slowly filling my mug and I will it to fill faster. "I bought donuts." I add, waving my arm towards the table.

"I saw. Think I'll make some scrambled eggs and bacon to go with them. Then, Hannah won't freak about the sugar," he adds with a smile.

My mug is finally full so I grab another and pop in a coffee pod to make Mr. O'Brian one. "That sounds delicious." I pause. "Want to split the extra with me?"

"Is it chocolate with sprinkles?"

I nod my head. "Always."

"Don't tell Anne. She says I need to watch what I eat." Mr. O'Brian grins conspiratorially at me.

"Your secret is safe with me." I laugh and go to cut the donut in half before plopping on the couch to sip my coffee and nap until everyone else wakes up.

"What time did you get here?" Hannah plops down on the couch next to me, already dressed. I can see the mock turtleneck of her favorite long-sleeved leotard peeking out from under the jacket she's wearing. Her voice drops down to a whisper, "I was really worried about you."

I eye her for a moment. The makeup on her face is light and natural. If I didn't know what she looks like without it I'd have a hard time telling if she even had any on. But I can tell she's got concealer on under her eyes. I grunt to myself, taking a sip of coffee so I don't have to answer. I bet she's mad at me for making her worry, not because she was worried, but because it meant she didn't get the good night's sleep she's convinced she needs. Perfect Hannah needs everything to be *just right*, and I've ruined the start to her day. "Breakfast!" Mr. O'Brian calls from the kitchen, saving me from Hannah's death stare.

Breakfast is a mixture of sleepy yawns and irritated glances being thrown my way. Thankfully, with Mr. and Mrs. O'Brian here, the girls can't voice their opinions of my decision to sleep at home without getting themselves in trouble for letting me go. Checkmate.

I FLICK HANNAH'S butt while we wait our turn. She turns around to glare at me, but I just grin. I swear she hasn't taken a full breath since we walked into the room an hour and a half ago. I throw in a wink just to make her mad, then I move up in line with the other girls in my group. I love this part of class, grand allegro is my favorite and this one is a doozy. It's so ridiculously hard and I'm dying to try it.

You could have heard a pin drop when the teacher, Marco Bethelo, started it, "And, relevé passé, close behind, then relevé passé close fourth en pointe. Then pas de bourre en tournant into a fouetté, a fouetté, a fouetté, and a double..." I mean, fouettés are hard enough, turning on one leg while whipping the other one around to start again will knock you off balance in a heartbeat, but to get into them with almost no preparation?

I. Love. It.

The turns go straight into a series of leaps, zig-zagging across the floor. Going from high speed spinning to literally flying across this giant studio is going to be a trip. It makes me almost glad I came today, although sleeping in would still have been better.

The group of four girls I'm part of is next up, so we arrange ourselves in a diamond shape in the corner and wait. Then I'm off, I bend both knees, then spring up onto pointe on one leg, then the other, before I throw myself into the series of turns. I manage to get two good turns in, before spinning out of control. I put my foot down quickly and do an ungraceful spin to catch up to the next part of the exercise. I jump, my legs gracefully pushing underneath me as I take off to leap. I can feel myself flying, my arms outstretched in front of me and for a moment I'm weightless, before I quickly head the other way for another leap. The girl in front of me didn't travel across the room as far as I did on the first side, I may have cut off the girl behind me to get past her, but she'll adjust. We finish and scurry out of the way. I turn and watch Hannah in her group. Katy is in her group too, but I don't bother watching her. Katy and I have a bit of a frenemy situation going on these days. Probably because I kissed her brother Hunter last Halloween. Whatever.

Hannah is definitely one of the best dancers in the room, especially when she stops overthinking everything and just dances. When she really dances, Hannah looks like she could explode with joy, it makes you want to watch her. Not that I would ever tell her. She manages to pull off the whole turn sequence with barely a bobble, although I think she probably could have done a triple turn at the end instead of a double, but she plays it safe, typical. I bet she only did two so she wouldn't be late on the music. Her long legs sometimes make that hard for her. I knew distracting her for a second was a good idea. You're welcome, Hannah.

Me? I'm a little more of an all-around pretty good dancer. I do a lot of stuff decently, but not one thing better than all the others. But my real strength is that I'm fearless. I'll try anything. I figure that the worst thing that could ever happen to me already did, so what do I have to lose now? Double pirouette into a somersault? Why not? A grand jeté landing into a roll on the floor? Done it a thousand times. Audition in front of a famous former dancer? No sweat. Not literally, I'm sweating like a pig right now, but you know what I mean.

We get a chance to try it again on both sides and I manage to do better on the second try. At least I don't spin out this time, even if I feel like my jumps aren't quite as high. This late in the class, my legs are heavy and feeling my lack of sleep last night. Hannah goes for a third turn and is late getting into the next step but she manages to catch back up. Katy falls out of her turns and crashes into the girl behind her. She's rewarded with a dirty look from the girl she knocked over as they take off leaping across the room. I notice Marco Bethelo raise an eyebrow at the woman sitting next to him at the table at the front of the room, I bet that girl just lost her spot in the intensive. No one wants to work with a bitch.

The audition finishes and we curtsey, thanking the teacher and pianist, like the good little ballet robots we are. The pianist was really good though, so I genuinely smile and make eye contact with her when we clap at the end of the class. Anyone who decides to play "Pokerface" for degagés is a-ok in my book.

"So, how did it go girls?" Mrs. O'Brian asks, tucking her finger in her book as we troop over to gather up our bags and clothes.

"Pretty good," Hannah says, dropping onto the floor next to her to gather up her stuff. "It was hard, but good."

"Oh my god, it was so much fun," I pipe up, pulling my sweats on and pulling a make-up remover wipe from my bag to wipe off my sweaty face.

"Ugh, I totally messed it up," Katy complains. "I hate fouettés on pointe." I offer her a makeup wipe, which she reluctantly takes. I manage not to roll my eyes at her. I wish she'd let it go already, Hunter and I would never have worked out. But I play nice because 1) Tyler and Jack are best friends and 2) the Quinn's house is where we all hang out, especially in the summer since they have a pool. As Tyler's girlfriend and a cheerleader, I have a standing invitation.

"Did you guys see that girl in the purple leotard? She did double, double, single, triple the first time we went to the left." Thank you Lisa, easing tensions since fourth grade. "It was crazy!"

"Yeah, she was really good," Hannah bites her lip nervously. This time I don't bother to hide my eye roll. I don't understand how she gets so nervous, she won the freaking Jean Field Award at YIGP when we were ten, or as I like to call it, the "Child Prodigy Award." Obviously she's an amazing dancer.

"Hannah Banana O'Brian, knock that shit off. You were one of the best dancers in the room." I can hear the eye roll in my tone as I say it, oops. I glance at Mrs. O'Brian out of the corner of my eye and mouth "sorry" to her when I see her looking. "Seriously, Lisa and Katy agree with me, right?"

At their nods, Hannah sighs and shrugs. "She was still really good."

"So what? Just because she was good doesn't mean you aren't," Lisa points out. How do they put up with Hannah's need for reassurance all the time? Has she always been this needy? I don't remember her being like this when we were younger. Maybe I just blocked it from my mind.

"I don't remember her at all, was she in my group?" Subject change so we can be done with the needy portion of this conversation.

"Yeah, she was behind you. You cut her off the one time in the grand jeté."

Oops. "Oh. Wish I could have seen it, it sounds impressive," I add.

We throw the rest of our stuff in our bags and head out to the O'Brian's SUV and pile in. "It was cool, but then she was late on everything else, so I don't know if they'll like that or not," Hannah points out slowly. Finally, she's showing some backbone again. "It's PSB, musicality is a big deal." she adds with a shrug as she buckles up in the front seat. I'm squished in the back with Lisa and Katy, but at least I managed to score a window seat.

We spend the rest of the hour drive home dissecting the audition class. I don't hang out with these ballet girls much anymore, but I have to be honest I'm enjoying it more than I expected, especially now that Hannah isn't fishing for compliments. I forgot how much fun these girls can be. My cheer bitches only ever want to talk about boys, clothes, and gossip—celebrity or otherwise. It's nice to have a conversation that actually uses a few extra brain cells. But I'd never tell them that.

CHAPTER 8

Hannah

TUTUS? CHECK.

Good tights? Check.

Spare tights? Check.

Pointe shoes? Check.

My English teacher drones on, but my mind is fully occupied with making sure I haven't forgotten to pack something. Someone is asking me about the symbolism of the green light. Green light? All I can picture are the bright stage lights that will be shining in my eyes tomorrow.

Extra pointe shoes, soft shoes, bandaids, second skin, and toe tape? Check, check, check, check and check.

Hair stuff, make up, emergency supplies? Double check.

A voice by my head is speaking in Spanish. "¿Donde esta la estacion de trenes?" With a start, I realize the question was directed at me. I quickly think back to what was said and pull an answer past the endless litany of checklists in my head. Where is the train station?

I quickly glance down at my Spanish book and grab the first building name I see. "Está al lado de la universidad." I just need to get through two more periods and then I can forget about school and focus on what's important.

Did I check all this last night before I went to bed? Absolutely. Am I convinced I forgot something? You bet.

The day is a blur until I sit down next to Lisa at lunch.

"Did you pack a nice dress for the awards?" Lisa has her own list in her hand, double checking she didn't forget anything either. At least she'll have a chance to go home and grab anything she forgot before Katy and her mom pick her up before driving down for the competition. "I have 3 leotards per day, is that enough?"

"I only packed two, one for the morning classes and a spare so I don't have to wear a sweaty leotard all day." I peer over Lisa's shoulder at her list to see if she has anything I forgot. Warm ups, pajamas, extra clothes, toiletries, phone charger. All there.

My mom is picking me up after school to drive two hours south to Orange County for the Youth International Grand Prix regional semifinals. Technically, the competition starts tonight with optional classes, but the real competition doesn't start until tomorrow morning. The whole weekend is a combination of master classes and onstage competition. We're performing our ensemble Sleeping Beauty excerpt, plus a couple of us are competing solos. Lisa is doing her Lilac Fairy variation, Olivia has a contemporary solo, and I'm competing three solos–Aurora's wedding variation, Kitri's Act One variation, and a contemporary solo. There's some younger girls also competing but I've been so worried about myself I haven't really paid attention to who's doing what.

"I wish I could have skipped school today," Katy says, flopping down next to us. "I'm surprised you didn't Hannah."

"I have tests today. My mom said I had to be here." By the time the bell rings for the end of lunch, the three of us have gone over everything we've packed. Only a math and a biology test stand between me and the most important weekend of my life. I can do this.

I'm waiting for my mom to pick me up after school, when Olivia crashes past me, Tyler in hot pursuit. "Sorry!" she calls over her shoulder. "Tyler, don't you dare! I have to go!" she shouts as Tyler catches up to her and tosses her over his shoulder. He smacks her butt, hard by the sound of it, and she shrieks with laughter as he jogs them both over to her car. Is it weird that seeing him touch her like that makes my breath catch and my stomach clench? Yeah, that's weird. Stop it, Hannah. He's not even breathing hard when he puts her down. I can't seem to tear my eyes away from them as he leans down to kiss her, caging her in between his arms as he leans against her car door. My breath is coming faster as he slowly pulls away from her, tucking a strand of hair behind her ear.

"Hannah!" my mom calls and I start. Oh my god, I'm such a creeper. My face on fire, I run over to the car and hop in, checking to make sure all my stuff is in the back. I keep my head turned to the back seat until I can catch my breath and feel my face cool off.

"Hey sweetie, how was school?" she asks. She pulls out of the parking lot and we hit the road to Orange County and my next chance at my dream. I tuck my hands between my thighs so I don't do something totally weird like fan my face.

"Uh..." I try to gather my thoughts. All I can see are the muscles of Tyler's back and arms flexing as he scooped Olivia up. "Good, it was good. Math test was better than I thought it would be." I manage to spit out.

"That's good. Gosh, it feels like it's been ages since I picked you up from school. I miss hearing about your day in the car," my mom grins at me. "So, ready for this weekend?"

"Yup. I think. I mean. Yes." I nod my head decisively. "I'm nervous, but I have to just do it now. You know?"

"This is always the hardest part, the waiting right before it happens. Walk me through what you're nervous about." My mom always does this when I say I'm nervous. She has me tell her all the things I imagine could go wrong and then we think of a plan to solve all of those problems. It usually helps. "What are you nervous about right now?"

"Well, we could get stuck in terrible traffic and get there late." I start.

"Well, there is definitely going to be terrible traffic, we are driving through LA at four in the afternoon. But, that's why we left now, remember? If there's no traffic we'll just get to the hotel super early and have time to shower. And if it takes longer we will still be there by dinner time. I'll take you to the master classes and then go check into the hotel without you. Absolute worst case, you skip the classes and get an early night. Good plan?"

I yawn and consider it for a second. "Yes. Good plan. Okay, so what if I have a terrible class tonight and it makes me anxious for tomorrow?"

"Well, did you talk to Ms. Parker about it?"

"Yeah, she said that I should take the class tonight easy. Focus on getting a good barre in and don't worry about anything. It's an optional class, no one is judging it." Technically, Ms. Parker said that if I got anxious I should skip class and do my own barre at the hotel, but I desperately want to take any chance I can to be seen by the teachers here.

"Well, that sounds like a good plan to me."

"What if I get a run in my tights?"

"You have extras packed. Worst case, I'll go buy you new ones."

"What if I get my period?!" Visions of the beautiful pale peach tutu I borrowed from Ms. Parker with a red stained crotch assault my mind and my breath starts coming faster and faster.

"Didn't you just have it a week ago? I packed tampons just in case, anyway."

Oh. "Um, yeah. Okay. I forgot." Trust my mom to remember the details.

We go back and forth like this as we slowly crawl through LA traffic. The sun is shining through my window, warming me. Leaning against the window to feel the warmth on my face, the gentle rumble and rocking of the car lulls me to sleep.

"Come on Hannah. Just leave it." Olivia pulls me away from the door. "Let's go make up dances in your room," she pleads.

"Okay, but why is my mom crying?" I saw my mom hugging Olivia's mom and crying while they were sitting on the couch. Even my dad and Mr. Beck looked like they were crying, standing there kind of helplessly. "What's going on Olivia?" I asked, pulling my hand free of hers.

She looks at me with her big blue eyes and shrugs. "I don't know, they won't tell me," she whispers. "My mom's been going to the doctor a lot, but no one will tell me what's going on. But I don't think she's pregnant again. They would tell me, right?" Olivia's voice drops down to a whisper. Her mom got pregnant a year earlier when we were in fifth grade and Olivia was super excited to finally be a big sister. I was too, but then her mom had a miscarriage. It was so sad.

Olivia and I had been planning all sorts of fun things to do as big sisters. I'm not sure which one of us was more disappointed.

We tiptoe into my room and close the door. "What kind of dance do you want to make up?"

"I don't know. Maybe I don't want to make up a dance anymore." Olivia flops on my bed and pulls a book out from under her.

"Give me that!" I squeak. "That's my diary, you're not allowed to read it!"

Olivia rolls over onto her stomach, a gleam in her eye. "Ooooooooo, does it have anything juicy in it?" She grins and starts to open the cover, moving in slow motion. I'm frozen and just stand there, staring at her.

"Fine," I huff, crossing my arms. "I just got it, I haven't really written anything in it yet." Sometimes, if I give in right away Olivia gets bored and stops doing whatever thing I just told her not to do.

"Hmmmmm," she starts reading, stopping to waggle her eyebrows at me over the edge of the book. "Gasp!" Yes, she really says gasp, like the drama queen she is. "Tyler Stanley?" Oh no. I was hoping she wouldn't get to that part. "You think Tyler is cute!" Olivia giggles and starts making kissing noises. "Hannah and Tyler, sitting in a tree K-I-S-S-I-N-G!" she sings at me like a lunatic.

"Ugh!" I flop down on the bed next to her. "I know, it's dumb. I just think he's cute. He looks kinda like Ross Lynch. I know he'll never like me back, okay? I just like looking at him." I sound so dumb.

"Ah, Banana, you never know! And he does look like Ross Lynch. Maybe you guys will be like Austin and Ally, except with dance instead of singing," Olivia says, handing me back my diary which I immediately stuff inside my bedside table.

"Um, I don't think Tyler can dance," I say, dead serious.

"Oh my god, I bet he totally can not dance at all," Olivia dead-pans back and we collapse against each other laughing at the thought of our awkward sixth grade selves dancing with a boy, let alone Tyler Stanley.

I wake with a start as Mom pulls the car to a stop. My mouth is dry and gross and my neck is sore from sleeping in the car. "Almost there Hannah. I'm going to drop you off at the venue, then I'll go check in okay? Ms. Parker is already here, she called about fifteen minutes ago. Go find her and I'll be back when classes are over, okay?"

We pull into the parking lot of a high school. I look up at the grey, stone building and take a deep breath. A dozen girls and a few guys are scattered around the entrance to the theater, some chatting, some stretching. You can tell they're all dancers since the girls almost all have their hair up in a bun and are wearing warm up suits, the colored embroidery on the back identifying which studio they're from. My black warm up pants and jacket with the simple white "Camarillo School of Classical Ballet" logo embroidered on the back is packed in my dance bag for later. I recognize some of the logos on the backs of their jackets from previous competitions. I think one of the girls with a black and red jacket was at the auditions last weekend, her face looks vaguely familiar. YIGP is a prestigious competition, so most of the dancers here are from pre-professional ballet schools all over Southern California and even Arizona and Nevada.

As my mom pulls up to the curb I lean back and grab my dance bag. "Should I leave everything in the car?" I ask.

"Do you have a leotard and tights in your dance bag?" I nod my head, of course I do. "Then leave the rest, I'll take it to our room. You don't need any of it, right?"

"Nope. Thanks Mom. Love you!" I lean over to let her kiss my cheek before I hop out of the car. I can see Ms. Parker talking to some other parents from the studio, so I head that direction.

When I get close, I stop just next to Ms. Parker and wait, bouncing my knee nervously, while she finishes up her conversation with the mom who was talking to her. She gives me a smile and gently lays her hand on my shoulder. My knee stills and I take a deep breath. As the mom starts walking away, Ms. Parker pulls me in for a hug.

"Hi sweetie, I'm glad you're here. You feel okay for tonight?"

"Yeah, I think so. Should I go change?"

"Sure, if you want to. You have about forty-five minutes before the class starts over there," she points to a building just next to the theater. "The classes are in the studio there, they have the bathrooms in there open for you guys. Why don't you go change and come back here so we can make a plan for tonight?"

After a quick nod, I take off for the studio building where there's a locker room with benches and a long mirror wall. I quickly change my clothes and throw my warm up suit on. I have leg warmers on underneath the pants, a ballet skirt hanging over it and a long sleeve shirt under the jacket. I park myself in front of the long wall of mirrors to do my hair.

I brush my thick red hair until there are no tangles, then I flip my head over and gather it up into a high ponytail, making sure to comb out any bumps or stray hairs. Once my ponytail is secure I divide it in two, then start twisting one half tight. Once it's twisted I start wrapping it around my ponytail, pinning it in with large hairpins as I go.

"Oooo, I love a good cinnamon roll bun," someone says, startling me. "Hi!" A tiny little dancer waves at me in the mirror.

"Hey," I say, eyeing her in the mirror as I keep pinning my hair up. I don't know what else to say, meeting new people is not my thing. I concentrate on doing my hair, pulling a hair net out of my bag and wrapping it around my bun so no stray hairs escape.

"I'm Mae Ngyuen," the pixie continues as she sprays her bun with hair spray. "Want some?" she says, offering me the can.

"Oh, uh, thanks." I reach for the can and give my hair a spray. "I'm Hannah O'Brian," I add. We grab our dance bags and head out the door. She seems to know where she's going so I follow her to the studio where the class will be held. We silently pull a barre into the center of the room and start stretching.

"You're the only person I've seen who looks older than twelve since I got here. You are older than twelve, right?" Mae asks from her spot on the floor. I glance around awkwardly, not wanting to be rude, but these barres only have space for four people on them. Katy, Lisa and I promised that whoever got there first would save spots for the others. I was including Olivia in my count, but with Mae at the barre there wouldn't be any space for one of us.

"Yeah, I'm sixteen. Is anyone else from your studio coming?" I hope the answer is yes, maybe she'll go join them once they get here.

"Nope, just me." Shoot.

"Hi Hannah," Ms. Parker says, coming inside the room, claiming one of the chairs along one wall.

"Is that your teacher?" Mae's voice is barely a whisper. I glance down, her mouth is hanging open, her eyes are wide like she's just seen a celebrity. "Your teacher is Leslie PARKER? Like, LESLIE Parker from CBC? THE Leslie Parker?"

I grin. These days I'm so used to Ms. Parker, I don't think about how famous she is. "Are you doing a solo?" I ask, anxious to change the subject.

"Yeah, one of the Paquita ones, the one from the pas de trois with the entreche quatres in the beginning." Oh, I love that one.

"That's a good one. I worked on that one a few summers ago, but that cabriole section was killer for me." I say over my shoulder as I stretch my calves in a down dog pose.

"Yeah, I know. Those cabrioles are the bane of my existence! I've got a contemporary as well. What about you?"

"I'm doing Aurora's wedding, Kitri's Act One, the one with all the pirouettes, and I have a contemporary too."

"Oh man, that Kitri variation is the best! Are you using castanets?" Mae exclaims. "I always wanted to do that one, but my teacher says I'm not old enough." Mae looks me up and down, trying to decide if I'm old enough for that variation.

"How old are you?" I ask. I mean, honestly, she could be twelve, but I have to assume she's older after what she said in the locker room.

"I'm fourteen. I know, I look like I'm ten," Mae grins, "but I'm in high school, I swear." I just nod my head in response, breathing deep as I hold a deep lunge, stretching out my hip flexors.

Since I'm sixteen, I'm in the senior division, for fifteen to nineteen-year olds. The twelve to fourteen-year olds compete in the Junior division and there's a Pre-Competitive division for nine to eleven year olds.

I have to admit, I'm relieved I'm not competing against her, she is so flexible and her balance is ridiculously good. I watched her hold a perfect arabesque for almost a minute while I was warming up my feet. Yup, really glad we're in different divisions..

"You feeling okay now, Hannah? I need to go get the other girls ready." Ms. Parker gathers up her things and waves to me before she heads out the door. She passes Katy and Lisa on her way out who wave and beeline for the empty spots on our barre.

"So, how early did you get here?" Katy asks before she sees Mae laying on the ground across from me. "Can I take this spot?" Katy asks before dropping her water bottle at the foot of the barre.

"Yeah, sure." Mae nods her head vaguely towards the empty spot. Her hands are currently occupied in pulling her left leg behind her shoulder. "I'm Mae," she adds.

Katy looks her up and down, appreciation for Mae's flexibility in her eyes. "Katy. What studio are you from?"

"South Coast Ballet Academy, are you from Hannah's studio?"

"I'm Lisa, yeah, we are. How do you know Hannah?" Lisa interrupts, sounding a little suspicious.

"Oh!" Mae laughs, "I forced myself on Hannah when she got here, since I'm here all by myself. You guys are so lucky to have Leslie freaking Parker as your teacher. Oh my gosh, if I was you, I would watch videos of her dancing like every weekend. Oops!" Mae's rambling is interrupted by her own leg swinging back down to earth and knocking over her water bottle. "Anyway, tell me how amazing it is to have Leslie Parker for your teacher."

Katy and Lisa are looking at me with eyebrows raised almost up to their hairlines. I cough uncomfortably, "Well, I mean. She's an amazing teacher. But we don't really obsess over her too much. She's just, I don't know. Ms. Parker to us." I shrug.

"There was definitely about a year though where I watched videos of her every weekend," I add, laughing. I can't deny the truth. I was starstruck when I realized who she was, but that was years ago. I was about eight when I realized how famous Ms. Parker had been back when she was a principal dancer at The Classical Ballet Company in New York. There are videos of her performing with them in different TV specials, and even a short documentary that was made about her before she took over the studio in Camarillo.

Leslie Parker had been a prodigy—accepted to CBC as an apprentice when she was fifteen, joined the corps de ballet at sixteen, and by her nineteenth birthday, she was promoted to soloist. A year later she was made a principal. She danced every leading role you can imagine, had ballets created on her and was going to be the most famous ballerina of her time. But when she was just twenty four, as she was crossing the road in front of Lincoln Center, she was hit by a motorcycle and was knocked into the curb. The doctors said she would never walk again after the way her pelvis was broken, let alone dance. I once heard her tell my mom her back still hurts her every morning, but you would never know it to see her in class. She doesn't ever lift her legs high, and she doesn't ever really jump, but I always forget she isn't doing those things because the rest of her is so exquisite when she demonstrates an exercise for us.

I keep looking at the door to see if Olivia is coming. Class is supposed to start in five minutes and she still isn't here. I wonder if she sent me a text? I'm about to cross the room and dig my phone out of my dance bag when a tall, lean man walks in the door. He crosses the room with confidence and a dancer's graceful walk. I do not want to be the girl who was on her phone instead of paying attention, so I stay put. The quiet murmur of conversation that had been filling the room dies down to an expectant silence as we all wait for the instructor to begin the class. No one wants to be the first person to start talking again.

"Hello everyone," the man says, pulling off his shoes and jacket, carefully placing the shoes under the chair set in the corner of the studio and precisely hanging his jacket on the back. He has a distinct French accent and moves with absolute confidence. "My name is Jean-Paul Phillipe. I am a former soloist with Vancouver Ballet, founder of the BalletIMAGINE and one of the judges for this weekend. Is everyone ready?" With that, he claps his hands and everyone scrambles to take off all the extra layers of clothes we're wearing while we watch and listen to him demonstrate the first exercise at the barre.

CHAPTER 9

Olivia

YEAH, NOPE. That man is an asshole and I do not want to take his class.

I've been hovering outside the doorway listening to him talk for the last few minutes and I don't feel a need to subject myself to that.

"No, no, no. Not like that. Like that…is a stupid way. Is not efficient, you see? Now, you try this way. This way is the right way." I'm late to the class and I just know this French dude is going to rip me a new one if I walk in now.

I mean, is it my fault if there was really terrible traffic? Or that my awesome boyfriend made me leave forty-five minutes late because he insisted on buying me Starbucks before I left?

I have two options right now—I can walk into this class, stand there like a meek and mild ballet robot while this asshole tells everyone how awful I am for being late, or I can go find Ms. Parker and watch the pre-competitive competition that's going on right now. I would add going to the hotel and hanging by the pool as option number three but 1) it's February and 2) Mrs. O'Brian has my hotel key since I'm staying with her and Hannah. My dad is only coming down on Sunday to watch the groups and the awards.

I don't know what time the pre-competitive competition starts, but I know that Haley, Anna, and MacKenzie are competing solos tonight. They're a trio of really cute ten-year olds that dance at Ms. Parker's, sometimes we hang out in the lobby between classes. MacKenzie and I like to make Insta stories together cause she looks like she could be my little sister. Fake little sisters are much more fun than real ones.

Mind made up, I head over to the auditorium, eyes peeled for Ms. Parker and the stage door. I wander through the door and find her surrounded by three little munchkins in tiny tutus all clamoring for her attention. I check my phone as I walk in the door.

TYLER: Hey babe, how's the competition?

Well, he tries, right? It's cute how he doesn't get it. When he took me to coffee before I drove down here, I tried explaining how the weekend worked to him but I wasn't sure if he really got it or not. I had to make him promise not to show up tomorrow night with signs or an air horn. The big sweet dummy.

ME: Going okay. The teacher was a real asshole so I'm skipping the class and helping the little kids instead.

"Ms. Parker, will you fix my hair when you're done with Anna's?" Haley pulls at her bun, a lock of smooth black hair trailing down her back, bobby pins sticking out in every direction. Her half Korean heritage gave her the most gorgeous thick black hair, but I know from Lisa how hard it is to get it up in a secure bun.

"Is my makeup okay?" MacKenzie asks, trying to push her face into Ms. Parker's space while she's busy pinning Anna's hair into a perfect bun at the nape of her neck.

"I got you Haley!" I say, pulling her in front of me and pulling the pins out of her bun. "Hi Ms. Parker," I add. "Need some help?"

"Hi Olivia." Ms. Parker pulls a pin out of her mouth to smile at me. She looks a little flustered, not that I can blame her with these three munchkins twirling around and pestering her with questions. "Help would be great. I sent their parents away so we could get ready in peace. I didn't think I might need an extra set of hands." I grin at her from behind Haley's hair.

"You girls being pests?"

"I'm just so nervous!" Anna says, wringing her hands together. "Olivia?"

"What's up?"

"Is Hannah here?" I want to roll my eyes so badly, but notice Ms. Parker eyeing me so I restrain myself. Barely.

"I think she's in a class right now."

MacKenzie's face pops up between Ms. Parker and me, a bouncing blonde blob in my peripheral vision. "My mom said we could watch you guys do your contemporary solos tomorrow. Is she before or after you?" I shrug.

"Olivia is up first tomorrow, Hannah is after. I'm so glad you girls are going to come support Olivia and Hannah, that's the kind of attitude I like to see." Ouch. Man, Ms. Parker is really dishing out the guilt trips today.

I keep pulling the pins out of Haley's bun, pretty sure there are more pins than hair. "Haley, who did your hair?" I ask.

"I did. It's my dad's weekend and he's even worse at it than I am." Haley looks embarrassed, her eyes a little glassy. I give her shoulders a quick squeeze before I start combing her hair back and re-doing the ponytail.

"Oh, trust me, I know how that is. When my dad had to do my buns, they were a mess until I figured out how to do it myself. And then they were a different kind of mess until Ms. Parker taught me how to do them properly." I don't tell her I only ever let my dad do my bun once while my mom was sick and I wouldn't let him touch my hair after she died. Only my mom was allowed to do my hair, not him. My mom had the most beautiful golden hair, just like mine. I remember how she would brush it for me when I was little and she never pulled when there were tangles. I've wished so many times that I hadn't made her stop doing it after my tenth birthday. I was so grown up, I thought only babies let their mom brush their hair. Now, I would give anything to have her back, so she could do it for me one more time.

Ms. Parker never said anything about my hair always falling out that year, but she would quietly squeeze my shoulders and fix it while she kept class going, never making me feel bad about it or stopping class to make a big deal of it. Once, I happened to get to the studio early and she saw me struggling to do it myself, so she patiently taught me. She even let me practice doing a bun on her own long silky hair.

"One of these days I'll teach you how to do it yourself, but for today we want it to be perfect so I'll do it for you." I tell Haley as I pull her dark hair through the ponytail holder. I look up to see Ms. Parker smile at me and mouth "thank you" before I go back to pinning Haley's hair.

MacKenzie bounces in front of me. "Smile!" She's holding her phone up and takes a selfie of her and me, my hands buried in Haley's hair.

"Hey chica, how you feeling?" I ask around the bobby pin I have in my lips, opening it up with my teeth before I slide it into Haley's hair.

"I'm so nervous!" MacKenzie's big blue eyes are wide and shiny, her stage makeup making them look even bigger than usual. Her hair is perfectly pulled back and her blue tutu glitters with rhinestones. "But I'm pretending I'm Hannah, she never gets nervous or messes up." She's bouncing on her toes and spinning like she can't keep still, while I can barely contain my sarcastic laughter. Hannah never gets nervous my ass. The girl is a walking, talking bundle of anxiety at these things.

"MacKenzie, go do pliés again," Ms. Parker eyes her with a raised eyebrow, jerking her chin towards a handrail in the hallway that is serving as a barre for several other girls.

"But…"

"Go. And this time do it slowly, pliés should take longer than thirty seconds."

MacKenzie scampers off to find a spot along the hallway and I finish up Hayley's bun. Ms. Parker hands me a matching purple rosette for her hair and I pin it in. "Thanks Olivia!" Hayley squeaks as she turns around and gives me a hug. Her long purple and white tutu swishes around her legs as she hurries off to join MacKenzie.

I feel my phone buzz in my pocket.

TYLER: Do I need to beat someone up?

This is followed by a gif of some MMA dudes going at it. He tries.

"Do you want to tell me why you're here helping me, instead of in class where you're supposed to be?" Ms. Parker asks me in a suspiciously casual voice once she sends Anna off to join her friends. "I'm grateful for the help, especially with these three, but you should be in class."

"I got here late. I didn't want to be rude." I explain with a shrug.

"And?"

"And I watched for a minute and he seemed like the kind of teacher who was going to yell at me and make me feel bad. So I decided I would rather come help you."

"And why were you late?"

"Traffic was bad and I left a little later than I planned on." Please don't ask me why I left late. I'm crossing my fingers behind my back, hoping. "Um, should I go help them warm up?" I venture, hoping to distract her.

"You can go do barre with them after you tell me why you were late."

Damnit.

"Tyler took me to Starbucks and it took longer than I planned. I'm sorry Ms. Parker, it won't happen again," I add, like a good little bunhead. But Ms. Parker sees right through me.

"Olivia, I know that doing this competition isn't the be all, end all for you. But you did commit to being here, so you need to see that through. Don't let yourself down by being distracted. By a boy or by anything else. I know you, if you give it 100% you'll be happy with the weekend no matter what, but if you know you're giving less than that, you will regret it."

Ugh, I hate it when she's right. And she's right so many times, it's not fair. I do want to do well this weekend. I don't want to be a dancer, I don't need to win anything this weekend to prove myself. But I want to do well because I've worked hard for this, even if some people think I haven't, and I want to get on stage and perform because that's the best part, All the hard work is only worth it when you get to go on stage and just dance your heart out.

"I'm sorry, you're right. I'm focused, I promise." And I am. I mean, I will be. I probably shouldn't tell her that Tyler is planning to come watch the competition tomorrow night. I wonder if I should warn Hannah? Nah, I'm sure she's over her little crush by now. It's been almost a month, right? Besides, she probably won't even see him, knowing her, she'll spend all her time backstage worrying and won't come out into the audience at all.

"I'm not trying to make you feel bad or guilty, I just want you to finish this weekend feeling good about yourself, not disappointed," Ms. Parker wraps her arms around me for a quick hug. "Go. They're too wound up to listen to me right now, but they'll copy you." she sighs. "Go be the good example they need, and give yourself a proper barre while you're at it."

I pull my phone out as I make my way to join the littles, smiling at Tyler's texts.

TYLER: You still want me to come tomorrow, right? What time? I have practice until 2

ME: Yes please, I need someone here to cheer me on. Text me when you get here and if I can sneak out I will, but no promises. You can sit at the back inside the theater.

TYLER: Do I have to sit in the back? Am I in trouble?

I send him a gif of Judge Judy rolling her eyes.

TYLER: Got it. Sit in the back. Don't bring a sign. Clap like it's a golf tournament. Don't make noise. Any other instructions, ma'am?
ME: Ha. Ha. Ha.

Should I say anything about avoiding Hannah? I think about it, but it will probably just make it worse if the big dope is trying to be stealthy.

ME: Nope, just can't wait to see you after xoxo

CHAPTER 10

Hannah

*D*ON'T CRY.
Don't cry.
Don't cry.

My throat is tight, my jaw is locked, and my eyes are burning. Everything I did was wrong. I can hear Lisa and Katy talking to Mae as we pack up our bags, but I don't listen. It's background noise to the pounding of my heart and the voice in my head.

Don't cry.

Don't cry.

Don't cry.

My eyes are burning, my head is pounding, and my breath is shaky. Why am I even here? I was the worst dancer in the room. Tears blur my vision as I pull my warm up pants on. I can't blink, if I blink the tears will spill over. Too late.

Don't sniff.

Don't sniff.

Don't sniff.

My cheeks are wet, my nose is running, and sweat is still dripping down my temples. I was so terrible Jean-Paul had to stop the class and correct me after almost every exercise. I pull a towel out of my bag and roughly rub it over my entire face, hiding the fact that I'm wiping my eyes, not just my sweat.

"Hannah?" Lisa's voice breaks through my silent litany.

"Huh?"

"Are you okay?" she asks, concern written all over her face.

I look around and realize that we're the last ones left in the studio. I shrug my shoulders, but don't say anything because I know I'll start crying if I do. I grab my bag and stand up to walk out the door. I hear Lisa following me but I'm lost in my own thoughts.

I can't believe I danced so terribly.

Jean-Paul Phillipe was right when he said we were doing it all wrong.

Why did I think I could do this?

My legs were shaking and heavy before we even finished the barre.

He kept picking on me, pointing out all the things I was doing wrong.

I couldn't even land a single pirouette.

No wonder Jean-Paul kept correcting me, I was doing everything wrong. That's what he kept saying.

I messed up every exercise, I couldn't get a single combination right.

"Are you even listening to me?" I stop walking when Katy and Lisa block my way. "That class was awful. I swear he was trying to make us dance badly on purpose," Katy says, exasperated.

I silently shake my head. If I open my mouth to speak, all the thoughts in my head will come tumbling out. I don't want to say what I'm thinking, I know if I do I'll see on my friends' faces that they agree. I couldn't bear it.

I pull a shaky breath into my lungs, a little hiccup at the end of it. Concentrate on breathing Hannah.

I take a couple more shuddering breaths, trying to calm my mind and focus on nothing else. I know the girls are talking but I'm not listening. I wish my mom was here.

"Hey girls," Ms. Parker calls to us as she walks up. "How was class?"

"Um…" Katy stalls. "Honestly? It was awful."

"What do you mean?" Ms. Parker sounds concerned. I can feel her eyes on me and I shrug.

"Well, he made the exercises really tricky. Like, almost impossible." Lisa explains. "And then every time we did an exercise, he told us we were doing everything wrong. He kept saying that our teachers taught us everything wrong." I hear a choked sound, then I realize that I made it.

"He was picking on Hannah a lot," Lisa adds. "He singled her out after almost every exercise to correct her. He was pretty mean about it."

Ms. Parker pulls me into her arms and I bury my face in her shoulder. I try taking another deep breath, but as I exhale the tears just come spilling out. I can't hold back the sob that breaks free. Ms. Parker is making soft noises and rubbing my back as I hold tight to her and cry. I don't want to cry, I don't want to show anyone how deeply that terrible class affected me, I'm supposed to have a thicker skin than this. I want to be a professional one day, I need to be tougher than this. But I just can't help it, the tears and sobs are ripped from my gut, I'm so disappointed in myself and how I danced. This whole weekend is doomed to fail if this is how it starts.

"Shhhhhh, shhhhhh, it's okay Hannah. One bad class isn't the end of the world." I hear her saying. My breath comes out wet, shaky and gross, but I can't control it.

I feel more hands rubbing my back and, as much as I love that my friends want to help me feel better, my shoulders scrunch up towards my ears unconsciously. Ms. Parker must know how I'm feeling because she pulls me in tighter, subtly pulling me away from the other girls hands. I squeeze her in thanks and take another breath to calm back down.

"Okay, let's just break this down for a second, girls." Ms. Parker starts saying over my head. I don't move but I listen intently. "One bad class isn't going to be the end of your week-end. I'm not happy that the first class you had broke you down, instead of building you up. That's not how it should be. So this is what we're going to do—you're all going to go back to the hotel where you will take a nice hot bath or shower. Then, you eat a good dinner and at nine, you're going to come meet me in my room, okay?"

"Do we need to wear dance clothes?" I manage to ask.

"Nope, come in your pj's." She smiles down at me, then smiles at each of us in turn. "Everyone got it?" We all nod our heads and I pull myself upright, sniffing hard. My face is flushed and blotchy and my eyes feel swollen and red but I don't cry.

Ms. Parker looks like she's about to say something else when Olivia appears with three of the little girls from our studio in tow. "What's up?" she asks, looking around at our glum faces.

"Was the class that bad? I knew he looked like an ass..." she catches herself. "Um, he looked mean." she finishes.

"Colorful language aside, you were right to sit this one out," Ms. Parker answers. "Excuse me girls. I think I need to speak to the organizers. I'll see you all at nine. Room 319." She looks down to the three littles bouncing at Olivia's shoulders, then quickly gives them each a hug. "You three danced beautifully, I'm so proud of you." She looks at Olivia. "Will you make sure they get back to their parents?"

Our group breaks up after that. Olivia takes the girls into the lobby to find their parents, Ms. Parker heads inside the theater with a determined look on her face. Lisa and Katy walk over to the parking lot to look for Katy's mom. They're probably trying to give me a moment alone to get myself together. I slump down against a concrete planter and bury my face in my hands. A cool ocean breeze blows over my sweaty hair, sending a shiver through me. I scrunch down tighter, wrapping my arms around my knees, face hidden.

Was I really that bad? Maybe I've gotten cocky, too full of myself, tucked away in our little studio. I know I won awards at competitions when I was younger, but I never thought I was any kind of prodigy. I did think I was maybe good enough to be a professional one day. It's what I've wanted since our moms took Olivia and I to see our first ballet. Would Ms. Parker truly encourage me to pursue this if she didn't think I was good enough? I never thought she would give me unrealistic expectations. My mind is racing so fast I feel dizzy.

I feel bodies plop down on either side of me, sandwiching me between them. When an arm pulls me sideways I collapse into it with a shaky sigh. "He was such an asshole." Katy says, squeezing me tight. "I know master teachers are supposed to be tough, but that was ridiculous. I mean, he was just being cruel, and I *cannot* believe he called that one girl fat!"

"He called someone fat?!" Olivia screeches from in front of me. "Oh, hell no. Hang on." Before I even registered she was standing there, Oliva turns on her heel and runs back towards the theater lobby.

"Huh. I wonder what Ms. Parker will think of that?" Lisa muses from my other side, rubbing my arm. I hadn't even felt it until now. "Do you remember that one guest teacher we had? The one from England? I remember her telling us about how Rudolf Nuryev used to purposefully make exercises impossible, just to make people mess up. And he would get *pissed* when they got them right. I think some people just need to feel superior." I sniff and sit up, checking to make sure I didn't drip snot or something disgusting on Katy.

"Yeah. But..." I start to say before Lisa shushes me.

"Nope, no buts. Katy's right. He was an asshole who just wanted to take down the best dancers in the room to feel superior. He didn't pay attention to anyone who wasn't super good. He barely looked at anyone else." Lisa points out. "He spent the whole class correcting you, Mae, and that guy in the blue t-shirt."

I hadn't noticed at all, actually. I'd been nervous, scared and struggling to keep up with what he was saying to me. When he wasn't talking directly to me, I was watching myself and practicing in the mirror, trying to fix all the things he said I was doing wrong. I didn't stop for a second to see how he was treating anyone else, other than to assume everyone else was feeling as crippled as me.

"Really?" I ask. "I'm sorry you guys, I didn't even notice." And now I feel awful again for being such a bad friend.

Someone kicks my foot. Hard. "Ow!" I exclaim, even though it didn't hurt. Looking up I see Olivia standing in front of me again, a little out of breath but grinning. "What?" I ask, suspicious. I know that grin. That's Olivia's "someone is in trouble but it isn't me" grin.

"Dude, Ms. Parker is in the lobby ripping the organizers a new one!" Olivia squeals. "She is so pissed! I've NEVER seen her this mad before, ever!" she adds with a bounce. "Come on!"

We scramble to our feet and follow her, but stop short in the doorway of the theater lobby. Ms. Parker's hair is coming out of it's loose braid and her face is deadly cold.

"...fat! Didn't you do any research at all? Anyone who knows anyone in this business knows that Jean-Paul Phillipe is a self-centered, self-aggrandizing, pompous ass who should never be left unsupervised around children! You know why he was available for your dates? Because *no one else will hire him!*"

An older woman is facing Ms. Parker, her eyes wide but steeled. Her silver streaked hair is pulled back into a low bun and she has the slightly gaunt look of a former dancer. She murmurs something to Ms. Parker but we're too far away to hear it.

"No, I will not keep my voice down, these parents should know what their children are being subjected to, under *your* watch. I expect an apology, in person, to my students and if he is teaching any other class this weekend, I will pull my students from every class and tell every other teacher I know to pull theirs as well. He will not go near my students again. Ever." Ms. Parker crosses her arms against her chest and stares at the woman, daring her to explain away the situation.

Wow. Ms. Parker is fierce. Part of me wants to hide and pretend that this isn't all my fault, and part of me wants to shout "Amen!" and stick my tongue out at the woman facing my beloved teacher.

There are about ten other adults in the lobby standing frozen, shocked at the outburst between the two women. I recognize a couple of parents from our studio when they slowly move to flank Ms. Parker in her standoff. After a moment, all but one of the other adults in the lobby join them, creating a formidable wall around the event organizer. I almost feel sorry for her. Almost. She pinches her lips together and puffs up, like she's about to argue. Ms. Parker leans in close, daring her to speak.

"The ballet world is a small one, and I'm not exactly a nobody. You wouldn't want it to get out that your event sanctions and harbors abusive teaching staff. Now would you?"

CHAPTER 11

Olivia

*J*UST BEFORE nine, I lead the way from our room, Hannah creeping along behind me. My stomach is stuffed full of the burger and fries I'd eaten at the hotel restaurant. I'd wanted to go to the diner on the end of the pier, but Hannah and Lisa were worried we'd be late getting back so I got out-voted. I texted the squad girls my irritation—the beach was *right there* and I'd really hoped to get my toes in the sand—but tucked my phone back in my pocket after getting a pointed glare from Katy's mom for having my phone out while we were eating.

At nine o'clock on the dot, I knock on Ms. Parker's door. I'm not waiting for Hannah to do it, she's barely spoken since we left the theater. Katy and Lisa are walking down the hall towards us, coming from the room they're sharing with Mrs. Quinn. All of us showered and in our pajamas, as instructed. I don't know what Ms. Parker has planned, but it better be good if she wants to get these gloomy grumps to cheer up before tomorrow.

"Hi girls, come on in," Ms. Parker opens the door, a smile on her face. "Feeling any better?"

I ignore the chorus of voices behind me. Damn. Ms. Parker went all out. Her laptop is plugged into the room's tv, boxes of Red Vines, Gummy Bears, and M&M's litter her bed and once I get inside the room, I can smell the freshly popped popcorn I spy in a tub on the table.

"Make yourselves comfortable," Ms. Parker sweeps her arm around the room. I shake my head at the nervous looks on the other girls faces and flop onto the king-sized bed in the middle of the room.

"Ms. Parker, you know how to throw a pity party, that's for sure!" I push aside the teeny bit of guilt I feel for having evaded the mind-games Jean-Paul put everyone else through and plaster an extra big smile on my face. I guess extra-perky Olivia is making an appearance tonight. Someone has to get these girls to cheer up and I have a feeling it's going to take both Ms. Parker and I to make it happen. Something crunches underneath my hip. Curious, I reach down and pull a set of face masks out from under me. I wave them in the air, one eyebrow lifted.

Ms. Parker laughs at my exaggerated face. "Yes, those are for tonight. Pick one for yourself Olivia," I take one then hand them over. "Here girls, you each take one." After staring at her for a moment, Katy reaches out to take them, handing one to Lisa and another to Hannah. Finally, someone else is acting like it *isn't* the end of the world.

"Here," I take the lead, reaching over to pluck Katy's from her hand and rip it open, scooping the jelly inside onto my fingers. Katy stiffens as I start smearing it over her face, then giggles. If I can pretend everything is ok for long enough, maybe I can get the other girls to relax and enjoy themselves. I've had plenty of experience at pretending I'm fine even when I'm not. Lisa laughs and pulls Hannah over to a mirror so they can goop up their own faces.

"Hold still or I'll stick it up your nose," I warn Katy when she doesn't stop giggling. Her eyes flick to the side and a tiny snort escapes her. "Ew, Katy! Don't you dare blow snot on me or I really will stick it up your nose." I glance over at my shoulder and see Ms. Parker smearing a neon orange mask on her face. She grins at us and glances over at Lisa and Hannah putting on their masks, laughing at each other.

"Where's Mr. Mike?" I ask, looking around the room for Ms. Parker's husband. He was her physical therapist after her accident—I think it's so romantic how they fell in love while he helped her recover. Hannah and I even got to go to their wedding when we were seven, Ms. Parker looked like an angel in her wedding dress.

"Oh, he stayed home. He's having a boy's weekend with his nephews. Come on girls, I found the perfect show to watch." I finish putting Katy's mask on and go to wash my hands in the bathroom before putting on my own. Maybe I won't have to pretend to have fun all night, if we can get Hannah out of her funk, then the rest of us might actually be able to enjoy the chance to hang out with our teacher.

We all pile on Ms. Parker's bed, careful not to get goop on her sheets, and watch a silly Canadian tv show about a competitive dance studio, laughing at the ridiculous drama, listening to Ms. Parker's stories about being in CBC and her time training at their school.

We're four episodes in and fully invested in the drama between Michelle and Emily, bursting into fits of giggles whenever Emily's

Canadian accent slips out, when Ms. Parker speaks up. "So, how are you feeling? Are you ready to tackle tomorrow?" Ms. Parker's voice is casual. Too casual. Hannah's face falls, her shoulders slumping, fingers toying with the gummy bears in her hand.

"I don't know." She stops to blow out a hard breath. She's silent for a bit, but I can see the wheels turning in her head. I bite my tongue, now is not the time to crack a joke, even if the tension in the room makes me want to. "It was hard to think about anything in the class. I was so confused and so determined to do what he wanted but I couldn't. My body just...wouldn't do it. And I couldn't think straight while I was dancing. It's just a blur." She sighs and leans against a pillow, closing her eyes. Honestly, I can't help feeling like she's overreacting. It's just one fucking class, not her whole life, but what do I know.

"It felt like my mind was screaming at me to do what he wanted, but I physically couldn't get my body to do it. It was like my brain and my body were in two different places. Like, my brain was listening and taking it in, but my body was somewhere else." Hannah shrugs again. I hadn't realized how upset she had been while she was dancing. That nagging feeling of guilt resurfaces, making me feel bad for missing out on the same traumatizing experience as the other girls. "I don't know how else to describe it. But that is the worst I have ever danced, I wish I had skipped it like Olivia. What if this ruins the rest of the weekend?"

"Ok, this goes for all of you, even you Olivia," I know she's digging at me for skipping the class, but I'm definitely not sorry now. "That man was not a teacher. He wasn't trying to teach you anything, he wasn't trying to share his knowledge. He was belittling you in order to make himself feel important." She looks at each of us in turn. "There's an old school of teaching ballet that believes the only way to teach is through bullying, belittling and guilting students into perfection. To weed out the weak, to toughen you up. Anything less than perfection is failure. This is how they were taught and the only thing they know. They are so impressed with themselves they don't believe there is a better way."

"But—" Hannah starts to say.

"Nope, let me finish. They get results, but at what expense? How many dancers quit because of the emotional and psychological abuse they've been put through? Dancers who could have been amazing, if their training hadn't broken their bodies and minds. But it's not the only way to teach." Ms. Parker shakes her head, looking sad. There must be more to that story. "Don't you think you work just as hard for me every day as you did for Jean-Paul Philippe? You work hard because I've taught you that the satisfaction of working hard *is* the reward, that the pursuit of excellence is the goal and whether you achieve it or not isn't the point."

Ms. Parker turns a fierce eye on us. I hold still, despite wanting to cheer for my beautiful, bad-ass teacher. "At the end of the day, I don't put my self-worth, my opinion of myself as a teacher or a person, in *your* hands. Whether or not any of you go on to be professional dancers isn't going to hurt my feelings. I only care that you leave me ready to go be amazing humans, no matter what you choose to do with your lives."

The tv plays in the background as we sit on the bed, absorbing Ms. Parker's words without speaking. I eye the other girls and Ms. Parker, guilt and thankfulness warring inside my chest. When I think an appropriately respectful amount of time has passed I grin before speaking up. "I told you he looked like an asshole." This sets us all laughing, Lisa throws a pillow at my head and I slide off the bed, onto the floor where I stay, giggling too hard to climb back onto the bed.

We watch one more episode before Ms. Parker makes us go back to our rooms to get some sleep. Hannah looks happier than before which is a relief since I have to share a bed with her. She's a restless sleeper when she's upset.

I follow Hannah back down the hall to our room, pulling my phone out of my back pocket, swiping on notifications. I need a little relief from the heaviness of Ms. Parker's speech. My phone is guaranteed to deliver some smart-ass content and a break from all the seriousness.

> **MEGAN:** Ditch those bitches babe and get your ass to the beach
> **MADISON:** Too cold for the beach
> **MADISON:** It's so boring without you here. Why'd you ditch us?

There's a text from Allyson separate from the group chat. I have to smirk at her cattiness. Reading it makes me glad I have Tyler and don't have to worry about getting on her bad side anymore. She has an annoying tendency to claim a new boy every week and god forbid one of us comes between her and her pick of the week.

> **ALLYSON:** At the Quinn's, the boys are playing Madden. Megan is trying to get Jack to notice her. Or is it Hunter? I can't tell from here. Doesn't matter. Could be either. Or both.

ALLYSON: Would telling her that her boobs are about to fall out of her top be being a good or bad friend?

That girl is ridiculous. Entertaining as hell, but ridiculous.

There's a message from Tyler checking on me. I pause in the hallway to take a quick selfie and send it to him before hurrying to catch up with Hannah.

"I think my mom's asleep already. Do you need the bathroom?" She pauses in the doorway, looking back at me before tiptoeing inside.

"Nope, I'm good. Just catching up," I wiggle my phone in her face before tossing it on the bed.

"I don't know how you keep up with everything. It would drive me crazy to have my phone blowing up all the time like yours." Our whispered voices remind me of countless sleepovers from our childhood. Everything about spending time with Hannah makes me miss how easy life was back then, but at the same time so frustrated that she expects me to still be the same silly girl I was then. I'm not and I don't want to be.

Anything I say is going to sound stuck up, so I keep my mouth shut and shrug. Hannah's phone hasn't buzzed once all night, everyone who would be sending her texts has been with her all weekend. I don't understand how she isn't bored to death, but what do I know? It took so much effort tonight to get her in a better mood, I don't want to be an asshole and ruin it now.

She's quiet as we get ready for bed, eyeing me when I pause to respond to a text or notification on my phone every few minutes. Fortunately, she goes to sleep pretty quickly, putting her back to me as I scroll through my apps, earbuds in so I don't disturb the princess's sleep.

Just before I go to sleep, an email arrives from the event organizers apologizing and letting us know that Jean-Paul Phillipe has been replaced for the weekend. I smirk. Ms. Parker wasn't kidding when she said she knew people.

CHAPTER 12

Hannah

THE STAGE is clearing and our thirty minutes of time to go on stage to feel it out and practice a few steps as the judges rest between sections is almost over. Open Stage is a crowded, competitive free-for-all. Girls practicing fouettés are kicking people right and left, guys are jumping and practicing landing that double tour en l'air or that double cabriole, just missing each other as they land. Since this is the contemporary division, it's even more dangerous—people rolling on the floor while others practice leaping and landing with a complicated turn or a huge extension. I hate this part, I hate the side-ways glances, the crossed arms and stares if you try to practice a difficult step, like everyone assumes you're showing off.

Now that there's a little more room, I quickly practice a sequence from my solo that finishes with a series of traveling leaps and rolls, praying I don't run into anyone. I couldn't practice it earlier since there was no space, but making sure I won't run out of space at the end helps me feel calmer. I've been surprisingly calm this afternoon, last year when I was getting ready for my solos I was a nervous wreck, but this year feels different. Maybe it's because I'm older, or maybe after five years of not winning the top prize again, I just want to do my best without thinking about how I'm going to place. Ms. Parker and I haven't discussed it once this year, just worked to make my solos the best they can be. It's been a relief to work just for the sake of working, without trying to win anything.

"Hannah?" Ms. Parker asks from her spot in the wings opposite me. I give Ms. Parker a thumbs up and she nods. I dash back to her side of the stage to give her a hug before she heads out to the audience to watch. "You got this sweetie. Remember what we talked about last night? Take deep breaths and really feel them inside your lungs. Dance big, dance bold, and dance with joy." I nod my head at her mantra, feeling confident.

I take a deep breath and smile at Ms. Parker. "Thanks Ms. Parker. I feel ready. I'm good." I give her a quick squeeze before she turns to Olivia to check in with her before leaving. Olivia and I are the only ones from our studio who are competing in the contemporary division, so it's just the two of us backstage this afternoon. Later tonight, when it's time for the classical variations, it'll be just me and Lisa.

Olivia is busy stretching, earbuds firmly in her ears, jacket zipped up to her chin. Her blonde hair is smoothly slicked back to a low ponytail, a deep part over her right eye, an olive green scarf tied around the ponytail to match her costume. In the darkness of the wings, her dramatic stage makeup makes her look older than sixteen. My hair is twisted tightly into a smooth French twist, my lips are bright red, my cheeks are contoured and the deep smokey eye makeup I'm wearing makes my blue eyes pop.

Unfortunately, one of my false eyelashes is just a little bit off and keeps poking the corner of my eye. Hopefully I have enough time to take it off and re-apply it before my classical variations later tonight, because it is really annoying.

Olivia and I are scheduled to go eleventh and twenty-ninth out of thirty contemporary solos. I'm bummed that Olivia gets to go first and I have to wait until almost the end, I hate being at the end, but it means I can watch her dance without feeling stressed that I'm next.

I sit down next to her and silently start stretching my own legs and feet. We don't talk, just sit in comfortable silence through the first four solos, each lost in thought and focused on getting our bodies ready. Occasionally, Olivia points to something on the stage and makes a face or mouths "Wow," and I shake or nod my head in response when someone does something impressive or cringeworthy. The second competitor, I recognize him as the guy wearing the blue t-shirt yesterday, is really amazing. He moves like liquid across the stage, then flies through the air like he's weightless. One of Olivia's silent exclamations is accompanied by her fanning herself, which makes me giggle. I mean, he is also pretty cute and his costume is just a pair of flowy silk pants which shows off his toned abs, which I won't complain about. I elbow her and she smirks, then leans in close to whisper in my ear.

"What number are they on now?"

I listen for the announcer as I see a girl in the wings across from us hopping up and down, getting herself ready to go on. A muffled voice comes over the speakers and she sedately walks to center stage and stops, twisting her arms above her head, knees bent. "She's number eight, I think." I whisper, nodding my head towards the girl who just started dancing.

Waiting is the worst part.

I alternate between stretching, hopping around to stay warm and fiddling with my shoes and costume while we wait. I'm wearing a plain navy blue leotard, no rhinestones, frills or skirt to hide behind. It's got long sleeves and a high neck with big patches of matching navy mesh criss-crossing my arms, stomach and back. I used special glue to stick the bottom to my butt so it doesn't give me a wedgie while I'm dancing, since I'm not wearing tights for this solo. My skin-tone pointe shoes feel hard against my bare feet.

When the tenth competitor gets called on stage, Oliva hops up, pulls her warm up pants off and unzips her jacket. I take them so I can hold onto them while she's dancing. I don't trust anyone else not to step on them backstage. I stand with her in the wings while she waits, bouncing from one bare foot to the other trying to stay warm.

The dancer on stage finishes, bows and runs off stage. As the audience applause dies down the announcer says Oliva's name and she steps out of the wings to take her place on stage, standing with her feet flat, arms relaxed at her side, chin up and gaze lifted to the back of the audience. She looks confident, poised, and utterly sure of her place in the world. God, I'm so jealous.

I hear a single, deep voice give a lone, "Whoop!" in the silence, then her music plays. She starts swirling, twisting and moving across the stage. Her movements alternate between smooth and sharp—twisted and broken one moment and almost sensual the next. She's mesmerizing.

Her solo finishes with an abrupt freeze, as if she's about to take off and run straight off the stage. It gets me every time. The audience erupts into applause and I hear that deep voice again. Is that her dad? I thought he wasn't coming today? Besides, he knows better than that. Ballet competitions are sedate affairs, there's generally not a lot of whooping and hollering in these theaters.

"You were fabulous," I whisper to Oliva as she comes off-stage. I hand her back her clothes. Olivia's sweaty and flushed, breathing hard but she doesn't meet my eyes as she pulls her pants on and shrugs into her jacket.

"Thanks," she whispers back, finally, zipping up her jacket. "I'm going to go grab my water bottle." Without waiting for me to reply, Olivia slips out the side door and disappears backstage, leaving me on my own.

I turn and watch the guy who's currently dancing on stage. He's okay, I guess. He doesn't look like he's been training for very long, maybe a year or two. He's really strong, but not very graceful, he still has that stiff hesitation that only goes away when you've been dancing for a long time, that innate confidence in how to move your body, the trust you have that your body will do it right without conscious thought.

Just as he finishes his solo, I feel a buzz in my pocket. I pull my phone out to see an instagram notification.

> **(HANNAHBANANABALLERINA):** marvelousStanley sent you a post by...

I unlock my screen to see a message from Trevor. It's a post from an account called @biscuitballerina, a video montage of dancers falling on stage. Part of me wants to laugh and part of me is cringing so hard it hurts. I don't know if I can find this funny right now, just as I'm about to go onstage myself. Watching all those falls is making me nervous, so I ignore the video to read the text he sent with it.

> **MARVELOUSSTANLEY:** I hoped this would make you laugh before your competition today. Break a leg! But not literally.

How does he know I'm competing this weekend?

I don't have time to think about it, I need to focus. I switch apps before it can distract me again, put my earbuds in, find the music for my solo and mentally go through it with the music, concentrating on visualizing myself doing it perfectly. I get distracted halfway through wondering how Trevor knew I was competing and have to start the music over. This time I check to make sure I have space then practice a section with sweeping arm movements, feeling my body stretch from side to side before wrapping up tight around my torso. I let the music play to the end, half listening and half wondering about Trevor. Ugh. Focus Hannah. Focus. This is why I don't date.

Starting the song over, this time I close my eyes and just listen to my song, *It's Fine, But It Hurts* by Nico Casel, the ethereal notes building to a crescendo and then falling back down to near silence. I love this piece of music, Ms. Parker and I picked it out together. The moment I heard it, I felt it in my soul—the building of the notes, the ebbing and flowing of the piano, the yearning it makes me feel. I love dancing to it, I feel like I'm being pulled and stretched inside my skin as I flow across the stage, hovering on the verge of exploding or collapsing.

I channel my yearning to pursue my dreams, the swooping sensation of riding a roller coaster, the nervous excitement I felt when Tyler sent me that first text, the peaceful feeling of curling up on the couch with my mom, the little hiccup of happiness I feel when I see a message from Trevor and the confusion I feel whenever he sends me a message. I even grab hold of the weird obsessive feeling I had watching Tyler and Olivia in the parking lot after school yesterday. I take all those feelings and listen to my music over and over again, finding places in the music and the movement that match each of those sensations until they're all interwoven in my mind and body. A swooping, stretching, building, sinking, breathless thing that is ready to pour out of me the second I step onto the stage.

I wait and watch the dancers before me, slowly creeping towards my turn. I turn my phone over in my pocket, debating responding to Trevor's message. Olivia's been gone for awhile, but maybe she's just relaxing in the dressing room. I wish she was here, I waited for her before she went on and kept her company, but maybe that was her dad after all and she went to go see him. My phone buzzes in my pocket again.

Do I want to check? What if it's Trevor again? But what if it's Olivia or Ms. Parker? I debate checking it and ignore three more buzzes from my phone until the end of the solo currently on stage. I only have four more to go until it's my turn. With a huff, I pull out my phone and check to see what it is.

> **MOM:** Break a leg sweetie!!!!! Dad and I are so proud of you, love you forever!!!
>
> **MS. PARKER:** Deep breaths, you got this Hannah. I'm proud of the work you've done, now's the time to dance big and bold.

KATY: Good luck, you're gonna be amazing!!!! (Lisa
is yelling at me to put my phone away but she says
good luck too)
OLIVIA: Sorry I bailed, my stomach hurt. Good luck chica!

Relieved and cheered by the messages, my thumb hovers over the Instagram app icon. Should I respond to Trevor? I open up the app and idly scroll through our message thread. It's mostly Trevor sending me random photos of dancers, dogs and pretty landscapes, mixed with memes and jokes. There are a few short responses from me and a photo or two I've sent back, but no real conversation. Today's text is the longest he's sent yet.

HANNAHBANANABALLERINA: Thanks for the vote of
confidence. It definitely put my mind at ease to watch that
right before going on stage.

I add an emoji with its tongue sticking out, then slip my phone in my pocket, unzip my jacket and tuck it in an out of the way corner of the wings, so I'm not tempted to keep looking at it. I wonder again how Trevor knew about the competition today. I know I didn't post anything about this weekend, and I know I never mentioned it in the few messages we've exchanged since our weird, almost date in January.

Focus Hannah. You have more important things to worry about right now. Boys are a distraction. I hear the announcer introduce the dancer right before me, so I push the worry from my mind and focus. Time to get my head in the game. I pull my warm up pants off and focus on breathing deeply, stretching my arms and shoulders out, bouncing up and down on my toes and jumping a few times to get my blood flowing and my heart pumping. I feel good, a bone-deep sense that this is my time, I'm ready.

CHAPTER 13
Olivia

"**B**ABE!" TYLER calls from near the front of the building as I emerge from backstage. I quickly glance to make sure no one from the studio is around before running and jumping into his arms. His strong arms wrap around my back, easily holding me up as he kisses me. "That was epic!"

I laugh, like this mountain of muscle knows anything about ballet. "Thanks," I say. "Sorry I'm still kinda sweaty." Tyler shrugs and bends to kiss me again. I briefly respond, loving the taste of his lips before I remember where we are and squirm to get him to put me down.

"So...we have about forty-five minutes before anyone misses me, what should we do?" I ask. "Wanna go get something to eat?"

"Honestly babe, that was so fucking hot, I kinda wanna just take you to my car and make out with you for the rest of the night. I didn't think anything could be hotter than you in your cheer skirt, but that was...." Tyler grins wolfishly.

"Buy me a coffee and then I'll make out with you in the car," I tease back. I know I promised Ms. Parker I would focus this weekend and I am. I swear. But have you seen the muscles on this boy? They're kind of hard to resist. Not to mention how sweet he is for driving two hours, in traffic, just to watch me dance a two minute solo. I can't ditch him now, that would make me a terrible girlfriend.

Besides, I can focus when I'm actually in the theater, I don't have to think about ballet every second of every day to be focused for this competition. "Let's go!" I laugh, jumping on his back like a monkey and pointing to his car.

Tyler runs to his car with me on his back, not even breathing hard, and we peel out of the parking lot to the nearest coffee shop. As he's driving, I study his face. I wasn't sure if he would really come all the way down here just to watch me dance. "What? Is there something on my face?" he asks.

"Nope, just admiring you,"

"Take a picture, it'll last longer," he teases, flexing his bicep for my benefit. "You're not dancing again tonight, are you?"

"Nope, I just need to be there to cheer for the other girls when they do their classical solos." Technically, I should be there right now for Hannah's contemporary solo, but she doesn't need me. Not really. She's so self-sufficient, she probably doesn't even realize I'm not there. Self-sufficient is being generous. Honestly, self-absorbed is probably more accurate, but ballet isn't a team sport. She's focused on herself because she has to be, even if it is annoying. Her goal this weekend has to be to stand out on her own, not be a perfect robot in the group.

True to my word, we get coffee and snacks, then head back to the theater where Tyler parks his car in the far corner of the parking lot and we make out like the teenagers we are. I'm glad it's dark already and everyone is probably inside. We alternate between sipping our coffee, kissing, snacking and listening to music, while I keep an eye on the time.

"So..." I say as Tyler pops a handful of chocolate-covered espresso beans in his mouth. "Do you want to stay and watch the next section? I could sit with you?" On the one hand, I don't want him to think he drove all the way down here just to see me for an hour, we don't get to see each other that much as it is. But on the other hand, I know Ms. Parker won't approve of him being here and I don't know what Hannah will think of him being here.

I know it wasn't exactly nice of me to invite her on that double date, but I'm not such a bitch that I would purposely sabotage her this weekend. But tonight would be so much more fun for me if Tyler stays. I don't want to be with the O'Brian's all weekend. I love Mrs. O, she's awesome, but being with her is hard. Every time I catch her looking at me with the same sad eyes my dad does, it reminds me that my mom *isn't* here. If my mom were still alive, this whole weekend would have felt more like a girl's trip than a ballet competition. I miss her so much.

"Nah, I think I'll bail, I can only take so much ballet," he winks, then pulls me in for a kiss. Equal parts relief that I don't have to make the decision and disappointment that he doesn't want to stay floods through me. I try to relax into the kiss, but it takes a few sweeps of Tyler's tongue against my lips to truly forget and just enjoy the moment, the sweetness and fire of his kiss. Tyler's hand is warm against the back of my neck, pulling me closer. His hand slowly drifts down my neck, fingers gliding across my collar bone. I squirm a little, not wanting him to explore any lower. The sweetness of the moment fades rapidly as self-consciousness creeps up on me—I have a leotard on, and it's not sexy. If Tyler's going to get his first feel of my boobs, 1) it's not going to happen in the parking lot of a ballet competition and 2) I better be wearing something sexier than the ratty, old, black leotard that I threw on when I changed out of my costume. His hand starts drifting lower, yeah, he's definitely trying to get to my boobs now.

A sharp tap on the glass startles us apart. I look up to see Hannah's confused face peering down at me through the window. The confusion turns to hurt as she realizes exactly where Tyler's hand was when she interrupted us. "Shit," I scramble to grab my bag and make sure all my stuff is in it. "I gotta go babe. Thanks for coming, I'll text you later, okay?"

"What? Uh, yeah, sure." Tyler shifts in his seat, adjusting himself as I quickly straighten my jacket and fix my hair.

I glance at Hannah, who's turned her back to me and looks like she's talking to someone across the parking lot. "*That's* Hannah, just in case you need a reminder." I needle him, annoyed at the world for interrupting, but relieved I didn't have to stop him myself.

"Huh. Trevor's girl, yeah? I can see the appeal. Ow!" He exclaims when I slap his arm for that. "Whatever, don't get mad babe, I was kidding!" As I'm opening the door and climbing out, he grabs my arm and pulls me back for one last kiss. "Dance good tomorrow."

I run to catch up with Hannah before she reaches the parents and Ms. Parker standing around outside the theater. "Hannah!" I call. "Hang on!" She doesn't slow down, so I sprint to catch her and grab her arm to stop her. "Hang on, just wait a second, please."

"How could you?" Hannah says, her voice shaky. Shit. "You knew! You've known since seventh grade and you don't care! This weekend could be everything for me and you're purposefully trying to ruin it. I thought you were my friend." I'm sorry, what? Anger quickly replaces the guilt I felt at her catching us. Does she actually think I invited *my boyfriend* here just to upset her? Yeah, self-absorbed is the right word for Hannah's view of the world.

"Hannah, seriously?" I'm so over this, I'm not going to be made to feel guilty over inviting someone to see me dance. "You really think I invited Tyler just to upset you? It's been *years* and he's never noticed you. You can't honestly tell me you still thought there was a possibility..." Oh my god, she did.

"No, I mean. Obviously not...." she trails off, watching as Tyler's car slowly backs out of the parking space. I can see her visibly pull herself together. "I just meant, you knew how I felt. And you invited him to come without stopping to think that maybe I might get upset?"

"Are you serious? He offered to come, because he's supporting me, *his girlfriend*. He's *my* freaking boyfriend, Hannah." I jab my thumb into my chest to emphasize my word. "Of course I wanted him to come see me. You know this is the first time he's ever seen me dance?"

I can feel the anger building in my gut. Fucking Hannah, never thinks about anyone but herself. "Did it ever occur to you that I might want someone here to cheer for me too? You have your mom and your dad and I have no one." I gulp. "I don't have anyone here for me." I didn't even realize I was upset about it until the words tumble out my mouth. It's so unfair, Hannah has everything—a mom who's awesome, a dad who spends time with her, the talent to be a dancer. It's enough to make a better person than me hate her.

"What are you talking about? You have my mom and Ms. Parker."

"Yeah, *your* mom. Not mine. God Hannah, sometimes you're so dense." I take off at a jog to meet up with our group. I hear her close behind and speed up so I can reach them first. I plaster a smile on my face as I get close and cross my fingers that no one asks what I was doing.

"Great job sweetie!" Mrs. O'Brian exclaims as soon as I get close. "You were beautiful up there. Your parents would be so proud, I know your dad was sorry he couldn't come."

"Thanks," I smile. Yeah right. My dad was probably too busy taking the monsters to the zoo or working to even think about me.

Ms. Parker pulls me in for a hug. "I'm proud of you Olivia. You nailed it, way to finish on balance at the end." I love that she's always honest with me, no fake exclamations or meaningless words. And I nailed that ending, like a boss. I'm glad someone was concerned about how I did tonight, since my supposed friend sure wasn't.

"Did you see Hannah's quadruple pirouette?" Katy pipes up from the group.

"Uh…" I stall. Nope, missed it completely. I was busy sucking face with my hot boyfriend. That brings a tiny smile to my face. Hannah may have the awesome mom and the perfect family, but I have the perfect boyfriend, the one she wishes she had.

"Yeah," Hannah bumps into me as she reaches the group. I'm pretty sure that was on purpose, who knew goody-goody had a little spice in her after all? "It was pretty awesome. Anyway, Ms. Parker, when do we need to get ready for the classical variations?"

"Oh, we probably have about an hour. You girls should relax and have a snack or something. I'm going to go back in and watch, the little ones have their trio coming up soon."

"Hannah, Olivia, do you want to go get coffee?" Lisa asks. She and Katy are edging towards the parking lot. I look over at Hannah, she's stone faced, arms crossed and stubbornly looking away from all three of us. I would have been happy to hang out with the girls but I don't think Hannah wants to see me right now. I'm mad at her, but even I'm not enough of a bitch to make it worse by going with them now. Hannah needs her friends so she can calm down before she has to dance again. Contrary to what she believes, I'm really not trying to ruin her weekend.

"Do you want to go?" I ask her quietly, not sure if she'll answer me. "I won't go if you want to." I add.

Hannah sniffs and shifts her feet, indecision obvious on her face. "I'm still mad at you," she mutters.

"You can be mad at me, whatever. Just go, you'll feel better." Should I tell her I already got coffee? No, that's probably just rubbing salt in the wound. Screw it, I'm gonna say it anyways. "I just had coffee with Tyler, I don't want any more. I'm going to go watch the littles with Ms. Parker." Maybe I am a little more of a bitch than I like to admit.

With a choked sound, Hannah runs off after Lisa and Katy and I turn to find Ms. Parker inside.

CHAPTER 14

Hannah

HOW COULD SHE? My jaw aches from being clenched so tight. I'm trying to touch up my makeup but it feels like it's just going to melt right off my face from the waves of heat radiating off my skin. How could she do this to me? She was just…just…sucking his face like a freaking vampire. And was he trying to touch her boobs? Another flash of heat washes over me at the thought and I grit my teeth against it.

Why did she even invite Tyler tonight? I blow an unsteady breath out my pursed lips and raise a shaking hand to put on a fresh coat of lipstick. My hand is shaking so badly, I'm afraid I'll end up looking like a clown so I set the lipstick down and focus on pinning my tiara more securely instead. Every bit of calm I had conjured up earlier is gone, evaporated in the heat of my anger.

Lisa and Katy took me to the coffee shop around the corner, but other than asking for a black iced tea, I haven't said a word since I walked away from Olivia in the parking lot. If I say anything right now, I'll scream at the unfairness of it all. I need to be focused, to find every ounce of self-control and calm I can muster so I can concentrate on my dancing right now. I stare myself down in the mirror as I pin on my tiara, one or two pins hitting my scalp with more force than necessary, making me wince. Get it together Hannah, you're mad at Olivia, not yourself. But I'm lying, I am mad at myself. I'm mad for letting this get to me. It's not like them dating is new, it's been weeks. I'm furious with myself for letting it still hurt this much. I have to get over it, Tyler isn't important. It doesn't matter that I still thought Olivia was my best friend. It doesn't matter if today hurt worse than all the times I've seen them together at school. It shouldn't matter that she invited him to watch her dance.

It definitely shouldn't matter that they didn't stay to see me dance. I swallow hard and fight the sting in my eyes. Tyler came to watch Olivia dance, not me. It doesn't matter that I wanted him to see me too. That I just want him to *see* me.

This weekend is too important to let anything distract me from doing my best. Come on Hannah, focus on your goals. I close my eyes and bounce on my toes, shaking my arms like a boxer getting ready to fight. New York, New York, New York.

I keep mentally chanting to myself as I fix the false eyelash that was bothering me and make a second attempt to refresh my lipstick. I manage to apply it this time without making a complete mess. I tap some more powder over my face to keep it from being shiny and start getting my pointe shoes on.

"Hannah? Lisa? Girls, are you ready for open stage?" Ms. Parker appears in the doorway. "Anyone need help with a tutu?" she offers, noticing that neither of us is dressed yet.

"Ms. Parker, can you help me?" I ask, as I pull my delicate peach tutu out of it's carry bag. I love the gold lace overlay that decorates the top of the tutu platter and the peach tulle ruffle stretching across my shoulders and back, accentuating my long neck. I pull off my pants and jacket and step into the tutu. I turn my back to Ms. Parker so she can start doing up the row of hooks and eyes. I grunt a little when she pulls hard to make it fit and blow all the air out of my lungs to squeeze my rib cage together to help her get it done up. Professional tutus are like corsets and don't have any stretch in them. But once it's on I feel like a dancer, like all my dreams are within reach. If I could wear a tutu every day of my life I would, no matter how uncomfortable they can be.

I put my jacket back on over the tutu and follow Lisa and Ms. Parker to the stage. I'm thankful that Olivia isn't backstage this time. I try to push her from my mind so I can focus on my classical solos. We crowd in the wings until the curtains close and the MC announces a break for the judges and our open stage time begins. A crowd of Junior Division competitors stream past us now that they're finished. Mae waves to us as she disappears with the crowd.

Lisa and I head for a patch of open space on the other side of the stage so we can practice. We take turns standing back to keep the space clear and running through the sections that make us nervous. Ms. Parker flits between us and some of the other teachers, offering quiet corrections, reminders and encouragement between chatting with her colleagues. Lisa is struggling with one of the steps in her Lilac Fairy variation, it's really difficult because you have to step backwards into a double turn, then finish on one leg, the other one extended in a long diagonal on the floor.

My Aurora variation is first and doesn't have any particularly tricky turns in it, it's all about the delicate quality and suspension of each movement. Until this second, I was glad that I had the calmer of my two solos first. Unfortunately, I'm not feeling particularly delicate right now. I'm in the perfect frame of mind for my second solo, the Kitri variation, since that's all about being vivacious, flirty and full of sass. The explosive jumps, lightning fast footwork and bravoura quality of Kitri are exactly what I want to dance right now. I want to stab the floor with my pointe shoes and let the flash of fire I can feel in my heart explode out of me.

Every time I think about Olivia and Tyler together heat flares across my skin. My shoulders tense when I recall the sight of them in his car, the way he cupped her cheek with one hand so tenderly, like she was precious. How my heart shattered when I heard Olivia say, "That's Hannah. In case you forgot," as I walked away, reminding me just how forgettable I am to Tyler. When I think about how Olivia ditched me backstage to go see him, I want to stomp my feet and shout how unfair it is.

"Hannah?" Lisa's question interrupts my angry thoughts. "Um…you okay?"

"I don't want to talk about it." I mumble. I roll my head in a circle, trying to release the tension in my neck. "You good?" I ask, trying to push my feelings aside.

"I think so. Are you staying here or going back to the dressing room?" The stage is starting to empty, only a few stragglers left desperately practicing, chatting to each other or eyeing the competition and aggressively practicing a flashy step. I ignore them.

"I'm number four this time so I'm definitely staying here." I respond, pulling my earbuds out of my pocket and finding my variation music on my phone. "You don't have to stay if you don't want to," I tell Lisa, my voice a little sharp. Her face drops for a second, like she's hurt. "Do whatever you need to, Lisa," I say, hoping to smooth things over. She hovers for a few more seconds as I put my earbuds in, then walks off to talk to Ms. Parker.

I let the delicate violin notes of my music wash over me, my eyes unfocused, as I visualize my solo, making small arm movements as I go through it. I try to imagine myself doing each section smoothly, gracefully, like a princess on her wedding day. I imagine dancing for my parents, who are smiling lovingly at me, for my imaginary prince who very specifically does not look like Tyler today, I imagine my arms sweeping through the air, my legs reaching and pushing me through the dance. Just as I get to the last notes, the lights backstage dim, our signal to clear the stage. I trot across the stage to join Lisa and Ms. Parker for a last minute pep talk before they make the teachers leave the backstage area as well.

"You feel ready, Hannah?" she asks, running her eyes over me to check I don't have anything out of place. Nodding her approval, she turns to Lisa and looks her over. "You feeling ready, Lisa?"

"Yeah." Lisa fidgets a little glancing around backstage. "I'm nervous though. I wish you could stay backstage."

"Sorry, sweetie, you know the rules. But you have Hannah, you girls look out for each other, okay?" Ms. Parker eyes me meaningfully. My residual anger and upset at Oliva is starting to turn to annoyance. I just want to do well this weekend, why can't everyone just let me do what I need to do? "Hannah," Ms. Parker gets my attention with a little tap on the shoulder. "I know you're up first, but you have quite a while after your first variation to change and get ready for Kitri. I know Lisa will stay with you until your Aurora variation is finished." She waits for Lisa to nod her agreement before continuing. "Since her's is just a couple after yours I want you to stay with her until she's done, then you can go get ready for Kitri." She pauses and stares me down a little. I feel like a bug under a microscope and a little niggling feeling of guilt creeps into my brain. Wasn't I going to stay and support my friend? I mean, I guess if I'd thought about it I would have said of course, I just hadn't been thinking about Lisa at all. I was so wrapped up in my own feelings, I hadn't even thought about my friend. I drop my eyes to the ground and nod. "You're my girls, I need you to stick together and look out for each other since I can't be here."

I fight the urge to tell Ms. Parker how Olivia ditched me backstage earlier to go hang out with her boyfriend. I sigh to myself because there's no point, really. I'll feel vindicated if Olivia gets in trouble with Ms. Parker, but I didn't even notice she was gone until after I finished dancing. I know that's not really why I'm mad. If I get Olivia in trouble, it will only make tonight and tomorrow even worse, she's still sharing a room with my mom and me tonight, and we have to dance together all day tomorrow. It's not worth it.

Ms. Parker pulls us both in for an awkward hug, tutus poking out and getting in the way, kisses us each on the head and gives us one more squeeze. "Have fun, dance big and bold and with joy. I'm so proud of you both." We hug her back before she heads off to sit in the audience.

"You okay?" I ask Lisa. She's busy looking around at all the other dancers hanging out backstage. There's a girl in a blue tutu standing in the wings swinging her arms up and down chatting with the guy I recognize from earlier and from yesterday's class. He was the guy in the blue shirt, the one Lisa and Katy said was one of the few people that Jean-Paul Phillppe corrected. Was that terrible class only yesterday? It feels like a lifetime ago. "Hey," I tug on her hand, forcing her to look at me. "Tune them out, okay? They'll only make you more nervous." I look around again. "I bet she's doing Bluebird," I whisper, jerking my chin at the girl in the blue tutu.

Lisa and I look at each other for a long moment before she giggles. "How is it that I'm the one who's so nervous and you're the one who's calm? You're always the basketcase." Lisa manages to get out between giggles.

I could tell her the truth, that I'm too angry to be nervous. That the intimate glimpse I got of Tyler and Olivia burned away all my nerves and left behind only the burning desire to kick ass tonight. I haven't thought once about if I'm wearing my good tights, if my shoes feel okay, if my hair or makeup are perfect. I guess being mad as hell at Olivia did one good thing for me today.

"I don't know," I shrug, not sure how to tell Lisa what I'm feeling. "I've been a little distracted this afternoon." The announcer starts speaking and the girl in the blue tutu runs out on stage to take her position. I tune her out as soon as I hear the familiar music. "Called it," I say to Lisa, which gets her to crack a smile. I nod my head towards another girl in a white and gold tutu. "What do you think, Paquita?" We spend the next few minutes trying to guess which variation everyone is doing based on their costume. It's a fun game to play, since there are only a limited number of possibilities, YIGP has a list of approved variations for each age group.

I keep working through my feet and stretching, trying to keep my muscles warm and ready to dance. The guy I recognized from earlier walks out onto the stage and I realize I'm next. His variation will be short, male variations are usually less than a minute long, so I quickly strip off my jacket and hand it to Lisa for safekeeping, then stand in the wings, waiting for him to finish.

I close my eyes and take a deep breath, setting the stage in my mind once more. I imagine my prince, who looks suspiciously like Trevor this time, dressed in a coordinating costume to mine. In my mind we've just finished the wedding pas de deux and now he's finished his variation, signaling that it's time for my solo. I'm a regal princess, awakened from a long sleep by the man of my dreams and everyone is here to celebrate our wedding. Instead of walking out onto a bare stage, I picture an elaborate gold and white scene, with magnificent chairs scattered around the edges of the stage, a stunning garden backdrop and a full orchestra in the pit, just waiting for me to float onto the stage and stand ready to begin. I don't think about the judges, I don't think about Olivia. Okay, I do think about Olivia, but I push it out of my mind as soon as the thought starts to invade. But not before the pit of my stomach goes hollow and the scene I carefully drew for myself wavers.

There's a smattering of applause as the boy before me finishes and takes a bow before running offstage. I hear the announcer start to speak and before I have a chance to second-guess myself, I begin a smooth, careful, walk to the center of the stage. My arms are poised, floating through the air and opening towards the audience, welcoming them and inviting them to watch as I take my starting position. I breathe deep, trying to calm my racing heart as I wait for the music to start. My stomach turns somersaults and it feels like I've been standing here for hours, even though it's only been seconds. My cheeks freeze, my smile locked in place.

Just when I'm about to panic that something's wrong, I hear the first few notes of my music. I let out the breath I didn't realize

I was holding and start moving. The first few steps feel wobbly and wrong, like my legs are half a beat behind my brain. My face is stuck in a simulation of a smile, my teeth clenched tight behind my frozen lips. I push up onto one foot, the other carefully touching my knee but as hard as I fight to stay in position, I can feel my weight is wrong and I have to come down too quickly instead of balancing for a beat like I'm supposed to.

I repeat the step on the other leg, fighting the panic rising in my chest, desperate to balance this time. Again, I come down too soon. Now I'm slightly off the music. What is wrong with me? Why can't I do this? This is the easiest step in the variation, if I'm having trouble now, what will happen when I get to the next part? My body is moving through the steps on auto-pilot while my mind spins.

The next section is a series of little jumps with a relevé and a balance. I always struggle with the timing of this part, the jumps are slow and it's hard not to get ahead of the music. I'm already getting ahead, how am I going to fix this? My legs feel stiff and heavy underneath me, jumping feels impossible. It's like my body forgot how to do this. I do the first series and try to hold the balance, it's on both feet for goodness sake, I should be able to hold this. But I feel myself wobble to the side and have to start the next series of jumps too soon. The next balance is a little better, but I still can't seem to get right with the music. It's like I'm listening to it under water. The jumps are getting harder and harder, but I push through for the third balance which I almost manage to hold for long enough. I bend my knees deep, push hard against the floor, and pray that I can get through this section. Just as I feel like I can't do any more, I hit the last balance and my leg is right underneath me. I stay, balancing on one leg suddenly effortless. My body and brain click together and I hold the position for two extra beats, long enough to correct my timing and hopefully impress the judges.

Joy and relief flood through me and I float through the rest of my solo—the delicate circles of my wrists, the joyful movements criss-crossing the stage, all the way to the triumphant series of turns at the end. I finish with a flourish and hold it for a moment before I curtsey and run off the stage. Lisa is waiting for me with my jacket and an excited hug. "Oh my god, I thought you were in trouble but that was amazing!" she whispers to me as the next dancer walks onto the stage.

I hug her back hard, relieved that it's over. "I thought I was going to completely flop it. The beginning was so bad," I groan. Lisa shakes her head, but I continue anyway. "Nope, you know it was bad, don't lie to me. But it's okay, I saved it. I think. I honestly don't remember what I did."

"You totally saved it, Hannah," Lisa assures me. She gives me one more hug before handing me back my jacket. I shove my arms through the sleeves, zip it up, then hold out my hands for hers.

"Okay, your turn. What number are they on?" I ask.

"I think I have two more?" Lisa says, peering out at the dancer on stage who is just finishing. We listen to the announcer calling on the next soloist and make our way to the wing where Lisa needs to enter. There is just one more dancer to go before it's her turn.

"You got this Lisa." I whisper encouragingly. She nods and stands on pointe with both feet, holding my shoulders for balance, then she slowly lifts one toe up to touch her knee. I can feel all the tiny adjustments she's making to try and find her balance in that position. Slowly, she lifts one hand up above her head, then the other. She balances in that position for a few seconds before coming down with a smile on her face. "Feeling good?" Lisa nods, looking relieved. We stand in the wing together, watching the girl on stage as she struggles to get through a series of Italian fouettés. It's a really hard step and I wince in sympathy when she loses her balance and has to do a couple of extra hops to get around, and then cringe as she kicks her leg up, her foot in the air loose and floppy instead of sharp and stretched. I feel awful for her, second-hand embarrassment for her making my stomach clench.

She wobbles to a finish and the audience claps politely. Lisa rolls her shoulders and I can see her spine snap to attention as she gets ready to go on stage. She waits for her name, tosses a smile at me over her shoulder, then calmly walks out onto the stage and takes her starting position.

I watch as she sweeps her arms over her head and steps into the first diagonal of the variation, her left leg sweeping up almost up to her ear before circling down in front of her as she travels from one side of the stage to the other. I cross my fingers and hold my breath as she steps backwards into the next series, the one she was struggling with earlier. She only does a single pirouette, instead of the double she usually does, but she lands cleanly. She does single turns three times in a row but on the last one she goes for the double turn. It's a little wobbly at the end but she manages to save it and continue on. I can see how tired she is by the end of the solo, but she gets to the end without any major mistakes. Her double pirouettes in the last section are beautiful, I know she'll be happy about that. I watch her curtsy and run off into the wing where I'm waiting for her.

"That was so good!" I whisper as we hug, relieved she's done. Lisa shrugs her jacket on and gives me a tight smile.

"It was pretty good. I'm mad I singled those turns, but I didn't want to fall."

"Yeah, but your doubles at the end were-" I kiss my fingers like an Italian chef and grin.

"Come on, let's get you ready for Kitri," Lisa laughs and pulls me towards the dressing room. We scramble to unhook my tutu and change into my Kitri costume. I love this costume. I take a second to admire the black velvet bodice with lace sleeves and the red flounced skirt. The triple tiered skirt is made for swishing. I grab my eyebrow pencil and add fake curls near my ears and one at my temple. Lisa unpins my tiara while I color in the fake curls, then grabs a giant red rose and pins it on the side of my head, nestled up against the edge of my French twist. Stepping back, I admire the whole effect, satisfied in my transformation from regal princess to flirty and vivacious Spanish maiden.

I have time before I need to get back to the side of the stage, so I scroll through my phone while Lisa looks at hers.

> **MOM:** Love you sweetie! Aurora was beautiful, you made me cry
>
> **MS. PARKER:** Great job Hannah! Proud of the way you managed to get back on track. Deep breaths for Kitri, and use your plie!
>
> **DAD:** Proud Dad! Love you!

There's a picture of Katy blowing us kisses from the audience in our group chat. I laugh when I notice Ms. Parker's disapproving face in the background of her photo. When I hear Lisa chuckle I know she saw it as well.

There's a notification from Instagram, but I ignore it. I'll look when I'm done dancing, I don't need any distractions now. My heart stutters, wondering if it was from Trevor. I have yet to respond to any of his messages with more than a couple of words, but every time he sends me one I get a tiny thrill. It feels nice to be noticed. I need to answer him properly one of these days.

I grab Lisa by the hand and pull her with me back to the side of the stage, ready for my next solo. I'm already imagining the scene in my mind. Gone is the regal gold and white of Sleeping Beauty, replaced by a gritty Spanish village, complete with Sancho Panza and Don Quixote. I imagine the raucous cheers of my friends, the smirk of Baslilio, my secret lover, and the excitement of a wild night out. I would come flying onto the stage this time, leaping and showing off for my lover, flirting with all the other guys in my imaginary scene, trying to make him jealous, just because I can.

The music and the steps tell me exactly what to do—I know just when to look coy, when to avert my gaze, when to wink or smirk. That's the beauty of being a dancer. On stage, I can put on a costume and transform. I'm free from the confines of my own personality, from the million thoughts constantly running through my brain. One moment I'm Kitri, full of fire and fun, the next moment I'm Odette, broken, trapped and full of sorrow. Or perhaps I'm simply the embodiment of the music, the notes moving in me and through me and out to the world from there, a river of emotion barely contained.

I let the heat of my anger fill me, settling into my core as I close my eyes. I imagine the fingers of a lover trailing across my skin, strong fingers wrapping around the back of my neck, cradling my face. I let the butterflies build in my stomach at the thought of being seen, being wanted, being touched like that. I welcome them, imagining each flutter as another caress, a secret look, a stolen moment. Keeping my eyes closed, I smile. This is my moment.

CHAPTER 15

Olivia

ELL, SHIT. Who knew Hannah had that kind of fire in her meek little body?

Her Aurora variation got off to a rocky start but in the end she was her usual, perfect princess self. You could feel the joy radiating from her as she danced, elegant and refined like a spun sugar ballerina. But when she came out for her Kitri variation, she exploded onto the stage, flirting with the audience like she'd been doing it all her life. I glance to my right where Tyler is sitting silently. Right now, I'm seriously regretting that I asked him to come back.

After Hannah took off with Lisa and Katy, I called and asked Tyler to come back, mostly because I was irritated at Hannah and I wanted to rub my boyfriend in her face just a little bit. Yes, I know, it was a bitchy move. Do I look like I care?

Of course, I had no idea she was going to come on stage and do…that. Tyler leans over to whisper in my ear. "Dude. That's Hannah?"

I silently turn to face him with one eyebrow raised. He shrugs and grabs my hand to place a kiss on the back of it. We watch in silence until finally the last solo for the night is finished. It's late and I'm starving—I can't wait to get out of here. Tyler threads his fingers through mine and leads me out of the auditorium behind Mrs. O'Brian and the other parents from our studio.

"Okay, so dudes in tights? Hard pass. But some of the other stuff was cool." Tyler is saying as we walk through the lobby. "I liked your solo best though, that was pretty epic. I liked that style better, tutus are kinda lame." He stage whispers the last bit, adding an exaggerated wink for effect.

I smack him on the shoulder even though I have to laugh. I mean, I agree, tutus are kinda lame. And so uncomfortable. "Oh my god, Tyler, don't say that too loud. You'll get me in trouble!"

"What? I only speak the truth," Tyler grins as we hover at the back of a crowd of bodies. All the other parents and dancers are waiting for the competitors to emerge from back-stage. "Okay, but seriously, I had no idea that was Hannah. She was…" he drifts off seeing the look on my face. He coughs uncomfortably, "Trevor is gonna be so pissed he didn't get to see it." He smirks.

"There'll be a video later, if it's any good I'll try and get her to post it." I offer. "Then you can rub it in his face that you got to see it live."

"Cool. So when can we eat? I'm starving," Tyler looks around at the crowd of parents. It's late, just past nine o'clock, and every-one is talking about getting dinner. I'm torn between wanting the satisfaction of having Tyler join us and rubbing it in Hannah's face a little, and not wanting to deal with the interrogation that I bet Ms. Parker and Mrs. O'Brian would love to give him.

"Hey sweetie," Mrs. O'Brian says sneaking up next to me. "We're getting dinner soon. Your friend..." she pauses, expectantly. Crap.

"Uh, Tyler. Tyler, this is Mrs. O'Brian. Hannah's mom," I add.

"Nice to meet you, Hannah was amazing." Tyler sticks out his hand and shakes Mrs. O'Brian's firmly. A rush of jealousy washes over me at his words. Logically, I know he's being polite, but it irks me after he was so blown away by how...ugh, I can't believe I'm saying this...how *sexy* Hannah was.

"Tyler is welcome to join us." She stops and looks at each of us in turn. "Do you still need to drive back tonight? I don't want to keep you out too late, it's a long drive."

"Oh no, that's okay. I'm cool to drive back after dinner." Tyler assures her, squeezing me against his side. "But I am starving, do we know where we're eating? Olivia and I could go ahead and get a table for everyone?" He offers. Damn, he's nicer than me. I wouldn't have thought to offer. Oops.

I tune out the conversation as Mrs. O'Brian and Tyler discuss the logistics of feeding us all and busy myself looking around for Lisa and Hannah. Irritation and jealousy are still warring with my rational mind. I have no reason to be jealous of Hannah, we don't want the same things, ballet isn't my life's dream like it is hers and I have no reason not to trust Tyler. I know he's just excited to needle Trevor about being the one who got to see her perform. But it's making me so mad to think that Tyler suddenly sees her as something other than just background noise. Damnit, I shouldn't have invited him to come back and watch.

I'm interrupted from my thoughts by Tyler's arms wrapping around my waist and his lips pressing a kiss behind my ear. Hmmm, that's better. I lean back against his solid body and sigh, just as Hannah and Lisa come around the corner, arms full of bags and costumes. Hannah's eyes go wide at the sight of us, but she blinks and beelines to her parents. Lisa stops and stares at me for a second, head tilted, lips pressed in a thin line. I lift my shoulders in a tiny shrug, Hannah's issues aren't my problem. Lisa shakes her head before passing her costume bag over to Katy to hold.

Mrs. O'Brian looks over Hannah's head at us, eyes a little sad. She jerks her head towards the parking lot, silently telling us to get going to the restaurant. "Come on babe, let's go," I say as I pull Tyler towards the parking lot.

"So how come your folks aren't here?" Tyler asks as we get buckled into his SUV.

"I told them not to come today. They'll be here tomorrow." I explain. "It's kind of a long and boring day," I grin at that, elbowing him. "Anyways, the monsters would never make it through the day, and since I'm their resident babysitter, there wouldn't be anyone to watch them while they're here." I will never admit this out loud, but I do kind of miss those monsters. Aiden and Marie are a pain in my ass, but they give good snuggles. "I wish my dad could have come but it's fine. He'll be here for the groups and the awards tomorrow."

"Where are you sleeping?" Tyler sends a wolfish grin my way as we pull into the restaurant parking lot. "Can I crash with you?" he adds with a cartoonish eyebrow wiggle.

I laugh and slap his arm, "Yeah, no. Not gonna happen. I'm staying with the O'Brian's. Hannah, her mom and I shared a room last night." I stop and think for a second as Tyler parks. "Although, I bet Mr. O'Brian is staying tonight so maybe they got a second room, you can go bunk with him." I wink and slide out of the car towards the restaurant doors. The aroma of fresh tortillas and carnitas drifts towards me, making my mouth water.

Tyler stalks after me, a mischievous gleam in his eye. "Maybe I will…maybe I want to try and sneak into your room in the middle of the night. I bet you could convince Mrs. O'Brian to bunk with her husband and leave you and Hannah the other room." He pulls the door open for me and we head to the hostess stand. "Nine, please, we've got more people coming," Tyler tells the hostess. She hurries off to get a large table set up for us.

Jealousy rages white hot through my chest. I grab Tyler's arm and pull him to face me. I stand arms crossed, hip cocked to the side. "I don't think so," I say in a steely voice. "You're kidding, right? First of all, if we got caught, we would both be in big shit. I wasn't even supposed to have you here, you know. Ms. Parker got mad at me yesterday for being late because of you."

"Babe…" Tyler tries to interrupt. I shut him up with a glare.

"Secondly, there is no way in hell I am sharing a room with you and Hannah. No, not going to happen." I mean, if I was really as bitchy as I pretend to be I would sneak Tyler in and make out with him right in front of her, just to prove that for once I won. She may have the perfect family and the talent, but I got the boy. The one she's always wanted and always been to chicken-shit to do anything but stare longingly at from across the quad. Yeah, I've seen the way she stares. It's pathetic. But there's a difference between being catty and being cruel. "You know she has a crush on you, right?"

"What?!" Shit, shit, shit, shit. I didn't mean to tell him that. "What do you…how do you know that?"

"Well, I mean, she did back in middle school." I backtrack. "I dunno if she still does. But whatever, that's not the point."

"You're jealous." Tyler says slowly, a smirk lifting one side of his lips higher than the other. Damn him and his sexy smirk. "Also, you knew that this whole time and you still set her up with Trevor? That's…" he assesses me with his cool hazel eyes. "I didn't think you had that in you, Liv."

"Whatever, it was a middle school crush. Who cares?" I shrug, feigning nonchalance, feeling uncomfortable. Inviting Hannah along on our double date wasn't my finest moment. "The point is, you're going home after dinner." I hear the door open behind me and voices drift through from outside. I grab Tyler's shirt and pull him close so I can whisper in his face. "Do not say anything about it." His eyes sparkle with suppressed mischief, but he plants a quick kiss on my lips.

"I promise."

CHAPTER 16

Hannah

"REALLY LIKED her tutu. The girl who did the Paquita variation right before Lisa. Did you get a chance to see it close up?" Ms. Parker asks me as we walk into the restaurant. My stomach growls at the thought of the gooey, cheesy enchiladas I'm about to devour. Or maybe I'll have fajitas. I'm so hungry, I could eat both.

"I didn't get a good look at it, she was standing on the other side of the stage from us most of the time. But it looked really pretty under the lights," Lisa answers for us. I follow the group through the door, just in time to see Olivia and Tyler standing by the hostess stand, his arms looped casually around her waist, pressing her against his chest. His very broad chest.

When he and Olivia left before us, I assumed they were going to go hang out by themselves. I wasn't prepared to have to sit across a table from them all night. Something flashes through me, flipping my stomach upside down, my breath coming in shallower and shallower gasps. Tears prick the back of my eyes but I can't tell if it's sadness, anger or a post-performance adrenaline crash. One more dip of the emotional roller coaster I've been on this weekend.

I follow as we walk back to the large table they've put together for us. The adults all sit together at one end of the table. I sit between Lisa and Katy on one side, Olivia and Tyler sit next to each other opposite us. Lisa surreptitiously squeezes my knee once we sit down. I bump her shoulder with my own and try to hide the shaky breath I take as I slide my phone onto the table next to hers.

"So Tyler, how come you stayed for the classical sections even though Olivia wasn't dancing?" Katy asks the second we're all seated. I haven't even picked up my menu yet. I freeze, eyes darting back and forth from Katy to Olivia. I desperately want to know the answer, but I just as desperately don't want to draw attention to myself right now.

"Geez Katy, what the hell?" Olivia glances over at the adult end of the table to make sure they haven't heard her. "Seriously, what's your problem?"

Katy just shrugs, doing a good job of acting innocent, "I don't have a problem, I was just asking. You couldn't pay my brothers enough to be here, even if *I* was the one dancing, let alone if no one they knew was on stage."

Tyler just laughs, twirling a bit of Olivia's hair around her finger. "Dude, please don't tell your brothers I was here. Hunter will never let me live it down. Liv asked me to come back and keep her company, so I did." He shrugs like it's no big deal. "I mean, the dudes in tights I could live without, but Lisa was really good and Hannah was…" he glances down at Olivia and seems to change his mind about what he was going to say. Tyler clears his throat but Olivia cuts him off before he can say anything else.

"Besides, I'm at all his football games, it's only fair that he comes to my thing. That's what a good *boyfriend* does, right?" Olivia adds in a steely voice. I don't miss the way she stares directly at me as she emphasizes the word boyfriend. I also don't miss the way her hands are wrapped possessively around his bicep.

I don't even flinch, my mind spinning in circles thinking about what he was going to say before he changed his mind. What was Tyler going to say? I was what? The need to know what he was going to say burns through me. I hold myself frozen, afraid to move and disturb this world where Tyler Stanley thought I was…something. Something he didn't want to say in front of Olivia. His girlfriend. Who I thought was my best friend. I'm so confused, my emotions jumbled and tangled up inside me.

I'm elated that Tyler finally noticed me. I'm angry that Olivia invited him here in the first place. I'm jealous of the way they are so comfortable with each other. I'm disappointed with myself for still wanting him, even though he's dating my best friend. Maybe disappointed isn't the right word. Ashamed. I'm ashamed of myself for being "that girl," the one who wants a boy who's already taken. Does that make me a terrible person? But doesn't it make Olivia a terrible person for inviting me on that double date in the first place, and for inviting Tyler tonight?

Something pokes my side derailing my train of thought. I look up, not realizing I'd been staring down at my hands as they twisted my napkin in my lap. "Huh?" I look around the table. Katy clears her throat meaningfully. The adults are lost in their own conversation, but everyone else is just staring at me. "Oh, um, thanks Tyler." I gulp, his name crossing my lips feeling alien and wrong. "Thanks for staying to watch, Lisa and I appreciate it." I add, hoping to get some of the attention off me.

Olivia is still glaring at me, but turns to Lisa to ask what she's planning to order. Right, we need to order. I look down at the menu in front of me but I can't focus on the words. I can feel eyes boring into me from across the table. Do I look up and see who it is? There's a 50/50 chance it's Oliva or Tyler who's staring at me and honestly I don't know which one would be worse.

I peek over the edge of my menu to see Tyler eyeing me thoughtfully and quickly look down again. I try to concentrate on reading it, but the swirling thoughts in my brain make it impossible. Why is Tyler staring at me? I can't have anything on my face, we haven't even gotten chips and salsa yet. I glance up again and he's busy doing something on his phone. It was just a momentary lapse on his part. I mean, I still have my stage makeup on, I probably look pretty crazy right now, that must be all it was.

Wait, did I take off both false eyelashes? Maybe that's why he's staring. I quickly blink my eyes a few times to see if I can feel the false lashes or not. Nope, I took them both off. I glance up again just in time to see the back of Tyler's phone as he takes a picture of me.

"What are you doing?" Olivia snaps before I can gather my thoughts to ask the same question myself.

"Nothing, don't worry about it babe," Tyler says smoothly. Then he winks. I'm not sure who he's winking at, it could have been Katy for all I know. It was just a general "I'm a hot dude and even though I just got caught doing something kinda creepy, you're not gonna get mad" sort of wink.

"You just took a picture of Hannah. What for?" Olivia won't let it go. "What the hell Tyler?" She looks genuinely upset. I'm too shocked to say anything, I just sit there like a dummy staring at him. Why did Tyler take a picture of me? There's no way he wants it for himself, I mean, it's not like we're friends or anything.

"Babe, it's nothing. I promise." Tyler tries to smooth talk his way out of it, but now he has four sets of female eyes staring him down.

"Tyler…" Katy pipes up. I always forget she must actually know him, since he's on the football team with her brothers. "Dude, don't B-C," she says in a fake deep voice with a funny little two-fingered salute. I glance over at Olivia who's sitting with her back turned to the rest of the table, pouting.

Tyler bursts out laughing, breaking some of the tension at the table, "Hunter teach you that?" I can't help staring at the way his arm is draped casually over the back of Olivia's seat, his fingers tracing circles on her shoulder. She shrugs him off, but he goes right back to it as soon as she's still again. God, now I'm being the creepy one. I force myself to look away and pretend to read the menu again.

"Cole started it, we've just continued it," Katy explains. Tyler leans down and whispers in Olivia's ear. Out of the corner of my eye, I see her shoulders hunch up towards her ears, like she's fending him off, then relax as she straightens and turns to face him.

"Cole started what? What does "don't bee see" mean?" Lisa asks, as Tyler shows Olivia something on his phone screen. What is he showing her? I must look awful in the picture, that's why she's not mad anymore. I'm desperate to know what it is and why he took it, but I can't bring myself to speak up. Even with Lisa nudging me in the ribs. I silently shake my head.

"It means 'Don't Be Creepy'" Katy explains. "It's the rule when everyone is at our house, especially in the summer."

"Hang on. Are you showing Olivia?" Lisa interrupts. "If Olivia gets to see, why can't we? At least show Hannah, it's her picture." Tyler doesn't say anything for a second. "Seriously Tyler, that's a dick move," Lisa whispers across the table, not wanting the adults to hear her.

"Oh my god, it's not that big a deal." Olivia yanks Tyler's phone out of his hand to show us. It's a picture of me peering over the edge of the menu, my blue eyes wide and exaggerated from my stage makeup. It's actually kind of a cute picture of me. The menu is covering most of my face so all you really see is my eyes. It's in a text conversation, which is weird—I don't want to read Tyler's private conversations.

Hang on. Who is he texting my picture to?

I look up at the top of the screen and see that he sent it to Trevor.

Who hasn't responded.

Wait. What?

Olivia starts to pull the phone back when I see the three little gray dots pop up. My hand shoots out to grab her wrist before I think about what I'm doing.

TREV: Dude, quit creepin on my girl.

His girl?

CHAPTER 17

Olivia

"HANNAH, EARTH to Hannah." Hannah blinks her big blue eyes and glances down at the death grip she has on my wrist. She quickly lets go and I dump Tyler's phone back in his hand before rubbing my wrist.

"Why did you send my picture to Trevor?" she asks quietly.

"Because he's had a crush on you since January," I blurt out before Tyler can say anything. It's the truth anyway. Tyler keeps complaining that his cousin has been bugging him about Hannah ever since Winter Break. In fact, that's why I made sure to tag her in that photo from the sleepover at her house. I figured Trevor would see it and could go stalk her Instagram and leave Tyler alone.

Just then, the waitress comes to take our order, by the time she leaves the conversation has turned to tomorrow and the ensemble competition. Ms. Parker pulls out her program and gets deep into conversation with Lisa and Hannah about who

competed today, what ensemble pieces they'll be in tomorrow and who might be the competition. YIGP awards only the top twelve dancers in classical and contemporary in each age division, everyone except Hannah is certain she'll place in the top twelve for the senior division.

Tyler is busy shoveling food into his mouth which leaves me stuck at the end of the table with only Katy to talk to. She makes a point of ignoring me and methodically eats her plate of rice and beans. Occasionally she or Tyler shares a profound piece of commentary on their food, but mostly they just eat. At one point there is a serious debate between them on the proper way to assemble a fajita. Exhaustion and boredom creep over me as I pick at my food. I rest my chin on my hand and take slow bites of my salad while the conversation swirls around me.

Finally, everyone is finished stuffing their faces and we head out to the door to our respective cars. I walk with Tyler to his car while the adults are still talking. "Thanks for coming tonight, I really appreciate it. It was really nice to have someone here just for me." I rise up on my toes to kiss the tip of his nose.

"It was kind of fun being your cheerleader this time, babe." He smiles that sweet, vulnerable smile that only I get to see and my heart melts. I may not have pursued Tyler with the most noble of intentions, but he's turned out to be way sweeter and more fun than I ever could have dreamed.

"Are you going to be okay driving home?"

"Yeah, I'll be fine. I'll text you when I get home, okay?" I nod and press one more kiss to his lips before settling myself against his chest, my arms wrapped around his waist. Tyler's arms hold me tight to him, his contented sigh tickling the top of my head. I steal a moment to let myself just rest against him, the stress and emotion of the day falling from me. We stay like this for a minute, until I see the O'Brian's walking towards their car.

"Drive safe, text me when you get home." I squeeze him once more before heading to Mrs. O'Brian's car. I hop into the backseat, eyeing Hannah. "You girls must be exhausted," Mr. O'Brian says from the front seat, buckling her seatbelt.

"Yeah," Hannah says, barely audible, her head down, scrolling through her phone. Is she texting Trevor? Why would she look so sad if she was? Irritation at her pathetic face creeps through my gut. Her dad is still turned in his seat, watching us expectantly. He must not have heard her mousy response.

I nod my head at him. "Yeah. It's been a long day." He smiles at me and turns to face the front. The rest of the drive to the hotel is quiet. The O'Brian's chat quietly to each other in the front seat, while Hannah and I stare out our windows, lost in our own thoughts.

"You girls have the room to yourselves tonight, make sure you don't stay up late," Mrs. O'Brian says as we pull our bags and costumes out of the trunk of her car. "You have your room keys, right?"

"Yup," I answer when Hannah just stands there, digging mine out of a pocket in my bag.

"Okay, we're just down the hall if you need anything. We'll meet you for breakfast at 7:30, alright?"

"Okay Mom," Hannah finally speaks up. I'm so annoyed at her 'woe-is-me' act and her tiny little squeak of a voice. I swallow it down and smile as we say goodnight and walk down the hall to our room.

Hannah stalks through the door and goes straight into the bathroom. "I need to take a shower," she says flatly, closing the door in my face. Rude. What if I had to pee or something? I mean, I don't, but still. I knock on the door as soon as it closes. It opens a crack and Hannah's annoyed face peeks through.

"Can I least wash my face before you take your shower? I'll take a shower in the morning," I add.

"Fine, just give me a minute." Hannah sighs and closes the door again. I pull a pair of shorts and a tank top out of my overnight bag and change while she does whatever it is she's doing in there. Just as I finish she stalks out of the bathroom. "All yours," she says, waving a hand towards the bathroom door. "Just like everything else," she mutters under her breath.

"Excuse me?" I blurt out, annoyance and irritation exploding out of me as I whirl around to face her. "What fuck is that supposed to mean?"

"Nothing," Hannah says, turning away from me to flop down on her bed.

Oh no, nope, she's not going to get away with that. "It obviously meant something or else you wouldn't have said it," I fire back.

"I don't want to fight, just drop it Olivia." she says to the ceiling. But I can't let it go, I've been spoiling for a fight with Hannah for weeks. Who am I kidding, this fight has been brewing for years.

"You can't seriously think I get everything?" I ask, incredulous. "Excuse me, who is the better dancer in this room?" I pause, waiting for her to speak up, when she doesn't, the words start tumbling out of my mouth. I couldn't stop them even if I wanted to. "Which one of us has the perfect family, the perfect feet, the perfect life? It sure as hell isn't me!"

At my outburst, Hannah shoots up on the bed, eyes flashing. "Whatever. Who got a new car for the sixteenth birthday?" When I don't respond she plows ahead, counting off on her fingers.

"You get new clothes all the time. You have perfect blonde hair. You even got onto the varsity cheer squad on your first try. Everyone at school wants to be your friend." Hannah clenches her fist, breathing hard. "You dropped us. Dropped *me*, the second you got popular at school. I don't even know you anymore."

I sit down hard on my bed, facing Hannah over the space between the beds.

"'You're mad at me for making new friends?" I fire back. "Newsflash Hannah, my life doesn't revolve around you. Not anymore. I'm so fucking sick of being Olivia—Hannah's best friend, or Olivia—the silly one, or Olivia—the one with the dead mom." My voice cracks on that last one.

At the mom comment, I see Hannah start to give in, guilt flitting over her features. Then, shocking me, I see her take a deep breath and fortify herself. If I wasn't steaming mad, I'd be impressed, that is, until she starts talking again.

"Don't even get me started on Tyler." She chokes on his name. Good. "You have the perfect boyfriend and *you knew* I liked him and you invited him to come this weekend anyway!"

I can't help snorting at that. "Oh my fucking God, Hannah. You never listen. I invited him for me. You were never part of the decision. My dad and Martha didn't want to come, do you know how shitty that feels? No, you don't. Your perfect mom comes to everything. Every audition, competition or performance. I'm lucky if my dad comes to one thing a year. I just wanted Tyler here for me."

"It sure feels like you were trying to sabotage me. You knew I'd be upset. You know how important this weekend is for me. What if seeing Tyler ruined my concentration and I totally screwed everything up tonight? That's not just messing with my weekend Olivia, that's messing with my whole future!"

"Don't be such a drama queen," I snap back. "You didn't even know he was there." Hannah opens her mouth to interrupt, but I plow on. "Did you really think I sat at home and plotted how to ruin your weekend? News flash—my world does not revolve around the great and wonderful Hannah O'Brian and her ballet career."

"Felt pretty deliberate to me." Her arms are hugging her knees to her chest as she sits on the bed. If I wasn't so mad I would care that she looks fragile and small. But I know her better than that. Hannah may be anxious, shy, and self-conscious, but she is far from fragile. I've seen her steel core and how she doesn't let anything or anyone get in the way of her goals. But right now, I don't admire that trait at all, right now I want to strip away her perfect facade and make her see that she's not as blameless as she thinks she is.

"That's because you're so self-centered you assume everything is always about you. No one gives a shit. The world does not revolve around Hannah O'Brian."

"I do not think that," Hannah protests, swinging her legs down to face me fully. Finally, she's ready for a fight, instead of sitting there like a kicked puppy. This just got interesting.

"Yeah, actually you do. Did you even notice anyone else from the studio today? Did you see MacKenzie, Haley, and Anna? They talk about you all the time and I bet you didn't even know they were competing tonight. MacKenzie idolizes you and you never even acknowledged her presence today, even though she was standing three feet from you."

"When you went off to sulk with Lisa and Katy? They were doing their trio on stage. Would it have killed you to wish them good luck? Do you know who *was* there to support them? Me. Flakey, irresponsible me."

I watch Hannah's mouth open and close several times, trying to figure out what she's going to say. I wait, I want to see how she's going to defend herself, because she knows I'm right. "You left to hang out with your boyfriend when I was doing my contemporary solo." Hannah points out accusingly. Interesting that she doesn't deny my point.

"I bet you didn't even notice until you needed someone to hold your jacket when you went on stage," I counter, feeling smug. "Admit it, you only stayed with me because I was before you."

"I would have stayed. I thought we were friends." I can't help but laugh. She's so full of bullshit it's unbelievable.

"Like how you would have ditched Lisa backstage after your Aurora solo unless Ms. Parker specifically told you not to? Yeah, you're a real good friend." I add, sarcasm dripping from every word. "You want to know a secret? I told Ms. Parker she should tell you to stay. I know you well enough to know that you would have left Lisa on her own, without a second thought, if she hadn't. 'Cause you don't want to admit it, but you can be just as self-centered a bitch as me."

Hannah just glares at me from her bed. Her spine so stiff one good shove would snap her in half. I lean back on my hands, smug and confident I've made my point.

"It's not just this weekend. And you know it," Hannah manages to get out. "You know I've had a crush on Tyler forever."

Tears are pooling in her eyes but I'm too mad to care. Let her cry, I'm not done with this conversation. It feels so good to finally tell her what I think, the more I say, the more I realize I've been holding onto this anger for years. All the times I've watched her and her mom together, grief for my own mom clawing its way through my gut. How many times I've seen her dad show up at events, even though he travels all the time. He always makes the time to come support her, while my dad chooses Aiden and Marie over me time after time. I push all that aside and focus on the issue with Tyler. It's time to finish this fight.

"Yeah, and you've been too chicken-shit to even say hi to him for years. You know he didn't even know who you were until January? How can you expect someone to like you back if they don't even know your name? God, you're such a baby." I huff, blocking her words and firing right back.

"I—" Hannah starts to say but I'm not done.

"No, you listen to me. You don't get to call dibs on someone when we're twelve, do nothing about it, and then expect him to magically know he's not supposed to like me back four fucking years later. Life doesn't work like that." I take a breath and tell her the truth. "You don't get to decide who Tyler wants to date. And you don't get to tell me what to do either."

Tears are running down Hannah's cheeks and she angrily dashes them away, staring me down. I can see she's trying to say something so I sit in silence, waiting for her to get it out. "I thought you were my best friend," she finally manages to get out.

"We haven't been for years, Hannah. Even before I joined cheer, if we're being honest. Really ever since…" I swallow hard, dammit I don't want to talk about my mom right now, this is about how Hannah is being a selfish brat, not about why I can't be her best friend.

"Since your mom died." Hannah finishes for me.

I nod. "Yeah. But Hannah, even if we were as close as when we were kids, it still doesn't give you the right to be mad that I have new friends, or that Tyler chose me over you. It's his choice to make, not yours. And seriously, you can't honestly expect someone to know you like them if you never do a damn thing about it." I add. I'm equal parts irritated and sad at this point. The adrenaline rush I was riding fades and I feel myself start to droop. This day has been a fucking roller coaster.

Hannah is silent for a long beat. "Did you remember I had a crush on him when you invited me on that double date?"

Shit. Now I feel about two inches tall. "Maybe," I say quietly.

Hannah rolls over to face the wall, ending the conversation. "Guess I'm not the only self-centered bitch in the room."

CHAPTER 18

Hannah

"DID YOU girls sleep okay last night?" My mom and dad are already sitting at a table in the hotel lobby, steaming mugs of coffee in front of them. No, I want to say. I slept terribly, tossing and turning all night long. Olivia's words running through my brain

The world does not revolve around Hannah O'Brian.

"I'm fine. Just tired." I set my bags down near my dad, dropping a kiss on top of his head. Olivia has already wandered off to the breakfast bar and is loading up a plate with bacon.

We didn't speak a word to each other for the rest of the night. By the time I got up in the morning, Oliva was already dressed, packed, and scrolling through her phone, ignoring me until it was time to meet my parents for breakfast.

Did you even notice anyone else from the studio?

I got dressed and ready for the day in the deafening silence of our room, a sick, hollow feeling in my stomach haunting me. It's not nerves, nerves wouldn't leave me feeling like I'm about to burst into tears at the slightest provocation. No, I know what this is. It's shame.

Am I really that self-absorbed?

You would have ditched Lisa backstage.

I silently load up a plate with scrambled eggs and fruit before heading back to our table and sitting down.

"Are you excited for the classes today?" My mom is trying so hard to act like everything is normal. If everything was normal, I would be chatting non-stop about whoever they'd hired to be the guest teacher today, or maybe what kind of classes were on the schedule. Normal would have me thinking only about myself and what I needed today.

You can be just as self-centered a bitch as me.

"Uh. Yeah. I guess," I mumble around a mouthful of food.

"How did you sleep Olivia?" My mom's question interrupts Olivia as she is walking by our table. She glances up from her phone, a piece of bacon dangling from her teeth.

"Fine. I got up early and walked on the beach a little." She doesn't stop at our table though, she keeps walking and squeezes in next to MacKenzie and Haley, laughing as she tries to fit in at their table. I'd heard her silently leave the room around five this morning, but I hadn't asked where she was going. I was terrified she'd have some other flaw of mine to point out.

My dad studies the scene at the other table, then eyes me. I hold very still, trying not to squirm. "Everything okay, pumpkin?"

"Yeah, you know. We just spent a lot of time together yesterday." When they don't look convinced, I wave my hand in the direction of the table where Olivia is goofing off with the little girls. "I guess she promised them she would eat breakfast with them this morning." I shrug. I have no idea if I just lied through my teeth or not, knowing Olivia it could go either way.

We haven't been friends for years.

The rest of breakfast is quiet, my mom assuming I'm nervous about the day of classes and competition ahead. I'm happy to let her think that.

The second we arrive at the theater I find Katy and Lisa, eager to stay as far away from Olivia as I can. I'm determined to do better today. The hurt in Lisa's eyes when I said I didn't care if she stayed with me or not haunted what little sleep I got last night. I can't think about Ms. Parker pointedly telling me to stay and watch Lisa's solo without feeling ashamed all over again. I can't even recall seeing the younger kids all weekend. Olivia was right.

If Katy and Lisa notice the tension between Olivia and I during the morning classes they are kind enough not to mention it. Instead, they manage to keep themselves between us, like a human wall. I appreciate not having to explain to them what happened, even though it makes me feel even worse that they don't expect an explanation from me. Am I always so self-absorbed?

Normally, I would spend the master classes obsessing over every correction, watching myself in the mirror, comparing my body to everyone around me, starstruck over whoever they had brought in to teach the class. Today, I'm just going through the motions. I silently bless the hours I've spent in the studio, my mind on auto-pilot.

Olivia is a constant presence in my peripheral vision, keeping to the edge of our group in both classes, occasionally chatting with Lisa. She doesn't try to stand out during either class, just quietly does what is asked of her. A subdued Olivia is disconcerting. I catch the other girls glancing at her curiously.

Finally, the classes finish and everyone from our studio gathers in a dressing room to get ready for the ensemble competition this afternoon. The groups from other studios around us are chatting and spilling over with nervous excitement, completely different from our hushed and anxious group. Even the younger kids in our group, who have no idea what's wrong, are quiet, shooting nervous glances our way from time to time, then whispering quietly among themselves.

Olivia finishes her makeup first, looks around and then plops herself down in the middle of the younger girls, deftly pulling a lipstick tube out of one of their hands and applying it for her. I watch in the mirror from the corner of my eye as she smiles and jokes with them. The tension eases from their shoulders as she takes over, encouraging them and making sure they do everything properly. I've never noticed how often she does that. I'm the one who assists with the little kids' classes at the studio, but she's the one who acts like she actually cares about them outside of class.

"Oh my god, I can't take it anymore," Katy bursts out when she finishes applying her eyeliner. "Whatever happened between you and Olivia last night, can we just let it go for now? This sad, mopey, silent treatment is making everyone nervous."

I eye her and Lisa, standing on either side of me, all three of us leaning close to the mirrors and bright lights as we apply the finishing touches of our hair and makeup. "I'm sorry. I'm not trying to be…" My throat closes up and I stop to take a breath. Do not cry Hannah. You just finished your makeup. Do. Not. Cry. I slowly blow out through my nose and a snot bubble escapes. I burst out laughing, "Ugh!" Giggling, Lisa hands me a tissue and some of the tension eases. I blow my nose, being careful not to smudge my lipstick, glad the urge to cry is gone.

"Hey," Lisa gets my attention. "You know we love you, right?" I nod, a tiny smile creeping across my face. "Okay. Now get your act together, we've got a competition to win."

"Yes ma'am," I respond, nodding my head sharply. "Seriously, you guys are my best friends, I'm sorry I'm such a..."

"Mess?" Katy provides helpfully.

"Yeah, sorry I'm such a mess today. But I'm good. We're gonna be great." I straighten my spine and head over to the rack where all our costumes hang. I'm flipping through the hangers looking for mine when Olivia starts looking for her costume on the other end of the rack. I pull hers off the hanger next to mine and turn to hand it to her. "Here," I say quietly, handing it to her. I clear my throat.

"Don't," Olivia snaps, holding up a hand in warning. "Thanks," she adds, acknowledging the costume in her hand. "But I don't want to get into it with you right now."

"I just wanted to say I don't hate you." I murmur. "Good luck," I add, for good measure.

Olivia stares at me for a beat. Then she shakes her head and starts to walk away. She gets about two steps before she turns back to say over her shoulder, "I don't hate you either."

I guess that's good enough for now.

Pushing my feelings aside, I finish getting my costume on and join the rest of my group so we can get on stage and perform one last time. It's time to get focused on why I'm here. Today my goal is to dance with my friends, to dance with the group, all of us creating a beautiful picture together on stage. Each of us has our part to do on stage, mine is to handle the pressure and not let my feelings mess this up for everyone else. One last dance and then it's time for the awards. One more dance and I'll be one step closer to my dream.

I'M STANDING on stage holding a plaque in front of my chest, in complete shock.

I can't wipe the grin off my face.

I won the Grand Prix award.

I won.

The Grand Prix.

My eyes roam over the audience as I stand there, grinning from ear to ear. My mom and dad are standing up, clapping and grinning right back. My dad does a funny little dance when he catches my eye and I stifle a giggle. Ms. Parker is standing up too, a few seats down, smiling and clapping, stopping occasionally to wipe her eyes. I see Katy and her mom, Lisa's family, even Olivia's dad and step-mom all clapping wildly. I turn and glance back at all the other dancers on stage.

I was excited when Olivia and I were both called up as part of the top twelve in the Senior Contemporary Division. We stood next to each other in the line of dancers, not speaking but softly bumping shoulders from time to time. I was overjoyed for Olivia when they called her name in a tie for third place, but secretly disappointed when I wasn't awarded first or second place in the division.

It's possible there was a tiny part of my heart, a part I don't want to admit exists, that pouted at the unfairness of it. That she can skip as many classes as she does for cheer, that she doesn't seem to want it as badly as I do, and still place higher than me. But I pushed it away and concentrated on being happy for my not-best-friend.

When they moved on to the top twelve of the Senior Classical Division and this time Lisa got called up with me, my heart started working overtime. Lisa and I stood side by side, holding hands, as they read the name of the third place winner, then the second place winner. I was trying to brace myself for disappointment, because I saw the girl who got second place and she was amazing. There was no way I placed first. I scanned the line of dancers, trying to guess who could possibly have won first place. It was hard to be sure, since I didn't get a chance to see every solo when I had to go change for my Kitri variation. I thought it could be that girl over there with the dark hair, I didn't remember seeing her classical solo, but I noticed her in class and she was really good.

They called out a name and the dark-haired girl stepped forward to receive the plaque. I swallowed my disappointment and clapped along with everyone else. I had hoped I would place in the top three of at least one category. I have enough self-awareness to know that I'm naturally talented, and I work hard every single day in class. I didn't think it was cocky of me to hope for something. My shoulders sagged, but we couldn't leave the stage yet. Lisa squeezed my hand and bumped her shoulder against mine.

As I stood there with Lisa, trying not to show my disappointment the presenter explained that they don't always give this last award at a semi-finals competition, it only goes to a dancer who impresses the judges in both Contemporary and Classical and rises above the rest of the competition as a truly outstanding dancer. I looked down the line of dancers. Maybe that one guy, the one in the blue shirt at that horrendous first class, won it. He placed first for the guys in both the contemporary and classical divisions. Lisa tugged on my hand, bringing my attention back to the presenter standing at the front of the stage.

"This year's Senior Grand Prix award for the Orange County Semi-Finals is…Hannah O'Brian!"

I stood stock still for a heartbeat, until Lisa shoved me forward and I walked on unsteady feet to the front of the stage to receive my award.

I still can hardly believe it. I'm standing center stage, knees shaking, heart pounding, cheeks aching from the smile I can't stop.

"That's not all ladies and gentlemen," I hear the presenter say over the microphone as the applause dies down. "As I'm sure you're aware, one of our judges this weekend was the incredible Marco Bethelo, who will be taking over as the Director of the Pacfic Sound Ballet School in the fall. Marco would you like to join us on stage?" She gestures to someone standing in the wings. The man who walks on stage is the definition of tall, dark and handsome. His square jaw is covered in a layer of scruff, his dark hair has a few touches of silver at the temples, but he walks with the grace and confidence of a prince. It's not surprising that he was known for dancing all the leading male roles in his time at CBS. Ms. Parker has often said he was her favorite partner to dance with. I recognize him from the judging panel at the audition last weekend.

"Thank you," he says to the audience, gesturing for them to sit. "I had a wonderful time this weekend," he turns to look at the dancers on stage behind him and continues. "Thank you for sharing your artistry and talent with us. I know how hard you all have worked in preparation for this competition. You should be proud of yourselves and be sure to thank the teachers and parents who supported you on your journey to get here today." He pauses and we take that as our cue to politely clap for our parents and teachers. I awkwardly juggle my plaque and try to clap, my eyes seeking out Ms. Parker and my parents in the crowd.

Marco clears his throat before speaking again. "As you heard, I will be taking over as Director of the school at Pacific Sound Ballet. While I don't officially take over until September, I have been given the honor of offering places to our summer intensive this year." I turn and grin at Lisa behind me. Oh my goodness, how amazing would it be if we got offered a spot right now? We still haven't heard back from the audition. "Several of you have received an invitation from me, you'll find it attached to your scoresheet. Congratulations," he adds with a smile at those of us on stage.

His eyes roam over the dancers on stage, stopping on a few with a smile. The dark-haired girl who won first place in our division, the boy in the blue shirt and Lisa too, which makes my heart squeeze with joy. Then he turns to face me and my heart stops. "I was also given one full scholarship to award. I am awarding it to Hannah O'Brian for her astounding artistry and exquisite dancing this weekend." My eyes are open so wide they ache and I think my mouth is hanging open in shock. "Congratulations, Hannah!" He finishes, handing the microphone back to the presenter, then he strides over to me, hand extended, a breath-taking smile on his face.

"Congratulations," he says again as he shakes my hand. He hands me a large manila envelope. "Here, this is the paperwork you need for the scholarship. You were just lovely. Who is your teacher?" He asks quietly as the presenter wraps up the awards presentation.

"Ms. Parker. Uh, I mean, Leslie Parker," I stammer out. "She says you were always her favorite partner," I blurt out, like a total dork. Oh god, I'm so embarrassed. I want to shrivel up and disappear. But Marco just laughs and turns to look out into the audience, a hand shielding his eyes from the bright stage lights so he can make out the people sitting out there. The house lights come up as the awards finish and the audience starts moving from their seats.

I point her out to him, she's in the aisle making her way toward the stage, "Ah, there." A grin breaks out on his gorgeous face and he rests a hand on my shoulder. "Thank you Hannah. I look forward to working with you this summer." And with that he turns away to speak to another dancer who has walked over to meet him.

I'm nearly bowled over from behind as Lisa throws her arms around me. "Oh my god Hannah!" she practically screams in my ear. I can't help myself and I join her in jumping and squealing. I can't believe I did it. This is better than I could have ever dreamed, a full scholarship to PSB and winning the Grand Prix. I might just explode from joy, it's leaking out of every pore. My cheeks hurt from smiling so hard and my heart feels like it might beat right out of my chest.

My parents are standing hesitantly at the bottom of the stairs leading up to the stage, grinning at me. Katy rushes past them to tackle Lisa and me in a hug, her excited squeals joining ours. I manage to pull my head out from the tangle of arms and see Olivia standing nearby, a sad smile on her face.

I extricate myself from Katy and Lisa, the pair of them standing side by side at my back. "Hey," I say. "Congratulations, third for Contemporary, that's amazing Olivia." I add. "I'm so happy for you."

Olivia snorts. "Whatever. Grand Prix and a scholarship? That's amazing Hannah." Olivia swallows. "I'm really happy for you," she adds after a moment.

"Hey," I say as she starts to turn away. I take a breath, I need to say this. "You weren't wrong. What you said last night." Olivia's eyebrows shoot up almost to her hairline. I cough, feeling uncomfortable, but glad I have Lisa and Katy behind me. They literally have my back and I've never appreciated them for it more. "Anyway. Thanks for caring enough to tell me."

"I said it was because I was pissed at you. But you're welcome," Olivia responds with a smile that doesn't quite reach her eyes. "And back at you." she shrugs and disappears into the crowd of adults and other dancers surging towards me. I'm surrounded by people congratulating me, shaking my hand and hugging me. It's a blur of faces, until suddenly my mom is hugging me tight, my dad's arms wrapped around the pair of us.

"Ah! Sweetie I'm so proud of you!" my mom is saying over and over in my ear. I can hear my dad rumbling congratulations above my head as I'm crushed between them. "You did it, you did it," she chants, squeezing me so hard I can barely breathe.

Just as my parents release me, Ms. Parker pulls me into an all-encompassing hug. "I'm so, so, so proud of you Hannah!" she whispers in my ear. Pulling back, she holds my shoulders and looks into my eyes. "You were breathtaking. And you made me cry," she finishes with a laugh, her eyes glassy with tears. My own eyes tear up in response and we laugh at each other, tears running down our cheeks as I hug her tight.

"Thank you" I manage to get past the giant lump in my throat. "Thank you for believing in me and for being the most amazing teacher in the world. I couldn't have done it without you."

"Teaching you is a joy, Hannah. You've earned this, be proud of yourself. You deserve it." With that, she steps back to make room for the crowd of dancers from our studio who rush in to hug and congratulate me. Looking out into the auditorium, I see Olivia and her dad walking out the door. Mr. Beck waves from the door and I wave back, but Oliva just stalks past him without stopping.

Until last night, I would have said she was one of my best friends, but now? I don't know what we are. Are we friends who are in a fight? Are we even friends at all?

CHAPTER 19

Hannah

A WEEK LATER I still don't know where Olivia and I stand. I'm exhausted from the roller coaster of emotions I've been riding. Every time I see Olivia or Tyler at school I'm overwhelmed with anger and sadness. But when my phone buzzes and I see it's another funny message or picture from Trevor, I get a bubbly rush of happiness. In my ballet classes I feel lighter than air, the high of winning the grand prix rushing back to me, while school leaves me feeling heavy and numb.

By Sunday, a week after winning at YIGP, I feel wrung out and limp, but I have to pull it together for one last audition. The Classical Ballet School auditions are the last event on my list, one last hurdle to clear before deciding where my future begins.

Lisa and I aren't quite the first people to arrive at the audition, but we are close enough. I'm number eleven and Lisa is number twelve. We pin our numbers to the front of our leotards and walk into the studio. A few other girls are already in here, already claiming spots on the barre along one wall.

"Are we going to save a spot for Olivia?" Lisa asks.

"No." I know I sound snarky, but I can't bring myself to care.

"Woah...You okay?" Lisa asks.

"Yeah," I sigh. "I'm just exhausted and right now I need to focus. I'll tell you about it later, promise."

Out of habit, I watch everyone who comes in the door, sizing them up—good feet, bad feet, messy hair, holes in the tights, interesting leotard. The sliver of confidence I'm holding onto after last weekend starts to slip as the room fills up.

At precisely noon, four people walk into the room and the quiet chatter dies. The class is direct and to the point without a lot of fancy choreography. Julie King, the teacher, walks around the room during each exercise quietly giving corrections as she goes. The worst part is when she gives someone a correction, then goes and leans against the table, quietly talking to the other three.

"Did you see Olivia walk in?" Lisa whispers, when they give us a moment to stretch halfway through class.

"She came?" I ask, looking around. There she is, sitting right at the back, putting a bandaid on her pinkie toe. I feel my heart sink into my stomach, a hollow, empty feeling. I can barely stand to look at her right now. "I wasn't paying attention," I admit. Focus, Hannah, focus. Don't let anything distract you today. Today is about your future, nothing else matters right now.

"Yeah, I saw her slip in when we started plies on the second side. I think she's the last number."

"Ladies, we're going to line up in groups of six, in numerical order please. Number one you start over here," Ms. King says, indicating where the front row should begin. "Let's begin, starting with the right foot in front, facing croisé..." Ms. King sets the next exercise. I have a photograph of her in rehearsal hanging up in my room that I bought at a CBS performance when I was eight. I even got my mom to wait at the stage door with me and had her sign it. It's been hanging over my door ever since. I look at it every time I walk out of my room, praying that one day that will be me.

Fifteen minutes before the class is supposed to end, Ms. King sets a batterié exercise—a series of small quick jumps where you switch legs multiple times in the air—that feels impossible. The doubt and anxiety I felt in Jean-Paul's class starts to creep into my mind, making it hard to concentrate. I keep missing one of the beats and ending up on the wrong leg, which messes me up for the next part of the sequence. Ms. King has given us all a minute to work it out for ourselves, we've tried twice already and no one seems to be getting it right.

I do it slowly with my hands, willing myself to remember the sequence. I do it twice more with my hands, then mark the steps with my feet. I pull an unsteady breath in through my nose, pushing aside my frustration at not being able to get this exercise correct, and try it again.

"Mark it with the other leg," a voice says near me. I look up, startled. Ms. King is standing just next to me, watching me and Lisa. "Mark the brisé with your other leg, and don't get frustrated, no one ever gets this exercise right. Christopher likes to set it in class every few weeks. It took me ages to get it right," she smiles. I look up and notice that Christopher MacKenzie, the school's director, is smiling as he watches us struggle with the exercise.

It's amazing how different this class feels compared to last weekend. Jean-Paul gave us exercises that were purposefully designed to trip us up, just like this one. But while his exercises left me feeling ready to give up, this one is just making me more determined to get it right. I guess the difference is in the teacher. Even though this is an audition, it feels like this is a challenge to see who can rise to the occasion, not an impossible feat intended to weed out the weak.

"I know this is a horrible exercise," Ms. King is saying. "It's famous at CBS and in the company for being a real pain to figure out. We'll try once again and see if anyone here can get it." We all prepare, standing in perfectly crossed fifth positions, arms rounded and low, ready for the music. The music begins and we start jumping, our feet a flurry of right and left, left and right, right, right, left and left. "Better!" Ms King calls above the music, "Keep going, you're almost to the end! Left, right, changément, changément."

We finish up the audition with a waltzing grand allegro, leaping and soaring from one corner of the room to the other. After the quick and detailed footwork of the last exercise, I revel in the push of the floor against my legs and dancing in big, broad strokes. I'm exhausted, but love the feeling of this one last push to the finish line. After we finish, Mr. MacKenzie has us line up again in numerical order to curtsy and thank Ms. King and the pianist for the class. After a smattering of respectful applause for the teacher, Mr. MacKenzie raises his hands to ask for silence. We all stand, waiting expectantly.

"Thank you very much for coming today ladies, if you're accepted to the program, or waitlisted, you should receive a letter from us in the next week or so. If you do not receive anything from us, then we thank you for your time and encourage you to audition again next year. Now, if you would please clear the room quickly, we have the men's audition starting in just a few moments."

NOTHER STRAINED week leaves me exhausted and looking forward to my first weekend in almost a month with no events and no drama. All I want is a quiet night in my bed, watching a movie and relaxing. There's nothing I can do now except wait to hear from CBS, then I have to start making decisions about my future. I thought getting through the auditions was going to be the hardest part, but it turns out mentally weighing my options while obsessively watching Olivia and Tyler at school is worse.

Trading memes with Trevor on Instagram has become my escape from reality.

(HANNAHBANANABALLERINA): marvelousStanley sent you a post by @YIGP

I swipe to see what Trevor's sent me now and gasp when I realize what it is. The official YIGP account posted a photo from last weekend's competition, a photo of me, mid-jump, back arched, arms reaching up over head, my legs perfectly split. It's the jump shot every ballet dancer would die for. And it's me. On their page. Unbelieving, I read the caption, "Congratulations to Hannah O'Brian for winning the Senior Grand Prix award and a full scholarship to PSB's summer intensive at last weekend's Orange County Semi-Final." There is a photo from my Aurora and my contemporary solos with it. I can't believe this is really happening.

As I'm holding my phone a message from Trevor pops beneath it.

MARVELOUSSTANLEY: Congratulations! I'm assuming this is the competition I heard about? I'm sure you were working really hard for this, it looks like you did what you set out to do.

I stare at my phone for a second, suddenly nervous. We generally just trade pictures, we haven't really chatted much. Well, Trevor's chatted more than me. I never know what to say, so I usually just respond with emojis. After what I saw on Tyler's phone, I've been too confused about what he meant by "his girl" to do more than that. But I should answer him, it would be rude not to. Right?

HANNAHBANANABALLERINA: Thanks, that means a lot. I can't believe you saw it before me.

I sound so lame.

MARVELOUSSTANLEY: Is it totally weird that I've been checking to see if they had any pictures from the competition? I swear I'm not trying to be creepy. You don't post very many pictures and I wanted to see you in action.

Is it creepy? Maybe a little. But he's not wrong, I don't post very much and almost never photos of myself dancing.

HANNAHBANANABALLERINA: It's a little creepy. But I'll allow it this time.

MARVELOUSSTANLEY: Thanks for the creeper pass. So how come I caught you tonight? It's Sat night, shouldn't you be out having fun? Isn't there some party somewhere?

MARVELOUSSTANLEY: I mean, I'm glad you're not at a party, then I wouldn't have gotten to chat with you.

Whoa. Is Trevor flirting with me? Am I flirting back? Olivia said he liked me, but she could have been lying just to get under my skin.

MARVELOUSSTANLEY: What are you up to tonight? Got a hot date with a pair of pointe shoes?

I actually laugh out loud at this one. Wow, Trevor is a bigger dork than I remembered. But it's kind of nice to feel on equal footing with someone for once.

HANNAHBANANABALLERINA: Nope, just me, my bed, and a movie
MARVELOUSSTANLEY: Whatcha watching?
HANNAHBANANABALLERINA: Promise you won't make fun of me?

Trevor's response is a gif of Duckie from Pretty in Pink pointing to himself mouthing "moi?"

HANNAHBANANABALLERINA: Teen Beach Movie. I know It's dumb, but I love It anyways.

I watch those three dots wiggle as he types a response. It seems to take ages for it to finally come through. What is he writing, an essay?

MARVELOUSSTANLEY: Promise not to tell Tyler, but my little sister is obsessed with that movie and makes me watch it with her all the time. I've probably seen it a dozen times.

This time I'm the one responding with a gif of Mack and Brady singing and dancing to "Make it Stop." Trevor responds with a clip of the girls dancing around in pajamas, which I counter with a dude dancing on the beach with a blow up shark. Trevor sends a series of crying laughing emojis in response followed by the famous Katy Perry dancing left shark with the words "I have no idea what I'm doing" underneath it.

I burst out laughing when I get a gif of Chris Evans with the words "allow me to seduce you with my awkward self" flashing underneath it.

MARVELOUSSTANLEY: Enjoy your evening with bikers and surfers. Night Hannah

HANNAHBANANABALLERINA: Night

I snuggle down into my cozy nest of blankets and press play. I'm half watching and half scrolling through my phone. On a whim, I scroll through Trevor's Instagram account, looking to see what he posts. There's a bunch of pictures of a dog, a goofy-looking mutt that he seems to take on a lot of runs. There are some photos of what look like track and field events and some really pretty shots of the harbor and water out in Seattle.

I switch over to scrolling through Tyler's account, to see if there's anything new. I don't know why I do this, it hurts me every time I see him post a new picture of him and Olivia, and there are a lot of pictures of the two of them. But I have this irresistible need to look. It's like a bruise, I keep poking it to see if it still hurts. The thing I would never admit out loud—I don't know if I want it to stop hurting or not.

What would it be like to let that go? I've had this crush on Tyler for so long, it feels like part of me—this angsty, unrequited feeling. Who would I be if I let it go? Would I still be able to conjure up that feeling of yearning, of wanting, if he isn't the object of that desire anymore? I've had it for so long, if I let it go would that space in my soul just be empty? Or would something else take its place? The fear of the unknown is what keeps me holding on. I know this pain, this particular pain is familiar and easy to live with. It's a safe kind of pain. What if whatever takes its place is bigger and scarier?

"Hannah?" My mom sticks her head in my door. "Is Olivia supposed to be here?"

"Um, no?' Confusion clouds my mind and I slide my laptop and phone off my lap. "I haven't spoken to Olivia in a couple of weeks." I say, still thoroughly confused.

"Can you talk to Dan please?" I take my mom's phone from her outstretched hand and hold it up to my ear.

"Uh, hi Mr. Beck." Please let Olivia be okay, please let Olivia be okay.

"Hi Hannah. Do you know where Olivia is? I was trying to check on her and she isn't answering her phone. She said she was at your house tonight."

What?

"Um, no. She's not here Mr. Beck." I say tentatively, tendrils of worry sneaking up my spine and settling in my gut with a heavy weight.

"What do you mean, she's not there? Olivia told me that she was spending the night at your house." My heart stops.

"Um. I don't know. We haven't really talked since YIGP. She never said anything to me about tonight. Are you sure she isn't out with Tyler?" I mean, that's the logical place for her to be on a Saturday night.

"Hannah," my mom interrupts. "If you know anything you need to tell us. Please." My mom's voice quivers, an answering quivering begins in my own voice.

"I really don't know, I swear Mom." My voice cracks on the last word. "I'm sorry, I don't know. I don't know where she is." I can't control the tears that spill over. My mom plucks her phone out of my hand.

"Sorry, Dan. I'll see if Hannah can help us find her. You should call the Stanleys. Do you need…" her words trail off as she walks away.

I sit on my bed, numbness battling with anger and worry. Is she okay? Where is she? Is Olivia with Tyler? What are they doing? Questions fly through my brain faster and faster, my brain already thinking of the next question before I've even had a chance to think of an answer.

I quickly send a text to Olivia.

ME: Hey, your dad just called looking for you.
Where are you?

I start scrolling through Instagram looking to see if I can figure out where Olivia is while I wait for a reply. There's nothing posted on Olivia's account, no surprise there. She's not dumb enough to post something showing she's not at my house. I click over to Tyler's account but I already know there's nothing there. I start looking through the accounts of other people at school. It's the only thing I can think of that might be helpful.

Where are they and what could they be doing? Why do they have to lie about where they are? I'm imagining cheap motel rooms and crazy parties, getting more and more worried by the minute.

I consider messaging Trevor again, if only to have someone distract me from my worry.

I'm about to message him when a Facetime call interrupts me.

"Hey Lisa," I answer.

"Oh my god! Did you see what Olivia is doing?" Lisa practically yells through the screen.

"Where is she? Everyone is looking for her." I'm practically hyperventilating. "Her dad called here looking for her, but obviously I have no idea where she is. She told her dad she was going to be here, so now no one knows where she is." I finally have to stop and take a breath.

"Go look at Jack's instagram." Lisa says cryptically. "Look at his latest post and tell me that's not Olivia in the background." Lisa clarifies.

I quickly pull up Jack's account and look at his latest post. It's a photo of basically the entire varsity football team, Jack and Tyler right in the center. They're standing on the beach, no, wait, that's not just any beach. They must be in LA because that's the Santa Monica Pier in the background. The sun is setting and there are a bunch of girls hanging around them, wrapped up in sweatshirts and sweaters.

I scan the picture, looking for whatever has Lisa so worked up and then I spot it. Almost hidden behind the group of guys, I see Olivia. She's wearing a too-large letterman's jacket, it must be Tyler's, over a bikini top and jeans, her long blonde hair hiding her face. The thing that obviously has Lisa worked up is the brown glass bottle she's taking a sip from.

"Oh my god," I breathe. "No...Lisa how did you find this?" I don't know what to do. I feel sick to my stomach, I can't believe this. "I have to go, I have to go tell Mr. Beck. Wait, how did you find that picture?" I ask.

"Just scrolling." Lisa doesn't sound concerned and I'm over here freaking out. "Hey, this is not your fault." Lisa's voice breaks through my fuzzy thoughts.

"Hannah, her bad decisions are not your fault. Okay?" Lisa reminds me. Yeah, okay. I can remember that. "See you tomorrow?"

"Yeah, see you tomorrow." I hang up and run down the stairs to show my mom what Lisa found. I pace the living room as she calls Mr. Beck to let him know. After a minute, my mom pulls me to sit down on the couch next to her, arm around my shoulder.

"Hannah, are you sure you don't know anything else?" she asks gently. "You're not in trouble, but if you know anything else you need to let us know."

"I swear Mom, I don't know anything else," I rub my hands over my arms, nervous and worried. "Olivia and I got into a huge fight at YIGP, we really haven't spoken since."

"I thought something must have happened, you've been pretty quiet ever since last weekend." Her phone buzzes and she glances at the screen for a moment, reading. "Her phone is going straight to voicemail. You don't have Tyler's number do you? Or Jack's?"

"I have Tyler's," I say in a quiet voice. "I don't have Jack's, but I can get it from Katy."

"That's okay sweetie, I can get Jack's from Nancy. Can you send me Tyler's please? And then you can go back to bed, there's nothing else for us to do. Dan and Martha will let me know if they need any more help." I send Tyler's number to my mom but I don't get off the couch.

"Mom?" My stomach feels like lead. "Are you going to be mad at me if Olivia and I aren't friends anymore?"

"What? Of course not, sweetie!" my mom grabs me in a tight hug, her arms wrapping all the way around me. I lean against her for a minute, eyes closed, letting my body go bone-less against hers, relaxing for the first time in what feels like months. I feel her press a kiss to the top of my head. "How I feel about Olivia, or how I felt about her mom, doesn't have anything to do with you. I loved Jenny like a sister and I miss her every day. I worry about Olivia, she's like a niece to me." I look up, worried I will see disappointment in her eyes. "But that's *my* relationship with her. You have your own relationship with each other."

"I would be worried if your relationship never changed. You aren't six anymore, we can't fix a fight between you with a time out and a shared peanut butter and jelly sandwich." She smiles sadly at me, tucking a piece of hair behind my ear. "Olivia's life and yours are very different, and that's okay. If you need to step away from each other in order to find friends that understand you better, that's okay. It's good."

"She said she can't stand seeing us together, cause it makes her miss her mom too much." My mom just nods. "I would probably feel the same way if it was me. I guess I remind her of everything she doesn't have anymore."

"Maybe it's time for you girls to move on. I'm sorry if I made you feel like you had to stay friends with her." I squeeze my mom again, drawing just a little more of her strength.

"You didn't, not really. It just feels like, that's how it's supposed to be? I don't know, I'm so confused. I want to be her friend because I care about her, but I don't want to be her friend because I don't really like her very much right now." I shake my head, not sure how to describe what I'm feeling. "I'm so worried about her. But I've been mad at her for so long now, it's like I don't know how to like her anymore. I don't think I can be her friend right now."

My mom doesn't say anything, just holds me tight, stroking my hair like she used to do when I was little. After a minute, I drag myself to my feet. "I'm going to go to bed. Love you Mom."

"Love you too, sweetie. Do you want me to let you know if I hear anything?"

"No, that's okay. I'm sure I'll hear about it one way or the other." I make my way back to my room, exhausted and ready to sleep.

Sleep doesn't come.

11:47PM. I hope Olivia is okay. Should I text her and check on her?

11:55PM. Don't text Olivia. She's not going to respond anyway.

12:01AM. I hope they don't drink and drive. I should just make sure she's okay.

I can't take it any longer and I quickly send her a text. Not knowing is killing me.

ME: Are you home yet?

I don't expect a reply, but I feel better for asking.

12:17AM. She isn't answering. What if they got in a car accident on the way home?

12:29AM. Stupid Tyler. Stupid Olivia. Why can't I let it go? I need to let it go.

CHAPTER 20

Olivia

I THINK I'M going to throw up.

"Hey babe, you okay?" Tyler reaches out a hand to gently rub my thigh, never taking his eyes off the curving highway ahead of us. He decided to drive home on PCH and my stomach is not happy about all the winding curves along the coast. I'm curled up in the passenger seat, Tyler's jacket wrapped around me, my head resting against the window sipping from a bottle of water. I can't remember the last time I felt so carsick.

"Yeah, I'll be fine. S'mores, hots dogs and excessive quantities of soda are probably not a good combination." I smile weakly, taking another sip of water. "Distract me?" There's sand in my hair and my feet are dry and itchy inside my shoes from the salt water.

Tyler's hand on my thigh is comforting. "Did I tell you about what Drew did in class yesterday?" I shake my head, keeping my eyes on the road and willing the churning in my stomach to settle and my skin to stop itching. "So we were sitting in English and Allyson was doodling in her notes, you know she's always doing that?"

"Yeah, she's really good actually. Did you know she drew all the stuff on her backpack?"

"Seriously? I thought she bought it like that. Anyway, she was doodling and Drew, being Drew, was trying to flirt by copying her notes."

"I bet she got pissed." I chuckle to myself, imagining it. I heard Allyson's side of this story earlier at the beach. "Did you see what she was drawing?"

"No, she started yelling at Drew, then Mr. Garcia yelled at them both before we could see it." Puffing up his chest Tyler does his best impression of Mr. Garcia. "Andrew. Allyson. Flirt on your own time, not mine." I laugh at his terrible impression, my car sickness fading.

"She was drawing Andrew's face. That's why she got so pissed, she didn't want him to see it." I happened to know that Allyson has a whole collection of portraits scattered through her notes. It's what she does when she's bored in class, but since she has a crush on Andrew "Drew" Park, I'm not surprised she didn't want him to see it.

I smile to myself as we drive home. Since we started dating, Tyler has turned out to be more than just my "cute boyfriend." We make a great team, sticking together in our friend group and the school in general. Plus, he encourages me to stay on top of my homework. Our coaches both insist that we keep our GPAs up to stay on the team and the squad.

The varsity football and cheer teams un-official party down at the Santa Monica Pier had been just what I needed after all the drama with Hannah and the ballet girls. Just a night with my real friends, laughing, being silly, not taking life seriously. I didn't even have my phone with me, it died right after we arrived, so I left it in Tyler's car. Not having it was as relaxing as the sound of the waves crashing against the beach.

One of the guys brought hot dogs, Tyler and I brought s'mores and as a joke Allyson brought these craft sodas called Apple Beer. They look like beer bottles, but are totally non-alcoholic. We definitely got some dirty looks, but since half those boys are counting on football to get into college, we weren't actually stupid enough to have open beer bottles on a public beach. We thought it was hysterical, but were super glad we didn't have any real beer when one of the beach cops came over to talk to us. Once he had a good look at the label, he laughed with us, but told us off for having glass bottles on the beach.

Tyler pulls up to my house just after midnight. I was expecting the house to be dark, but the lights are on downstairs.

"Shit, I gotta go," I scramble to get out of the car, tossing Tyler's jacket in the back seat. "Pray my dad doesn't kill me." I toss over my shoulder as I close the car door. Before I get two steps, the front door opens, silhouetting my dad standing in the doorway, his arms crossed over his chest.

"You have some explaining to do." My dad's voice is cold. I try to wipe my feet on the grass as I walk past the driveway.

"Uh..." I start. My dad turns and leads me into the house, our voices dropping so we don't wake anyone up. I drop my bag at the front door.

My dad doesn't say anything, just gestures me to sit at the kitchen table. I sit, not sure how much trouble I'm in. I was late getting home and I lied about where I was, sure, but my dad seems angrier than those things deserve. There has to be something else and I don't know what it is. I don't like not knowing. I fidget in my chair, nervous.

"I tried to call you, but your phone went straight to voicemail."

"My battery died." I pull my phone out of my pocket to show him the blank screen. I even try powering it on, letting the battery symbol flash so he knows it's the truth.

"I was worried so I called Anne O'Brian to check on you." I swallow. "Want to explain why she had no idea where you were?"

I open my mouth but nothing comes out, not sure if I can talk my way out of this.

"I know you weren't at Hannah's." He interrupts me before a lie can cross my lips.

I sigh, my shoulders slumping. "I was at Santa Monica pier with the squad." My dad's eyebrow shoots up. "And the football team," I add.

"Why did you tell me you were with Hannah?"

"So you would give me a later curfew."

"What?" My dad looks confused.

"Whenever I say I'm going out with Hannah, you go easy on my curfew," I say quietly.

"So, all the times in the last few months you've told me you were going out with Hannah, or at her house, were a lie?" My dad growls. I'm in really big trouble now.

I swallow. "Um, not every single time." I get a look. "Not the first time. And I was kinda there when you and Martha went to Santa Barbara."

"What do you mean, 'kind of there'?"

"Um…I was there for a while, then I hung out with Tyler for a little while. But then I went back."

My dad's face is getting red. "Are you serious? Olivia, what were you thinking? I have been sick with worry for hours and now you're telling me you've been lying to me, abusing my trust, not to mention using your friend, for *months*?"

Well, when he says it like that, I guess it does sound pretty bad. I've been feeling guilty about what I said to Hannah at YIGP, but this is ten thousand times worse. I just look at him, feeling terrible, but I have no words to explain myself. There's nothing I can say that will make this better.

We stare at each other in silence for a minute. When I don't offer up any explanation he holds out his phone. "Want to explain this?" There's a screenshot of someone's Instagram post on the screen. I look closer, it's from Jack Quinn's account. It's a photo of the entire football team on the beach, Tyler and Jack in the center, the distinctive outline of the pier in the sunset behind them.

"I told you, we went to Santa Monica. We were just hanging out Dad. I'm sorry I lied to you about where I was." I begin, not entirely sure what I'm supposed to say.

"Look closer," my dad's voice has gone icy. His cold disappointment is worse than if he would just yell at me. I take the phone from his hand and examine it. I spot myself, barely visible behind the guys, sitting on the sand, drinking my soda. And then it hits me.

"Dad, I swear, that was soda. It's not what it looks like!"

He just looks at me. "I swear Dad, Allyson brought it. I know it looks like beer but it's *just soda*. I promise. I can show you." I use his phone to pull up a photo of the label, where it clearly states that it is non-alcoholic. I sigh. "It was a joke." I debate telling him, but decide that full-disclosure is the best policy. "One of the bike cops that patrol the beach came over to yell at us, but when he saw what it was he thought it was funny too. I swear!"

"I don't think it's particularly funny, Olivia. How can I trust that you're telling me the truth right now? You've apparently been lying to me for months."

"Let me get my charger and I can prove it." For once, I'm thankful for Allyson's penchant for texting us every ten minutes. I run and grab my charger from my room, plugging my phone in as quickly as I can. I fumble in my hurry, my dad's angry stare sending goosebumps down my spine. Finally my phone powers on and I pray Tyler sent me the photo he promised. I open up my texts and hand it over to my dad to read.

> **ALLYSON:** OMG, just found the best thing EVER!!!!!
>
> **ALLYSON:** I'm totally getting my mom to buy these for tonight, it's going to be HILARIOUS!

Attached is a photo of the Apple Beer, the label identical to what I showed my dad.

> **MEGAN:** Hell yes, those are amazing.
>
> **MADISON:** I had those at Thanksgiving last year, they're so good. Do it, it's gonna be hysterical!

There's a bunch of crying laughing emojis and a gif from me of a baby laughing so hard they fall over.

"See?" I tell my dad when he gets to the end of the messages. "Allyson's mom bought them for us," I add, in case that wasn't clear. I take my phone back and open my message thread with

Tyler, looking for the photo he was supposed to send me. I breathe a sigh of relief when it's there.

I hand my phone back to my dad so he can see it. It's a photo of Tyler, me, and Allyson with the cop who came to talk to us, each of us holding a bottle, clinking them together. Of course we gave him one, once he saw what they were.

"Well," my dad clears his throat. "Okay then. I can see that you didn't do anything quite as stupid as it looked." I grin. It was funny, even he has to admit it. "But that doesn't excuse the fact that you have been lying to me and Martha about where you are for months."

My grin falls. Damn, I was hoping I'd distracted him from this conversation.

"I don't know if I can trust you to keep dating Tyler if you've been lying to me about going to see him." I start to protest, but my dad holds his hand up to silence me. "No, you need to listen to me. Olivia, this serious. If you really like this boy, then you'll do what it takes to earn back the trust you've broken."

At my dad's words, it hits me. I really like Tyler. The idea of not being able to see him leaves me breathless, like my heart is breaking apart inside my chest. Worse, he doesn't deserve this, he never once lied to *his* parents about where we were or when he was out with me. I did this to myself. I did this to us and for what? To get my curfew extended by an hour?

"Please, Dad! I'm so sorry, I promise, it won't happen again," I say quickly, my throat tight and my eyes filling with tears. What have I done? "Please, it isn't Tyler's fault. You can ask the Stanleys, he never lied to them, it was only me, I swear. I just…" I hiccup, the words getting stuck in my throat. "I don't know why I did it. It was so stupid. I just wanted to feel like I was in control of it all." Now that the tears have started, I can't stop them. God, I'm such an idiot.

My dad's arm wraps around my shoulder, hugging me to his chest. "I'm not going to make you break up with him, Olivia. But there will be consequences." At his words, I manage a deep, albeit wet and snotty, breath. "For one, you're definitely grounded for the next two weeks."

I probably deserve more, so I bite back my impulse to argue with him.

"And until I feel like I can trust you again your curfew is nine o'clock sharp. Not a minute later. We can negotiate extending it at a later date. And I'll need you to check in and send proof of your location any time you go out. If you go somewhere new, you'll have to let me know and send proof." Is he serious? I have to check in with him every single time I go out? This time the urge to argue with him overpowers me, but as I open my mouth and make a noise, the look on my dad's face stops me. I close my mouth, still fuming inside. I know arguing right now is only going to make things worse, but the words bubble up inside me anyway.

I take a slow breath, fighting down the angry words that are dying to get out. "Fine." I get the single word out, gritting my teeth against the rest of the tirade in my mind. It's not as bad as it could have been, I'll just have to keep reminding myself.

"One more thing."

"What is it?" I ask, willing myself to stay calm. Am I going to owe him babysitting on Friday nights for the next month?

"You owe Hannah an apology."

Damnit.

"What?" I ask, that was not what I was expecting. I lean back in my chair, crossing my arms over my chest. "Why?"

My dad's incredulous look leaves me squirming in my seat. "Olivia Rose Beck, you used your best friend to lie to me. When I called there looking for you tonight, she had no clue what you had been doing. She was worried sick about you."

"She's not my best friend anymore, Dad." The idea of apologizing to Hannah has my stomach churning. Or maybe that's leftover from the car ride. Or it could be the guilt I've been fighting off all week, the guilt I can feel below the surface of my anger.

"Do you really believe that?"

"What do you mean? Of course I believe it." I say, annoyed. If I focus on being annoyed at Hannah and angry at my dad for punishing me, then maybe I can keep the guilt at bay.

"If you were in trouble and you didn't want me to know, who would you call?"

I mull it over for a moment, the guilt doing it's best to make me acknowledge its presence.

"Hannah," I spit out, reluctantly.

"If you were scared, who would you call, besides me of course."

Guilt is winning out. I shrink down in my chair, fingers fiddling with a stand of wind-tangled hair. "Hannah."

"When you need help solving a problem, big or small, who would you trust to actually help you get it done?"

"Ugh! Hannah, okay?"

"Do I have to keep going?"

"No. I get it. It doesn't mean that I like her right now, though." I point out. It's the truth, I don't like her right now. I keep my eyes down, not meeting my dad's eyes, my fingers absently picking at a new tangle.

"I don't care if you like her or not, you owe her an apology. What on Earth possessed you to think it was okay to use her like that?"

"Because she never does anything wrong!" I can't contain the words, or my anger any longer. "Stupid Hannah is so fucking perfect, with her perfect mom and her perfect dancing and her perfect never-breaks-the-rules attitude." My dad looks shocked at my language, but once the words start flowing I couldn't stop them if I tried.

"It's not fair! When I told you she was coming on my first date with Tyler, suddenly, just because Little Miss Perfect was coming, you go from the Spanish Inquisition to 'have fun, sweetie, here's an extra hour on your curfew while you're at it.' Just because *she* was coming too." I take a shaky breath, the tears I've been fighting spilling over. "I hate her for always being right."

My dad is silent for several long minutes while I hiccup and try to catch my breath. "Do you think that maybe you started being mad at her years ago, because she didn't understand how you were feeling about your mom? And in her defense, how could she? You guys were twelve when your mom passed, neither of you knew how to deal with it. She tried to be your friend the best way she knew how and I think you're mad because she wasn't exactly the friend you needed." He pauses expectantly. I glance up to see him looking down at me, making sure I'm paying attention. "Because she couldn't understand what you needed. And the one thing you really wanted was impossible for anyone to give you. It's not her fault your mom isn't here."

I let my dad's words soak into my mind. Maybe he's right.

"Olivia, it's okay if you never go back to being the best friends you were as kids. I don't think you can expect to, but you owe her an apology. What you did wasn't right, even if she's not your best friend anymore."

"I'M SERIOUS Olivia, I was worried sick! How could you do that to me? What were you thinking?" I tried to catch her before our next class, but she never even gave me a chance to speak before she started laying into me.

"I got it Hannah, it won't happen again. Promise."

"Really?"

"I solemnly swear I will not say I'm with you when I'm not." I answer sarcastically, hand on my heart. We're alone in the dressing room at the studio. "Let it go, I have the worst headache," I add, wincing as she drops her water bottle with a clang.

"Serves you right," Hannah says, a little nastily, which takes me by surprise. "I'm so mad at you right now. That was a stupid thing to do Olivia. I know you think that being sixteen is all about making dumb decisions, but there's dumb and then there's really dumb."

"Oh my god, Hannah, stop." I cut her off, my eyes flashing with anger. "What exactly do you think we were doing?" I don't wait for her answer. "We went to the beach, roasted hot dogs and s'mores. And drank," her eyes open wide at this and I know I've nailed it, that's exactly what she thought. "We drank fucking soda Hannah, nothing else. That was the entire varsity football and cheer squads, do you really have such a low opinion of not only me, but Tyler and Jack and Hunter that you think we would be on a public beach, where there are *cops* patrolling every hour, drinking alcohol? Not to mention we all had to drive home again? Wow, some friend you are. I bet you were the one who sent my dad that photo."

"Then why did you lie about where you were, if you weren't doing anything wrong?" Hannah huffs, arms crossed over her chest.

"Honestly? Because my dad lets me have a later curfew if I say I'm with you," I tell her with a shrug. "Like I said, you're making a big deal out of nothing."

"That's it? You just wanted a later curfew?" Hannah looks ready to spit fire. "I'm done." What? Meek and mild, bland banana Hannah is actually standing up for herself? I'd be impressed if I wasn't so irritated. "Get a new sucker to cover for you."

"Seriously? You are such a baby. For god's sake, nothing happened." Hannah just stands there staring at me. "Whatever. I promise I won't ask your goody-two-shoes ass for help again." She grabs her shoes and stalks out the room without a word.

Whatever. I know I'm supposed to be apologizing, but Hannah's accusations are making that really hard right now.

Our next class is so tense that you could slice the sweaty air with a knife. The more I focus on being mad at Hannah, the better I dance. I attack each step with an energy I haven't been able to muster for the last two weeks. It feels so good to throw my legs up in the air, to swing my arms wide, to turn as fast as I can and crack my hips and shoulders from side to side as we dance. I find myself staring into the mirror, my eyes intense and glittery. Today I feel like fire and lighting is crackling under my skin and the harder I dance, the bigger I dance, the better it feels.

When class finishes I collapse on the floor, glad to have a break for the next hour before our ballet rehearsals begin. "You okay?" Lisa, peers down at me.

I smile up at her. "Yup, just tired," I say. She still looks concerned.

"Um, I heard you and Hannah in the dressing room. You want to talk about it?"

"Nope," I say, rolling over and climbing to my feet. "We'll work it out eventually," I add. I assume so. I know I owe her an apology, but I don't think today is the day it's going to happen.

CHAPTER 21

Hannah

EVERY FEW MINUTES, another wave of emotions brings a lump to the back of my throat. Each time my cheeks burn with embarrassment remembering what I said to Olivia, tears prick at the corner of my eyes. I can't meet anyone's gaze. Even Ms. Parker's.

"Hannah, your spacing is off again. Come on sweetie, get it together." I nod, quickly moving to the center of the group, feeling everyone's eyes boring into my back. I don't want to be the reason rehearsal runs late.

Lisa tries to catch my eye but I keep my gaze fixed on myself in the mirror, not seeing myself but too afraid that if I meet her or Katy's eyes I won't be able to stop the tears from falling. The only thing worse than keeping everyone in rehearsal late because I can't get the spacing right, would be keeping everyone late because I'm a big cry-baby.

"You sure you're okay?" Lisa asks at the end of class. Olivia slips past us and into the dressing room, I want to say something,

199

to explain, or apologize. I want things to be back to normal, but that's not possible.

"Hannah, I have to go. My mom's waiting, but promise you'll text me if you want to talk?" I nod my agreement and begin my rounds of the studio, picking up trash, sweeping and wiping down the barre and mirrors. The monotony of the tasks helps, but it also gives me time to think. I don't know if I want to cry because I'm embarrassed for making such unfounded accusations or sad that it feels like our friendship is truly over. I feel lost, like I just broke a part of my soul.

I fish my phone out of my bag as I climb in my car to drive home, hoping for a message from Trevor. Something to distract me from the weight of my thoughts. My mood starts lifting at the sight of a notification waiting for me.

> **(HANNAHBANANABALLERINA):** marvelousStanLey sent you a post by russianballerinas
>
> **MARVELOUSSTANLEY:** This is gross. Please tell me your teachers don't do this to you

Well, Trevor never disappoints, I'm definitely distracted from my thoughts now. I cringe at the video he sent. It's from a Russian rhythmic gymnastics school. The teacher is standing on the legs of a little girl, probably 6 or 7 years old, while pushing her torso down over her splits.

> **HANNAHBANANABALLERINA:** That's disgusting, and no, my teachers would never. There's an old joke in the ballet world "no matter how good you are there's always a Russian fetus out there who's ten times better"

Trevor responds almost instantly, as usual.

> **MARVELOUSSTANLEY:** That is equal parts funny and sad. How was your day?
> **HANNAHBANANABALLERINA:** Terrible, how's yours?
> **MARVELOUSSTANLEY:** Terrible? What happened?
> **HANNAHBANANABALLERINA:** I don't want to talk about it. How about you send me something funny instead?
> **MARVELOUSSTANLEY:** Funny, cute or both?
> **HANNAHBANANABALLERINA:** Both?
> **MARVELOUSSTANLEY:** Your wish is my command Twinkle Toes (I still want to know what happened though)
> **HANNAHBANANABALLERINA:** I'll tell you later, I don't have the energy for it right now. About to drive home from dance. So. Tired.
> **(HANNAHBANANABALLERINA):** marvelousStanLey sent you a post by puppiesrcute
> **(HANNAHBANANABALLERINA):** marvelousStanLey sent you a post by dogfails
> **(HANNAHBANANABALLERINA):** marvelousStanLey sent you a post by puppywalks
> **(HANNAHBANANABALLERINA):** marvelousStanLey sent you a post by labradorsssss
> **(HANNAHBANANABALLERINA):** marvelousStanLey sent you a post by D0gm3m3s
> **(HANNAHBANANABALLERINA):** marvelousStanLey sent you a post by ball3tpupp1es

My phone buzzes with incoming notifications the whole way home. I wait until I park, then sit in my car in the driveway laughing at the onslaught of silly dog memes. By the time I get to the end, I'm feeling much better.

"I'm home!" I call out as I walk in the door, poking my head in the kitchen to see my mom slicing up an apple. "Hi," I say, swiping an apple slice from her plate.

"Hey honey, how was dance?" she asks, slapping at my hand as I reach for another slice. "Get your own!" I grab another apple slice from the plate with a grin. "There's an envelope on the table for you," my mom adds, faking nonchalance.

I rush to look and there it is, a long white envelope, the letters "CBS" in big red print in the upper left corner. This was it, Classical Ballet School of New York. Any lingering worries about my conversation with Olivia disappear in an instant. This was either going to be the worst day of my entire life, or the beginning of my future dreams. I pick up the envelope, swallowing my bite of apple, nearly choking on it.

Dear Hannah,

We are pleased to inform you that you have been accepted to the Classical Ballet School of New York's summer intensive. Additionally, we are pleased to offer you a 50% talent-based tuition scholarship based on your audition. Below is an outline of the tuition and….

"Ahhhhhhh!" I scream, clutching the paper to my chest. "Mom! Mom! Dad!"

"What? What happened?" my dad yells, running down the stairs as fast as he can.

"Well? What does it say?" my mom calls, stepping quickly out of the kitchen behind me.

"I got in! I got in!" I cry, jumping up and down until my mom wraps her arms around me, hugging me tight. She starts jumping with me, the acceptance paper in my hands squished between us.

"I'm so proud of you baby!" my mom cries, giving me an extra squeeze before letting me go. My dad immediately gives me a hug too. "I knew you could do it," she adds, reaching out to read the paper for herself.

I collapse on the couch, my knees turning to jelly. "Oh no," I groan, hanging my head between my knees.

"What sweetie?" my dad says, taking the paper from my mom to read the details I hadn't bothered with. My mom sits down next to me on the couch, wrapping her arm around my shoulder and pulling me into her side.

"How am I going to decide between my two dream schools?" I groan. "CBS has been my dream for forever. But PSB…" I trail off.

"You don't have to decide tonight sweetie. How about tonight we just enjoy the fact that you have two wonderful places that want you. Decisions can wait, at least for a couple of days. I think this calls for a celebration, don't you?" my mom says looking up at my dad. "Why don't you see if any of your friends want to come and we'll go out for dinner."

"Can we get sushi?" I ask, already digging through my bag for my phone.

"Absolutely," my dad says, "Let me know when you're ready to go." He disappears into the kitchen, dropping a kiss on my head as he passes.

I grab my phone and immediately text the group chat.

ME: I got an acceptance letter from CBS!!!!!!!!!!!!!!!!!!!!!!!!!!!!!!!
!! Did you get your letter Lisa?

My phone explodes in a mass of gifs from Katy, making me giggle.

LISA: Congrats Hannah! I knew you would get in. I got waitlisted

Lisa sends a few smiling emojis after her message. I barely have a chance to see them before Katy sends another series of gifs, each one more ridiculous than the last. The flailing Kermit one is my personal favorite.

KATY: Ok, I'm done. For now. On a side note, I just got an acceptance letter from PSB, apparently it got lost in the mail. I'm as shocked as you, lol
ME: You guys!!!!! I'm so happy for you both. Not shocking at all Katy, don't be like that. We're going to Noriko to celebrate, can you both come with?

While I wait for them to respond, I debate sending a text to Olivia. My thumb hovers over her name in my text messages. Normally I would have invited her without question, but after everything that's happened, I don't think she'd even respond to my text. I debate for another moment. Do I invite her? Or will she think I'm trying to rub it in somehow? Do I owe her an apology for making assumptions about last night? Heat stirs in my belly at the thought. I don't want to apologize, who can blame me for making that assumption when that's exactly what it looked like? No. I'm not going to apologize.

In fact, maybe she's the one who owes *me* an apology. I check my phone to see if there's an answer from Lisa or Katy.

> **KATY:** We're already on our way to Cole's game. It's the playoffs, gotta cheer him on!

This is followed by a selfie of her, Hunter and Jack in the back seat of her dad's Suburban. Jack is holding a sign in his lap with Cole's name on it and Katy has his jersey number painted on her cheek. Hunter's face is painted the blue and yellow of UCLA's colors. They're ridiculous but adorable.

> **ME:** Have fun and cheer for us too! Lisa?
> **LISA:** Yes! My mom said I can go! I'll have her drop me off at your house but I NEED a shower first.
> **ME:** Yes, showering is essential. See you when you get here.

Twenty minutes later, I am showered and dressed in my favorite skinny jeans and cozy sweater. I'm determined to forget about Olivia and focus on the good things in my life. My dreams are literally coming true right now, I'm not going to let Olivia ruin my mood. I tuck the sadness that threatens to ruin my celebration away, I'll deal with it later. Not tonight. Tonight is about celebrating.

Besides, I have two true best friends who have earned the title and Lisa deserves to be celebrated tonight too. She placed in the top twelve at YIGP, and she got accepted to PSB and wait-listed to CBS. No matter how prestigious the school, her parents don't see it as an accomplishment, but I sure do. They just don't see ballet as more than a hobby for her, no matter how talented she is. Even if she had gotten a scholarship, Lisa told me her parents aren't letting her go anyway. They want her to do this intense Japanese exam prep class over the summer. One that's actually *in* Japan.

I hear Lisa's mom dropping her off outside so I tuck my phone in my pocket and run downstairs, throwing my hair up in a ponytail as I go. "Mom! Dad! You ready? Lisa's here!" I open the front door and throw myself at Lisa, grabbing her in a giant hug. "Congrats!" I say, stepping back. Lisa smiles, shrugging her shoulders.

"It's not like I'm going to get to go anyway," Lisa's smile turns sad and I pull her to my dad's car, determined to make sure Lisa celebrates tonight, even if her parents kind of suck. It's time I started acting like a real best friend. We climb into the backseat, getting buckled. "Hey," Lisa pokes me in the ribs. "Are you ok? I heard you and Olivia in the dressing room…" She looks at me expectantly.

"It's a long story, but I'll tell you later. We're celebrating you and me, no Olivia allowed." I glance back at the house to see my parents locking the front door. "I'm so tired of it, I don't want to think about her anymore. It's exhausting and I'm over it."

"Hey Lisa, congrats sweetie," my mom says, climbing into the front seat.

"Thanks Mrs. O'Brian," Lisa says. My dad drives while me, Lisa and my mom talk about the CBS and PSB summer intensives. My phone buzzes a few times while we're talking and I pull it out to check.

MARVELOUSSTANLEY: Did you fall on your butt like this guy? Is that why your day was so terrible? Has it gotten any better?

(HANNAHBANANABALLERINA): marvelousStanley sent you a post by epicfails

HANNAHBANANABALLERINA: OMG, did his teeth get knocked out? That's disgusting! And yes, it got better. Just found out I got accepted into CBS!

MARVELOUSSTANLEY: Rockstar!

HANNAHBANANABALLERINA: Hahaha, thanks! Going to dinner to celebrate

(MARVELOUSSTANLEY): hannahbananaballerina sent you a post by isushinomnom

MARVELOUSSTANLEY: *drooling* I love sushi

"Who's that?" Lisa whispers in my ear.

I jump and almost drop my phone. "Oh! Uh. No one." I whisper back. I mean, it's not like it's a secret, but I don't want to talk about Trevor in front of my parents. That's weird.

"Is that Trevor?" Lisa's leaning over my shoulder to see my phone screen. "Come on Han, let me see. He's kinda cute, I looked the other day," she adds with a wink.

"What? Why?"

"Katy and I were doing our best friend duty and stalking him back. You never tell us anything, so we did a little sleuthing. " She winks. "He's related to Tyler Stanley, right?" I'm relieved to hear Lisa call herself my best friend. Since I realized how oblivious I've been to my true friends, I've been secretly worried that they resent me for it after all this time. Hearing her say it so matter of factly puts my mind at ease.

"Yeah, they're cousins. Trevor lives in Seattle." Lisa smirks. "What? Why are you looking at me like that?" I huff in a whisper. My parents are busy talking to each other about some work thing, I don't want to draw their attention.

"Hannah, how oblivious do you think Katy and I are? You've been messaging each other ever since YIGP, don't lie. It's also very convenient that Trevor lives in Seattle, seeing as how PSB is also in Seattle..." She starts scrolling up through the message thread and I dive to grab my phone away from her. She laughs and holds it high and out of my reach.

"Lisa! Give it back!" I shriek. My parents both snap their heads back to look at us.

"Hannah!" my mom says, "what on Earth?"

"Sorry Mom," I reply, head down, glaring at Lisa from under my lashes. Lisa meanwhile is happily scrolling through my phone and reading Trevor's messages to me.

"Hannah, he liiiiiiiiiikes you." Lisa says with a smile. "That boy is crushing on you."

"No he doesn't, no he isn't." I protest. "He's just being nice or whatever. He knows I li..." I trail off. I was going to say I like Tyler but I stop, not sure if it's true anymore. Lisa raises an eyebrow at me.

"Knows you like Tyler, his cousin?" she finishes for me. "Do you really? I mean, we all know you've been pining for him for years. Do you really still like Tyler, or do you just like the *idea* of liking Tyler?"

I scrunch down in my seat, arms crossed over my chest, staring straight ahead. I don't appreciate that Lisa is calling me out on the very thoughts I've been trying to avoid ever since YIGP. "Shut up. I don't know. It's weird, okay?" I sigh, frustrated. "I mean, I did. I kinda do. I don't know anymore." I finish and I know I sound ridiculous even to myself. I hold my hand out for my phone. "But I *definitely* don't like Trevor, okay? He's just a friend." My dad pulls into the parking lot at Noriko, my favorite sushi place, and we climb out of the car and head inside.

Lisa is still teasing me about Trevor while we follow my parents through the door. I'm pretending to ignore her by looking all over the restaurant, anywhere except at Lisa, when I freeze. At a table in the corner, I spot a mop of perfectly messy sandy blonde hair. Tyler is here with his family, chatting and talking animatedly. He's....honestly? He's still adorable. He's laughing at something his sister said and his perfect cheekbones are highlighted by the overhead lights as he throws his head back, letting out a deep guffaw. He's fiddling with the wrapper from his straw, leaving bits of shredded paper on the table.

Lisa tugs on my arm and I turn to follow her and my mom to the table and plop down in the booth next to Lisa. My mind is racing. There is no denying that Tyler is handsome and most of my fantasies about him have involved me looking at his face and feeling his strong arms around me. But Olivia may have had a tiny point, I've never really had a conversation with him. The closest I've ever come was when he had dinner with us at YIGP, but if I'm being honest he and I still barely said two words to each other. When I imagine going out on dates, texting and hanging out, do I imagine myself doing that with Tyler?

"What's wrong?" Lisa asks quietly. I shake my head, lost in my own thoughts.

If I'm truly being honest with myself, I don't. I have an easier time chatting with Trevor and I've only known him for a few weeks. If I was really meant to be with Tyler, surely we would have found a reason to hang out before now? He and Olivia are perfect for each other and no matter what I think of Olivia, I would never want to come between a happy couple like that.

If I truly let this crush go, what do I have left? I picture Tyler and Olivia together. Thinking of Olivia makes me sad, but the idea of them together doesn't hurt my heart like it used to.

"Nothing, just thinking," I glance at the table where the Stanley's sit. I look at the way they chat and I don't feel sad. I look at the mess of shredded paper Tyler made on the table and I admit it isn't actually adorable. In fact, I would be kind of annoyed if that was my table. I test my heart again. It still doesn't hurt, Tyler Stanley is just a good-looking guy, sitting at a table eating dinner with his family.

This is supposed to be a celebration and I refuse to be upset. Everything is supposed to be perfect right now. I got into CBS, I got into PSB, and I got offered scholarships to both. Marco Bethelo himself picked me for a scholarship. I just won the Grand Prix prize at YIGP. All of my dreams are on the verge of coming true and, dang it, I will not let a boy ruin this for me. Boys are nothing but a distraction.

"So, Hannah sweetie, Lisa was just telling us about the cram school in Japan her dad wants her to go to," my mom says. I squeeze Lisa's knee under the table. I know she doesn't really want to go. "It sounds pretty intense. Who would you stay with out there Lisa?"

"My grandma lives just outside of Osaka. I'd stay with her and my uncle and go to the cram school near them." I sneak a glance at Tyler and am amazed to find I still feel fine. I concentrate on Lisa, my best friend. My actual best friend who is bummed that even though she got into PSB, she isn't going to get to go because her parents don't think ballet is a real career.

"That will be nice," my dad says. "How long will you be out there?" Tyler is trying to eat his sushi but can't get a good grip with his chopsticks and keeps dropping it. It's adorable how bad he is at it. But also, he keeps splashing it in the soy sauce, making a mess. Gross.

"I think about a month?" Lisa says. "My parents haven't really decided yet."

"I still think you should try and get your parents to let you go. If I decide to go to PSB, it would be so perfect if you were there too."

"I wonder if they'd let us be roommates?" Lisa asks as we peruse the menu together.

"Wanna get the onigiri? We could share?" I point out the rice balls that are my favorite. Noriko makes them with either plums or salmon in the middle and I can never decide which kind I want. "Also, being roommates would be amazing."

In the end we get the onigiri, seaweed salad and a variety of different rolls to share with my parents. "What if you got straight A's?" I ask, still thinking about how to get Lisa's parents to let her go to PSB.

"I already have straight A's. Don't you remember what happened when I got a B on that test last year?"

"Was that when they took your phone away for a week?" Lisa nods in response, popping a piece of tuna sashimi in her mouth. "Ok, you can't really make your grades any better. How are we going to convince them to let you go? Is there some other study class you could take that isn't in Japan?"

We keep chatting about different ways to convince the Hamasaki's to let Lisa go to PSB while we eat. I'm so focused on making my best friend feel better, I don't even notice the Stanley's leave.

My phone buzzes in my pocket again but I don't look, assuming that it's probably some funny video from Trevor, I wonder if it's one with dogs? I like funny dog videos. When I finally get home and flop on my bed, belly full of sushi, I grin when I read the message from Trevor.

MARVELOUSSTANLEY: You'll never guess what movie my sister is forcing me to watch with her right now. Send help!

CHAPTER 22

Hannah

I CATCH THE bannister as I fly down the stairs, my bag bouncing against my hip. "Bye Mom, bye Dad!" I call as I head to the front door.

"Bye love, have fun!" My mom calls from the couch.

"Have a good time Banana!" my dad calls from beside her. "See you tomorrow!"

I toss my bag into the passenger seat of my car and buckle up, ready to relax. My bikini is on underneath my tank top and plain black leggings and in my bag are a couple of face masks I picked up at the drug store on my way home from the studio. I am ready for girls' night.

The sun has been shining all day, tempting us through the studio windows while we sweat our way through hours of rehearsals. Things are still tense between Olivia and me, but even that can't ruin my mood today. It's the end of March, spring is on its way, and in SoCal that means seventy-five degree afternoons and sunny skies, it's my favorite time of year.

Between the perfect weather, my relief at having been accepted to both of my dream summer intensives, the scholarships and winning Grand Prix, I feel something akin to unstoppable. Everything is happening exactly how I dreamed it would. Since our visit to Noriko, I've been testing how I feel whenever I see Tyler Stanley at school. There's the tiniest bit of regret over what could have been, but I keep surprising myself by not feeling much of anything else. When I see him and Olivia together, I'm more upset over our lost friendship and the Olivia-shaped hole in my heart than any lingering feelings I have for Tyler. The tension with Olivia is the only cloud in my otherwise perfectly sunny sky.

I haven't decided yet where I'm going to spend my summer, but I'm determined not to worry about it today. Today I am going to have fun. When Katy suggested that we come over after class today to swim and have a girls' night, I was the first one to say yes.

There's a crowd of cars parked on the street as I pull up, so many that I have to park four houses down from the Quinn's house. I pull my bag over my shoulder and walk up the street to Katy's front door. Someone on the street must be having a party, I can hear music playing and people talking from here. It's only when I stop in front of her house that I realize the noise is coming from the Quinn's backyard.

Just as I lift my hand to knock on the door, it flies open, startling me. "I got it," Jack calls over his shoulder as he barrels out the door and crashes right into me, knocking me flat on my back. "Are you okay?" Jack reaches out a hand to pull me back onto my feet, concern written all over his face.

"I'm okay," I say automatically, rubbing the sting out of the hand that broke my fall. The palm is a little scraped up and my butt hurts from hitting the ground, but otherwise I'm okay.

"Let me see your hand," Jack commands, pulling my hand towards him to inspect it.

"I'm fine, really." I insist, pulling my hand back. "Um, can I come in?"

"Jack!" Katy's voice comes from somewhere behind him. "Let Hannah inside and go away," she adds, shoving him aside. "Hey Han. Come on." She pulls me inside and straight up the stairs to her room. Lisa is already there, flipping through a collection of lotions, cleansers and assorted spa-like goodies.

"Ugh!" Katy groans, flopping backwards onto her bed. "Hunter and Jack invited all their friends over to swim." That explains the noise and all the cars on the street. "I thought they were going to Nicole's house this afternoon and we would have the house to ourselves. If we want to swim, we have to put up with them, I'm sorry." She looks up at us apologetically.

"It's fine, we don't have to swim," Lisa says with a shrug. "We can hang out up here." All three of us pause and listen to the noise coming from Katy's backyard.

"Yeah, we can just stay up here," I add quickly.

"I hate my brothers!" Katy groans. "They always do this." She pouts.

"Do what? Have people over?" I ask.

"Yeah, they're here all the time." Katy shakes her head. "It's been like this since Cole was in high school, so like, basically my whole life. The worst is when I come home from dance all sweaty and disgusting, to find my living room overflowing with beautiful people playing video games or watching a movie and the whole room turns to look." Katy shudders.

"KATY!" a deep voice thunders through the open window. "Kaaaaaaaaaty! Come hang out!"

She jack-knifes up off the bed and shouts right back, "Shut up Hunter!" Lisa's wide eyes meet my own. I send mental thanks up to whoever is in charge up there that I'm an only child. "I'm sorry. You guys don't have to stay."

"No, no, we're staying," I say quickly. "Come on, I brought masks." I pull them out of my bag and toss them on the bed. Ten minutes later the three of us are giggling at the green, pink and yellow goop on our respective faces as we watch YouTube videos on Katy's laptop.

"Hey Ka-" Hunter cuts off in a choked laugh as he throws open her door.

"Oh my god Hunter, don't you know how to knock!" Katy yells, chucking a pillow at his head.

"Sorry," he says, sheepish. "Hi Hannah, hi Lisa," he adds, nodding at us. We wave back from the bed. "Uh, Dad's ordering pizza, he wanted to know if you guys are eating, too."

"Of course. Can you make sure he orders salad too, please? And a big one, enough for the three of us, plus whatever girls you have downstairs." Hunter sticks out his tongue at Katy, then heads down the stairs without another word.

We pass the next thirty minutes scrolling through our phones, washing off the facemasks and watching random videos together. My stomach growls loudly just as the scent of pizza comes wafting through the window.

"Let's go. If we don't get there quick, there won't be any food left," Katy hops up and thunders down the stairs, Lisa and I trailing behind.

"Um, this is weird, right?" I whisper to Lisa as we hang back from the crowd of bodies huddled around a table that I assume has food on it. We can't actually see anything from where we hover in the sliding glass doorway.

"Yeah. I had no idea this was a thing that happened in real life," Lisa whispered back. We watch in awe as Katy elbows her way through the crowd, plate in hand.

"Excuse us." Allyson and Megan push past us, taking a moment to snicker at my tank top and leggings.

"Why are *they* here?" Megan asks, tossing her thick brown hair over her shoulder. We make eye-contact briefly, long enough for her to see I heard her words, before I look away.

"Ignore her," Lisa says.

I pull my gaze from their denim cutoffs and tiny bikinis. Not before I get a good look at Allyson pressing her palm to Jack's naked chest. I glance at my own leggings and t-shirt, realizing for the first time that everyone here is half-naked. The yard is a sea of tanned skin and brightly colored swim trunks and bikinis.

I rub a foot against my calf, feeling self-conscious in my covered up state. "Do you guys want food?" Katy calls to us from deep in the crowd by the table. Like a scene from a movie, every head in the backyard turns to look at us. Okay, not every single person, but all the ones nearby, which feels just as bad. Like a spotlight has flared to life over my head, sweat breaks out between my shoulder blades and I gulp, my throat suddenly dry.

Lisa pushes me forward towards the table, using me as a human shield. I try not to squirm under the scrutiny of the most popular and beautiful people at our school. People who I would have happily lived my whole life never hanging out with. I grab a paper plate, shove a second one in Lisa's hand, then make my way over to the salad sitting on one end of the table.

"Hey Hannah," someone says from across the table. I look up, startled to see it's Tyler talking to me. "Hey Lisa," he adds, with a nod.

"Hi," I say quietly. I fumble with the salad tongs, spilling lettuce on the table.

"So…" Tyler clears his throat. "Uh, you guys hanging out with Katy?"

I nod, my eyes wide. I can't seem to make words leave my lips. This seems like a good test of my resolve to think of him as just any other guy. I can do this.

"Yeah," Lisa pipes up, saving me.

"Katy invited us over after dance." I add, growing confident as I speak.

"Cool. Yeah. Olivia said rehearsal was rough today." Right. Olivia. Is she here? I look around and spot her sitting at the other end of the backyard with Allyson, Megan, and Madison. Tyler follows my eyeline and waves to her. She blows him a kiss, pointedly ignoring me. "You done with those?" he asks, indicating the tongs hanging uselessly from my fingers.

"Oh, uh yeah. You eat salad?" I blurt out. Stupid. I want to slap my palm over my face and die right there on the spot.

Tyler just laughs and shakes his head. "Na. It's for Olivia." I hand the tongs over, silently congratulating myself for speaking actual words to him without turning into a babbling fool. I turn to snag a slice of pizza, feeling a little cocky. I'm reaching for the last slice of pepperoni when a very masculine hand snakes in and snags the slice I was inches from claiming.

"Hey!" I exclaim, annoyed. "That was my slice." I lean back to see Andrew Park mid-bite, cheese dripping from the hot slice. Water is dripping from his jet black hair and swim trunks onto the concrete patio. I watch, wide-eyed, as he runs a hand through his short wet hair, leaving it sticking up and pointing in all different directions. I avert my eyes, embarrassment flushing thorough me, my new-found confidence dripping away with the water dripping down his chest. Andrew Park plays both football and baseball, his chest and shoulders prove how much time he must dedicate to each sport.

He shrugs, unapologetic. "Nevermind." Irritated, I pick up the now empty pizza box to take a slice from the box keeping warm underneath it. I look around, unsure of where to put the empty box so I can grab my slice, when it's plucked from my hand.

"Here, I got it," Andrew says, sliding in next to me and reaching to put the empty box on the ground under the table. "It's Hannah, right?"

"Yeah. We had Algebra together last year." I add, like a dork.

"Oh yeah, I knew you looked familiar." Andrew says with a grin. "Here, let me," he reaches into the pizza box I'm holding open and pulls a slice out and onto my plate. "I thought ballerinas only ate salad?" he smirks, nodding at my plate.

I look at my plate, half of it is taken up by salad. I raise an eyebrow at his stupidly pretty face. Dark brown eyes, defined cheekbones and a square jaw—yeah, I was serious when I said stupidly pretty. I stay far away from the gossip at school and even I know he has a reputation as a player, that he's dated almost every girl on the softball team, volleyball team and half the varsity cheer squad.

There was a rumor going around school that he was an extra in *Crazy Rich Asians*, which he denies, but didn't stop almost every girl in school watching it multiple times hunting for him.

Almost every girl. Not me. I only watched it once, like a normal person. "I eat pizza too." I shrug and turn to go back inside.

"Here," Andrew's hand is on my elbow, gently steering me towards an empty space at the edge of the pool. I look around wildly for Lisa, but she and Katy are sitting together in a pair of lounge chairs grinning at me. Katy salutes me with her slice of pizza.

Andrew drops down to swing his legs over the edge of the pool, dangling his feet in the water. He pats the patch of concrete to his left like I'm supposed to sit there.

"Uh…"

"Sit down, Hannah. I don't bite." Now it's his turn to raise an eyebrow at me, a cocky smile on his face.

"Fine." I say, handing him my plate. I peel my leggings off and toss them into a patch of dry cement near the house, glad I already had my bathing suit on. My hunter green bikini is pretty tame compared to some of the other ones on display here, it has a high waist and covers my entire butt, not just half, but I love the deep green color and the geometric design accenting the waist and edge of the matching halter top. I leave my tank top on, too self-conscious of my pale skin to expose any more of it to this crowd.

"So, how come I've never seen you hang out at the Quinn's before?" Andrew says as soon as I'm sitting. I left a good foot of space between us when I sat, but he turns to face me, leaning on one arm, bringing his body closer to mine. I'm grateful for the open space at my back as I lean away from his smile. Andrew grins at me, like he knows I'm nervous.

"Well," I swallow. "I guess we usually hang out at my house. I mean, we're all really busy with dance, so we don't have a lot of free time anyways," I babble, Andrew is making me nervous, I squirm under his single-minded attention. "Um, do you hang out here a lot?" I ask out of desperation. I don't know what to say, how do normal people have conversations with boys? If I had to rank them, I'm less nervous talking to Andrew than Tyler, but way more nervous than chatting with Trevor. I wish Trevor was here.

"Yeah, they're really cool about letting us all hang out here. My parents would never be cool with having so many teenagers hanging out all the time, but I'm glad the Quinn's don't mind. Besides, their pool is awesome."

I nod in agreement. "Yeah, it is. I never realized that Katy's brothers had people over here so much, but I guess that explains why Katy never seems intimidated by you guys."

"Do I intimidate you?"" Andrew asks, grinning.

I nod my head, my messy bun bobbling on top of my head with the movement. "A little," I admit. I shove a forkful of salad in my mouth to force myself to stop talking. Andrew throws back his head and lets out a laugh. I'm fascinated by his confidence. He just started talking to me as if it never occurred to him that I wouldn't immediately want to continue the conversation. I guess I proved him right by sitting here. "So," I ask, swallowing my food. "Um, how's baseball going?" I manage, feeling brave.

Andrew leans back on both hands, lifting his face up to the sun, and starts talking. I'm half listening, trying to eat my salad and pizza without looking like a slob, and occasionally admiring the smooth expanse of his chest when I think he's not paying attention. A mental image of Trevor crosses my mind and I wonder what he's doing this weekend, but Andrew distracts me with a question and I let the thought go.

I relax as we chat and eat, the sun warm on my shoulders, the water cool on my calves. I slowly kick my feet back and forth in the water, enjoying the resistance and the relief from my hours of pointe work in rehearsal. I'm still wary, but it turns out Andrew is nicer than I assumed he was. He keeps me laughing with his witty observations of everyone sitting around the pool. I'm just finishing off the crust of my pizza slice, when I'm startled by a wave of water sloshing over us.

"Nice one dude!" Andrew laughs at Tyler as his head pops up from the water, a huge grin on his face. This seems to be some sort of signal, because suddenly half a dozen other boys go flying into the pool, legs tucked up in the air and bellows of "Cannonball!" and "Look out!" ringing out. I'm drenched by at least three more waves of water, my tank top soaked and stuck tight to my skin.

I'm startled by the sudden sensation of a pair of hands gripping my calves tight as I'm busy wiping water from my eyes. "Hey," Andrew says looking up from the water, his hands holding my calves. "You coming in?" When I hesitate he tugs on my legs, grinning. "Come on Hannah. I promise not to bite."

"You already said that," I point out as I peel my wet shirt off and wring it out. I toss it in the same direction as my leggings. Before I have a chance to push myself off the pool ledge Andrew's hands are on my waist, lifting me into the water.

"I know. And I haven't bitten yet, have I?" His voice drops an octave and leans in close to whisper in my ear, "I thought you might need a reminder." Andrew's eyes are roaming over my face, the skin of my waist still warm from his hands. I blush and look away, hands absently moving through the water, careful to avoid brushing against his arms. I gasp when he cups my jaw and runs a thumb over my cheek and into my hairline. My eyes open wide, my heart races and I know my mouth is hanging open like a fish, I'm so taken aback by the intimate gesture.

"You had a little…" he holds out his thumb and I see a smear of green. It must be a bit of mask that I missed washing off earlier. He grins like he knows exactly what I was thinking, then he winks and cocks a finger at me, before pushing off the wall and swimming out to the center of the pool where the boys all seem to be trying to drown each other.

I gulp and take a deep breath, trying to calm down, my stomach jumping and my heart pounding. That was…weird. I can't deny that having someone like Andrew pay attention to me made me feel powerful, like I just won a competition I didn't even know I was part of. I kind of like it. It was almost as good as YIGP, but without all the hard work. I push away my worry about what it means. I told myself tonight was about having fun with my friends, not worrying.

I turn around and hook my arms over the edge of the pool, looking at Lisa and Katy. "You guys coming? And no, we're not talking about what just happened." Katy gives me a look and I sigh. "Later, okay? Not now." They're already standing and pulling off their layers as I speak. They slip into the water on either side of me, squeaking a little at the coolness of the water.

"Do they always try and drown each other like that?" I ask Katy, before either of them can start asking me about what just happened between me and Andrew. I don't even know what it was.

"Yup. And the girls hardly ever actually get in the water," she nods her head towards the other end of the pool where all the other girls in attendance are gathered, whispering furiously amongst themselves. "It's been like this since I was a kid and Cole would invite all his buddies over. When I was little, they used to toss me around the pool like a football."

"You don't hang out with the girls?" Lisa asks. Katy just scoffs at that.

"Um, no. They are exactly as catty and superficial as they look." Katy looks over at the group. The girls are stretched out in the sun, their limbs artfully arranged for the boys sneaking glances from the water. "Olivia is the only somewhat tolerable one."

"Katy!" Jack calls. "Go get the ball!"

"And the nets!" Hunter adds.

"Get them yourself!" Katy bellows back, crossing her arms over her chest and leaning back against the edge of the pool.

CHAPTER 23

Olivia

"WHO DOES that little bitch think she is?" Allyson growls. I follow her gaze to Andrew and Hannah, sitting cozily on the other side of the pool. He's running a thumb across Hannah's cheek. Now, I can't even get away from her at the Quinn's? I move to defend Hannah from Allyson's attack, then I remember Hannah isn't my problem anymore.

"Seriously, what the hell does he see in her?" Megan pipes up from the other chair where she and Madison are artfully stretched out, ready to throw fuel on the fire as always. Megan has an amazing ability to start drama between other people without ever getting her hands dirty. "She's not even that pretty," she adds for good measure.

I stop and assess the trio across from us, trying to look subjectively. Hannah's long, lean limbs are perfectly toned by her hours in the studio, her fire red hair piled up on her head in an effortless messy bun. Her wide blue eyes are completely innocent and her pale, creamy skin would tempt any boy who wasn't blind.

She may not be my favorite person in the world right now, but I know Megan is full of shit. Hannah has always been pretty. More than one guy paused to watch her pull her leggings off, transfixed by the allure of her long, slim, legs. Not Tyler though, I checked. He was busy hunting for a water bottle for me.

"She's just a shiny new toy, he'll be bored of her goody-two-shoes ass in an hour," I say, fake disdain dripping from my lips. "Andrew has been eyeing you for weeks Allyson, maybe he's just trying to make you jealous." Today is the first time my dad's let me out of the house since the beach incident, no way am I going to waste it on stupid drama. Especially drama with Hannah.

The conversation with my dad hovers at the back of my mind. Technically, I still owe her an apology. I'm surprised at the protective streak I feel towards her hearing Allyson and Megan. I don't want to be her best friend, but I can't stand back and watch these girls chew her up and spit her out.

Allyson huffs and crosses her arms over her chest, elbowing me in the arm, conveniently pushing her boobs up a little. I glance around and see that Andrew happens to be looking our way. Of course. I shove her off me, "Go get in the water and claim your man if you're that worried."

Allyson swings her legs off the lounger, but turns to face me, pulling her sunglasses down to look me in the eye. "Bitch."

"That's Queen Bitch to you," I fire back without hesitation. "Go on, go get your man." I make a shooing motion with my hands, then slap her butt as she stands up. "Go get 'em, Tiger," I add, laughing at her outraged face. "Love you!"

Allyson stalks towards the edge of the pool, eyes on her prey. I slide my sunglasses down my nose to watch as she carefully sits on the edge of the pool closest to where Andrew is rough-housing with the other boys. She leans back on her hands, deliberately stretching her torso out to expose a smooth expanse of golden skin between the top and bottom of her little red bikini, the perfect lure. I stifle a laugh as Tyler dunks a couple of baseball players, including Andrew, who quit paying attention, distracted by Allyson.

Hunter and Jack appear from the side of the house carrying a large net and a water polo ball. Jack tosses the ball to Katy with a cry of "Quinn Ball!" before he and Hunter start attaching the net to some anchors on the sides of the pool. "Liv!" Tyler calls from the middle of the pool. "Come on!" he yells again, motioning me to come get in the pool.

"You better come too," I say to Megan and Madison, standing up and pulling off my shorts. "If I have to suffer through this, you guys do too."

"I'm out. I got my hair done yesterday, no way am I ruining it," Megan replies, shoving Madison out of the chair and sprawling in it so she can't sit back down.

Tyler is waiting for me at the edge of the pool, chatting with Allyson. "Come on babe," he says taking my hand. I sit on the edge of the pool while he turns his back to me. I drape my legs over his shoulders and push myself off the edge and onto his shoulders. I tuck my feet securely behind his back as he pushes off the wall and wades back to the center of the pool. I look across the pool and see that Katy is already perched on Jack's shoulders, tossing the ball up in the air and catching it. Hunter is getting Lisa up on his shoulders with Hannah's help.

"Quinn's can't be on the same team!" someone shouts from behind me, followed by a chorus of agreement from the other guys.

"I'm coming, hang on," Hunter shouts from his end of the pool. There's six of us girls in the pool. I eye Allyson. I better not let her be on the same team as Hannah, who knows what she'll do. I'm not trying to protect Hannah. I'm not. I swear. I just don't want to deal with more drama than necessary. Really.

"Come on babe, let's go be on Jack's team." I say, leaning a little that way to force him to move.

Tyler ducks down in the water so I can slide off and cross under the net. Two bodies torpedo past me in the water as I leisurely make my way over. I'm surprised when it's Andrew's head that pops up next to Tyler's in front of me. Well, I tried. Sorry Allyson.

Tyler spots me, grins, and dives back under the water. I feel his hands grip my thighs a second before I'm lifted up in the air, his head firmly between my legs as I sit on his shoulders. I laugh at the ease with which he picks me up and reach my hand down for a high-five. A less dignified squeak sounds from my right and I turn my head to see Andrew has done the same thing to Hannah. She wasn't prepared for it like I was and the look of shock on her face is hilarious.

I laugh to myself, this is probably the first time a boy has ever touched her thighs like that. Her arms and feet flail for a moment like she doesn't know what to do with them. I can just imagine the panic in her little anxious brain right now. I enjoy my superiority for a minute, but I feel bad for Andrew. Okay, I feel bad for her too.

"Hannah!" I call out. "Tuck your feet back like this, and sit a little higher" I smack Tyler's shoulder so he turns to show her how I have my feet tucked behind his back. She hesitates for a second, then snaps her feet back, those long legs making it easy for her to get a good grip, and sits a little higher on Andrew's shoulders. Immediately she looks more comfortable and Andrew lets go of her thighs. She gives me a little smile and I smile back. I glance at Katy to see her eyeing me quizzically. I shrug. I'm not being nice, I just don't want to lose.

I don't have time to think about it again because the boys start playing in earnest. It's a mash up of volleyball and chicken that's been lovingly dubbed Quinn Ball. There are three of us girls on a side, clinging tight to whoever has us on their shoulders, the rest of the boys split themselves between each side. The boys do most of the work blocking and spiking the ball, although occasionally one of us girls will spike it from our advantage. Points are earned every time a girl falls into the water.

Hannah is the obvious target on our side, since she's never played before, not that I don't get targeted either, but Tyler and I are a good team. He's quick to place a steadying hand on my hips or waist if I start to fall. If I'm being honest a couple of those times were not because I was falling, he just wanted to grab my butt. But every time Andrew touches Hannah, she flinches and knocks herself off balance. If it wasn't for all her dance training, she would have hit the water twice as often.

No one even attempts to knock Katy off anymore, especially when she's with one of her brothers. She's been playing this game since Cole and his friends made it up when she was little. I've never seen her get knocked off. She and Jack are an unbeatable team and even though Hannah is a liability, our team still ends up winning. Although, I'm pretty sure Allyson accidentally knocked herself into the water a couple of times when she was gunning for Hannah.

Jack dumps Katy backwards off his shoulders as soon as the game is over, laughing at her outraged yells. "Don't. You. Dare." I tell Tyler as he reaches up to grip my calves. I have no problem with him touching my legs, he's touched a lot more of my body than that while we made out in his car, but I don't want to be dumped in the water like a sack of potatoes.

"I wasn't going to do anything," he says with a wink.

"Yes you were," I laugh, tickling him in the side with my toes. Instead he squats down and I step on his thigh, swinging the other leg around his back so I can jump off myself without being dumped in the water. Once I'm clear, he slides a hand around my waist under the water and pulls me against his side, my legs automatically wrapping around his waist. "Good boy," I tease.

"Do I get a treat?" he asks, mischievously. I lean forward and give him a quick kiss before wiggling out of his arms and swimming away. "That's it?" he pouts.

"Later," I call back over my shoulder, making a beeline for Allyson and Madison, ready to get out and dry off. The sun is setting and it's going to get cold soon. Spring in SoCal might mean sunny and warm days, but it's still too cold to hang around in a wet bathing suit once the sun goes down. Plus, I feel a need to head off whatever scheme I can see brewing in Allyson's mind.

CHAPTER 24

Hannah

"**Y**OU'RE NOT going to dump me in the water like that are you?" I ask from my perch on Andrew's shoulders, eyes glued to where Jack just dumped Katy into the pool.

"Only if you want me to," Andrew laughs back at me. "Here," he bends down in the water. "Did you see how Olivia got down?"

"Uh no…" I respond, leaving out the part where I was completely distracted by his hand rubbing up and down my leg, straying from just above my knee down my calf. I can't help squirming just a little, and he turns his head to look up at me and grin. That grin has trouble written all over it.

"Here," he says, bending his knees and taking my hand in his, gently tugging me sideways. "Step on my leg and climb down." I unwrap my legs from behind his back and gingerly place my foot on his thigh. A very muscular thigh. Andrew reaches out a hand to steady my waist as I swing my other leg from behind him. I can't help my reflexive twitch when his fingers wrap around my rib cage, his thumb brushing the bottom of my bikini top. It sends my foot flying off his thigh and I fall backwards, my leg making impact with something as I go down. I'm braced for the rush of cold water, but instead land cradled in a pair of strong arms.

"Ah! Oh gosh, I'm so sorry!" I blurt out, instinctively. I reach up to touch his cheek, it's a little pink from my leg hitting him in the face as I fell. "Are you okay?" I ask, turning his face to see if I did any damage. I'm fully expecting him to let go and I squirm a bit, but he just tightens his grip, that "Trouble with a capital T" smile firmly in place. The smiles and attention were fun before, but the way his hands are lingering on my skin is making my heart race and my stomach turn flips. And not in a good way. As exhilarating as his attention was earlier, the more he touches me the more uncomfortable I am.

"No damage. I guess we shouldn't have worried about me being the one who bites," he adds, laughing at me. I cringe and extract myself from his arms, swimming a little way away. I need space, my heart is pounding hard and the water is suddenly much colder. Goosebumps prickle over my skin and I start to shiver in the water. "You okay?" Andrew asks, looking concerned.

"Yeah, yup. Just cold," I babble. "I'm getting out now." Without waiting for him to respond or looking where I'm going, I swim to the pool ledge and pull myself out. I grab the first towel I see and wrap it around myself. It's already wet, ugh. I stay wrapped up in the towel as I look around for Katy and Lisa and my clothes. I spot them at the other end of the pool, drying off and getting dressed again. I start walking in their direction when I feel a hand on my shoulder.

"That's my towel."

I turn, startled. Allyson and Megan are standing very close, obvious irritation in their expressions. "Oh, uh, sorry," I mutter and hand it over. The wet towel wasn't exactly warm but now that I'm standing here in just my bikini in the cool breeze and setting sun I'm freezing. The goosebumps are back and my teeth clench so I don't start chattering.

"You shouldn't take things that don't belong to you," Megan says, pointedly. Not sure why they're so upset about a towel, I murmur another apology and start to walk away again. Allyson strikes, quick as a snake, her delicate hand holding my wrist in a surprisingly strong grip. I freeze, shocked.

"Listen, bitch. Andrew Park is mine. You should leave before you get hurt." Venom drips from Allyson's voice.

"I wasn't…" I stammer.

"He's out of your league, you can't handle someone like Andrew Park. Go home to Mommy before you get your feelings hurt," Allyson snears, still gripping my wrist tight.

I can feel myself crumbling under the weight of their stares. Madison and Megan flank Allyson, screening us from view. "I…I…" swallow hard. "I didn't do anything on purpose." I take a deep breath and find my courage. This is ridiculous. Olivia's words from the hotel come back to me. "You don't get to call dibs on someone. Who he likes or doesn't like is up to him to decide, not you." With that I wrench my hand free and walk away. I don't bother telling her I'm not interested in him anyway. That's not the point.

My hands are still shaking when I get back to my friends and my clothes.

"I can't believe I just did that," I tell them as Lisa hands me a dry towel. "I think I'm gonna be sick."

Katy just laughs, "I am so proud of you. We couldn't hear from over here, what did she say to you?"

I recount the confrontation to Katy and Lisa as I dry off. Their shocked and proud expressions accompanied by congratulatory high fives help settle my stomach, but I still have to sit down to pull my leggings on, my legs are shaking so much. I pick up my tank top but it's still soaking wet. With a sigh, I try to wring out some of the water. The cool breeze snakes up my back and I shiver again.

"Here," a deep voice says, almost in my ear. I jump, then freeze as something warm and soft is draped over my shoulders. I whirl and almost crash into Andrew. I stumble backwards and he catches my shoulders, keeping the sweatshirt from falling off and me from landing in an ungraceful heap on the cement. "You looked cold," he says, pulling me a little closer.

I can hear Katy and Lisa snickering behind me, some best friends they are. "Th-th-thanks," I stammer, not sure if my teeth are chattering or if my brain is just mis-firing from how close Andrew is standing.

Andrew carefully threads my arms into the sleeves of his sweatshirt, then zips it up to my chin. Grinning, he flips the hood up over my head, his finger sliding down my cheek to tap my chin. It occurs to me we're the last two people left in the backyard, everyone else is already inside. "Better?" he asks, rubbing his hands up and down my arms to warm me up. The hoodie is enormous on me, dangling off the ends of my hands. "Looks good on you," I can feel his eyes roaming up and down my body, it makes me want to squirm again. I feel like a worm on a hook. He leans in close, his lips almost touching my ear, "You should wear my clothes more often."

I choke on a gasp pulling back from his reach. He did not just say what I think he just said. Did he?

"Yo, Andrew, we're playing Madden, you in?" Tyler calls from inside the house.

"Save me a controller!" Andrew yells back. "You coming?"

"I'm not sure. We were supposed to be having a girls' night."

"Drew! Get your ass in here!"

"Coming!" he yells back. "Come on," he adds, tugging on my hand. I pull it back, annoyed by how pushy he's being. Andrew just shrugs and heads inside the house.

I stand outside in the dark, mulling the afternoon over in my mind. I had no idea Allyson was interested in Andrew. In my defense, how would I have known? I'm not friends with them, I've never had a conversation with either of them before today. The attention from Andrew was flattering, but the more Andrew flirted and got touchy-feely, the more uncomfortable I felt. I could see how I'd gone from confused by his attention, to flattered by it, and even enjoyed it for a little while. But after the way he kept touching me during the game and that confrontation with Allyson, I feel more sick about it than anything else.

I wonder if I would have felt the same if it had been Trevor? I'll probably never know.

I wonder if he felt that same combination of power and novelty that I had? Maybe that's why he was paying attention to me. If I was flattered and charmed by being the center of his attention, I wonder if he felt powerful by wrapping the innocent ballerina around his little finger all afternoon. I know that I'm not interested in him myself, before today he had never crossed my mind as anything other than the subject of other people's gossip. How can you have a crush on someone you don't even know?

I laugh to myself at the obvious irony.

No wonder Olivia was so annoyed with me.

I can see Katy and Lisa squished together on a loveseat, Hunter sitting on the arm next to Lisa, sneaking occasional glances at them. Katy is shouting and waving her arms, clearly directing the guys playing whatever video game is on the screen. Boys are strewn around the room, some on the couch, some standing behind it, others sprawled on the floor. They look absolutely comfortable, obviously at home here. Olivia and her friends are standing in a little knot by the front door. Allyson looks like she's complaining about something and I have a pretty good guess what it is.

This is what I'll be giving up if I get my dream. My summer will be spent in a hot, sweaty studio with dancers who are as dedicated and talented as me, not at a pool surrounded by other teenagers just wanting to have fun. Is it worth it? Is my dream worth giving up the chance to do what every other teenager in the world does?

Through the sliding glass door, I hear a faint round of good-byes from the boys as the girls leave, closing the door behind them. I keep watching through the glass, not ready to go inside. There's a wave of cheers from some of the guys and groans from the others as something happens in the game. It's like watching a movie, I see what they're doing and I'm happy that they seem to be having fun, but I'm outside of it.

Standing there in the dark, I know that as wonderful as this is, it isn't enough for me. I want that sweaty studio and giving this up doesn't feel like a sacrifice, it feels inevitable.

"Hey," Olivia says, quietly sliding through the glass door. "You okay?"

"Hey," I respond automatically. "Um, yeah?"

She stands there, rubbing her arms. Olivia looks, not exactly nervous, but like she's not sure if she's going to stay or leave.

"Allyson can be a real piece of work," she finally says, "I'm sorry she picked on you like that."

"I would have thought you'd think I deserved it. Karma and all that." I shrug. "I get it now," I add. "You were right, I was self-absorbed and I wasn't being fair to you. I wasn't being…" I search for the word I want. "Realistic."

"You weren't wrong either. I did invite you on purpose, back in January." She clears her throat, looking uncomfortable. "I knew. I remembered your crush. I just wanted to…" she seems to be searching for the right word just like I had. "I just wanted to win."

"I kinda get it now. It's a rush, huh?" I pull out one of the lounge chairs and sit, patting the spot next to me. Olivia perches gingerly next to me.

"Hannah, I owe you an apology, for real. That was a shitty thing to do to you, you were right. I invited you on that date because I thought it would make me feel good that Tyler picked me over you." She takes a deep breath and lets it out, sagging into the chair.

"Yeah, it was. But I forgive you." I bump her shoulder with mine. "I know you didn't do it for the right reasons, but it was time for me to wake up and move on." I pause, pushing the too-long sleeves of Andrew's sweatshirt up to my elbows. "My crush on Tyler gave me something to draw on when I'm dancing. That vague kind of 'artistic pain' I thought I needed, since I'd never really had anything else like that to draw from." Olivia makes a sad sound at that. "Sorry," I whisper, swallowing the urge to apologize a hundred more times. "But it was a safe kind of pain. I knew, really, that it was never going to happen. So my long-standing crush was pain I could control. It wasn't real pain, not like yours," I add. "And I know that makes me an awful person, but I saw how hard it was when your mom…" I can't bring myself to say it.

"Died," Olivia supplies for me.

"Yeah," I clear my throat. "I saw how much you hurt and I was afraid of it. I was afraid of something happening that would make me hurt like that too. Maybe somewhere in my head I thought if I could choose the thing that was hurting me, it would somehow keep anything else bad from happening to me." I shrug, I don't know if any of this makes sense, but I've had a lot of time to think about it over the last few days.

"So wanting Tyler from afar was safer," Olivia says quietly. "I get it. If I could choose between a crush who didn't know I existed and losing my mom…well, that's an easy choice." Olivia laughs a little at that.

We sit in silence for a minute before Olivia's voice comes out of the darkness. "I owe you an apology for more than that. I'm sorry I told my dad I was with you when I was really out with Tyler. The first time it was true, when we went on our double date. But my dad was so happy to let me stay out later, he wouldn't grill me on where I was going if I said I was with you." She shrugs. "It's not a good excuse, but it's the truth. I shouldn't have used you like that. I'm sorry."

"I guess I'm so lame, even our parents don't think I'll get up to any kind of trouble." I wince at my own words. Is that really what I think? Kind of.

"You're not lame. You have goals, you know what you want and you know what you have to do to make them happen. I'm kind of jealous, I feel like I'm just making shit up as I go most of the time."

"So what happens now?" I ask quietly. "I know we're not best friends anymore. You were right, we haven't been for a long time. But you've always been there. I don't know how to not think of you as my best friend."

"You have Katy and Lisa. They've been your best friends for ages now, even if you didn't realize it."

"I know, I guess I've known for awhile. It's weird to hear you say it though," I add, bumping her shoulder with mine.

"I meant it when I said I don't hate you." Oliva says, sitting up straighter. "Just because we aren't each other's best friend, doesn't mean we can't just be regular friends. We'll still be together at dance."

"Yeah. The last few weeks have really sucked not hanging out with you at dance." I admit. "I miss you there the most."

"Same." Olivia admits. "So. Not a truce. I don't think there's a name for this. Just…" Olivia seems stuck, looking for the right word.

"Just friends." I say, holding out my hand like we're going to shake on it.

Oliva bursts out laughing at my lame offer of a handshake, instead giving me a quick hug. "Yeah, just friends." she says. We sit awkwardly in silence for a minute. I study the scene inside, smiling at Lisa when she makes eye contact with me through the window. I feel lighter than I have in months, just sitting in here in the dark with my friend. I forgot what that felt like.

"So… what's up with Trevor, huh? Should I warn him he's got competition from Andrew?" Olivia's words echo in the dark.

"Ugh, no. Definitely not," I laugh with a shudder at the thought. "Trevor's…good? I don't really know what I'm doing, to tell you the truth." I turn to face Olivia, glad to see a genuine smile on her face. "Does he really...I mean, do you know for sure what he told Tyler?"

Olivia just laughs at me and pulls me towards the house. "Okay, let's grab Lisa and Katy, we're having a girls' pow-wow upstairs. I know exactly what he told Tyler and I'm gonna help you out."

Lisa

I DO MY best to keep an eye on Hannah and Olivia through the glass door, although Hunter's thigh pressing against my arm is completely distracting. It looks like they're clearing the air between them, finally. Of course, every time Hunter moves I have to stop myself from glancing at him. Instead, I keep my eyes glued to the tv screen, not that I know what I'm looking at, with the occasional glance behind his back to the backyard.

I'm relieved to see Hannah and Oliva working things out. Frankly, the tension between them has been exhausting. Katy and I have been doing our best to keep things quiet so Ms. Parker and the younger kids at dance don't know how bad it is, but since Katy can't stand Olivia, for some reason, it's really been me acting as the go-between.

Between the tension at dance, AP classes, and Japanese school on Sundays, I feel like all I do is go, go, go. I just want a day to do absolutely nothing. Just one whole day. Tonight is the first time I've spent a Saturday night *not* studying since Winter Break. My parents expect me to spend all my time at home downstairs at the kitchen table where they can see me working—I learned a long time ago to pick my battles, and school-work is not a battle I will ever win.

But I have a plan.

I'm not going to cram school in Japan this summer, I'm determined to go to the PSB summer intensive with Hannah and I think I know how to convince my parents to let me go. It's not going to be easy, but I think with Hannah and Katy's help, I might just have a chance.

I hope you enjoyed getting to know Hannah, Olivia and the gang! Hannah's story continues in Head to Head, available at this link:

https://books2read.com/u/mq0OL8.

Want to know what happened when Olivia "bumped" into Tyler that fateful morning? Sign up for Penelope's newsletter for a special bonus prequel!

https://sendfox.com/penelopefreedbooks

If you enjoyed this book, the best way to thank the author is to leave a review. Thank you!

ACKNOWLEDGEMENTS

Hey beautiful, we made it! What a journey this has been. Hannah's story started percolating in my mind way back in 2014 and it's been quite the journey to get here. We've grown up together, Hannah, Olivia, Lisa, Katy and I. And now here you are, joining our little squad. If you're reading this, I want to thank you from the bottom of my heart for allowing my story to be part of your life.

There are so many people who have helped to get me here that I need to thank. Alina Lane for creating the RWR group and for being my cheerleader and ass kicker. Lasairona McMaster for taking me under her wing and pushing me or cheering me on as needed. Stella, Tamara, Robyn, Claire, Norma, Breanna, Hattie, Bellamy, and all my fellow RWR authors, thank you for being on this roller coaster with me, holding my hand when I needed it, laughing with me on our ridiculous Zoom calls, and helping me do this crazy thing in the middle of this crazy time.

A huge thanks to my amazing editors Caitlin Fitzgerald and Sax Gray who made this book better than it had any right to be. You pushed me to make this story the best it could be and I am so grateful I found you! All mistakes are my own, don't blame those two lovely ladies for my comma catastrophes.

So many people in my life have encouraged me to tell my stories: Melissa, Patti, Daniel, Brody, Katy, Ryan, Dianne, Sheryl and Dr. Phelps. My amazing parents, who read to us every night after dinner, and didn't yell at me for staying up late reading all summer long. Thank you for your words of encouragement, your support, and for the courage to pursue this dream. My amazing husband is my #1 cheerleader, my rock, my champion. Thank you for always having my back, I couldn't do this without you babe.

And lastly, I can't write this book without acknowledging my inspiration—my beautiful daughter and my former students. All you kids out there who are ready to change the world, I wrote this book for you. So you know deep in your souls that you are seen and that you matter. You are worthy of love. I see you. Keep kicking ass and being better than the generations before you.

ABOUT THE AUTHOR

Penelope Freed lives in the Pacific Northwest where you can find her learning how to drive in the rain, walking her dog and making a mess in the kitchen. Her husband and daughter think she's a little bit bonkers and really hate it when she dances embarrassingly in public.

Which she does, often.

After a lifetime in the ballet world, Penelope decided to start writing down the stories in her head instead of narrating her ballet classes with them—her former students are very thankful for this decision. Now, Penelope writes stories about dreamers, just like she is, who are willing to do whatever it takes to make those dreams come true.

www.ingramcontent.com/pod-product-compliance
Lightning Source LLC
Chambersburg PA
CBHW071557110726
47908CB00007B/2146